# FIRST TRACKS

# FIRST TRACKS

## Catherine O'Connell

This first world edition published 2019
in Great Britain and the USA by
SEVERN HOUSE PUBLISHERS LTD of
Eardley House, 4 Uxbridge Street, London W8 7SY.
Trade paperback edition first published
in Great Britain and the USA 2019 by
SEVERN HOUSE PUBLISHERS LTD.

British Library Cataloguing in Publication Data
*A CIP catalogue record for this title is available from the British Library.*


ISBN-13: 978-0-7278-8873-0 (cased)
ISBN-13: 978-1-78029-598-5 (trade paper)
ISBN-13: 978-1-4483-0189-8 (e-book)

*All Severn House titles are printed on acid-free paper.*

Severn House Publishers support the Forest Stewardship Council™ [FSC™],
the leading international forest certification organisation.
All our titles that are printed on FSC certified paper carry the FSC logo.

Typeset by Palimpsest Book Production Ltd.,
Falkirk, Stirlingshire, Scotland.
Printed and bound in Great Britain by
TJ International, Padstow, Cornwall.

*This book is dedicated to Cindy Burke, Trish Schreiber, Maria Armstrong, Teri Christensen, Lori Spence and all the other amazing women ski pros and ski patrollers at the Aspen Skico who teach us how it's done and keep us safe while we're doing it.*

# ONE

I heard it before I saw it. There was a crack followed by an unmistakable whoosh signifying disaster. A quick look over my left shoulder confirmed my fears. An immense slab of snow had broken loose and was barreling toward me like a white locomotive that had jumped the track. I skied for the trees in an attempt to outrun the monster, but the slide was on me faster than thought and I only made a couple of yards. It slammed me with an angry surge, tossing me skyward before sucking me back down. I ended up riding its surface, a snow surfer at the front edge of a crystal tsunami that, like batter in a blender, kept threatening to pull me under. All my senses were on alert as the world flashed past in a river of white, trees folding like dominos, immense walls being carved into the terrain to either side.

Trying to keep my position atop the monster was like trying to leash a rabid dog. Pulling to mind every survival technique in my reservoir, I started swimming, which was like trying to do the breaststroke in mud. But I had to do something to stop it from towing me under and encasing me in a concrete coffin. My frantic mind recalled how they found Billy Rineheart's battered body last spring after the melt, his legs tucked behind his head in a morbid backbend, his spine but a memory. I swam harder, fighting to hold the surface, my frantic paddling like that of a non-swimmer thrown into a pond.

Thankfully, the force of the avalanche had knocked off both skis, so my legs were tracking directly behind me instead of being pin-wheeled into spiral fractures. Something hard hit from behind and bounced off my helmet. A moment later a tree branch swept past in the debris. My captor had funneled me into a chute and we were plummeting towards the valley below at mind-bending speed.

Ahead of me, the wave plumed upwards, crystals of snow turning to explosive white clouds. My helmet ripped off and then one of my gloves along with my left ski pole. My right pole was still attached and while I feared the strap might break my wrist, I also hoped it would stay with me so there might be something poking through the surface to let people know that a possibly breathing creature lay somewhere in the area.

I'd heard stories about a person's life travelling before their eyes when they know they are facing death, but that sure wasn't the case for me. There was no such luxury of time to recount my life, though I did think of my brother and wondered how he would take the news of my demise. Down and down we went, the white bronco trying to buck me off while every fiber of me struggled to stay on its back. My eyes flicked up to the clear blue sky that lay on the other side of the crystal fog. It looked so tranquil with the mountains carved into the blue and the rays of the late-afternoon sun slipping around the peaks.

And then, as quickly as it started, the slide came to a halt. My efforts appeared to have paid off, allowing the possibility of survival to occur to me. I was on the surface. Well, part of me anyhow. My legs, left arm and torso were encased in a snow cast, but my head, right shoulder and right arm were free. I was looking at Castle Creek Road winding lazily through the valley below. Miraculously, my right ski pole was still with me and I waved it in hopes of attracting the attention of some passing vehicle. In January, the sun set early, and if I wasn't rescued before it went down the chances of survival were slim.

My braid rested in front of me, a thick blond snow-packed piece of rope that I pushed aside to reach around my neck. I felt a surge of relief as my hand took hold of my avalanche beacon. Being on patrol, I always wore it. It was in the receive mode. I turned it to transmit and went back to waving my ski pole with an exhausted arm. A car in the valley flashed its lights and a wave of euphoria swept me. I was going to live.

The small glimpse of optimism was short lived, however, as another crack echoed through the valley followed by the sound of the locomotive bearing down on me again. The second slide took longer to hit, but this one knocked my ski pole free and shoved me from behind, taking the slab of snow that encased me along with it. I was travelling downhill again, the creature claiming victory as it pulled me underneath and enclosed me. When it came to a stop this time, I was in complete darkness. But somehow I'd had the presence of mind to keep my right arm in front of me. My right hand was inches from my face, protecting the world's smallest pocket of air. I said my prayers and tried not to panic. Panic meant hyperventilating and oxygen was precious enough as it was.

I wasn't cold or aware of any pain, but I was completely immobilized. I took miserly breaths, holding them in as long as I could, having no idea how long the air pocket would last. Time went into suspension, and an odd sense of acceptance came over me as I lapsed in and out of consciousness.

I was deep in conversation with the powers that be when a dull thump broke the absolute silence. I would have gasped had there been enough oxygen. The thump was followed by another thump and then another. The thumps started getting louder and more regular until it dawned on me it was a shovel I was hearing. And then a weak crack of light penetrated my tomb. Gray dusk brushed the sky above like variegated layers of smoke settling down after a fire.

A dark mustachioed face wearing a red ski cap was hovering over me.

'Are you an angel?' I asked.

Fierce dark eyes glared at me. 'Dammit, Westerlind. If you hadn't already got yourself buried alive, I'd do for you.'

# TWO

When I woke up, I was alone in a hospital room with all kinds of tubes and cords protruding from my bruised and battered body. A beeping monitor behind me only made my already intolerable headache worse. Though my vision was blurry, I managed to focus on the far end of the bed and could see the outline of two feet poking up beneath the sheets. That was a good sign. I wriggled my toes, and the sheets moved. Even better. My arms lay exposed atop the blanket and I played imaginary scales, first with my right hand, then my left. Another victory. I tried to raise my right arm. That hurt like hell, but with some effort I was able to bring it up above my head. The left was no problem.

A doctor came in, a good-looking one I might add. He had a light complexion and was clean-shaven with short straw-colored hair, a square jaw and small, oval-shaped wire-rimmed glasses. That his face wasn't familiar puzzled me. Since I usually stopped at the hospital to check on the skiers I'd brought down the hill, I thought I knew just about every doctor in that ER. But the season was early and I hadn't been to the hospital a whole lot yet, so I figured him to be new.

The doc gave me a smile that momentarily overrode the feeling that my body had been pummeled by a rock in a sack. It was a warm and heartfelt smile with evenly spaced white teeth, except for one side tooth that was charmingly crooked in a Hugh Grant sort of manner. His nametag read Dr Duane Larsen.

'Well, you're a miracle,' he said. 'Remind me to book my next flight on your plane.' He huddled over me and I noticed the eyes behind the wire-rimmed glasses were mismatched, one green, one brown. His mounded muscles beneath the green scrubs told me that aside from practicing medicine, the doctor practiced body building as well. He put his finger to my right eyelid and raised it, shining a light into it, flicking the light off before repeating the procedure on the left.

'Why am I here?' I asked.

'You don't remember?'

A shake of my head caused my brain to volley painfully against the sides of my skull. 'No,' I said, suppressing a grimace.

'You were in an avalanche, a pretty major one, I understand. The good news is all your parts are still in the right place. But you've been out of it for twenty-four hours. You've had a pretty severe concussion.'

*No kidding*, I thought, my head banging like those little hammers on those old aspirin commercials. A moment of panic followed as my thoughts turned to Kayla waiting for me at the front door. Then the pain in my head relocated to my heart upon remembering there was no need to let her out anymore.

'Are you up for a visitor?' Dr Larsen asked.

'Why not.'

He left the room, closing the door behind him. I turned my head toward the window and tried to make sense of what had happened, but my brain was a wall. The mountains were bathed in the pink of the sunset sky, turning the white-capped peaks inviting and foreboding at the same time. One good thing to be said about being in the hospital in Aspen: every room had a view.

The door opened and Neverman stepped in. He was in street clothes, jeans and a down jacket, his graying curls tucked under a beat-up old cowboy hat. An image flashed and retreated, a slide and then Neverman's stern face peering down godlike from above. My only regret about being in one piece was having him to thank.

My nemesis, mentor and boss, Mike Neverman was a true enigma in my life. A mountain man in the truest sense, he lived in a cabin on the backside of Aspen mountain and snow-mobiled or snowshoed to work most days. When he first started in patrol the day after God was born, there were no female patrollers and the only correlation he saw between women skiers and patrol was having to load us into toboggans for the downhill ride to waiting ambulances. And though things had changed a lot since ancient history and there were plenty of fully fledged women patrollers nowadays, it was no secret he wasn't happy about it. Luckily he had the good sense to keep his resentment simmering below the surface, only allowing it to boil over occasionally when dealing with Meghan and me and the other women. The only one he didn't mess with was Lucy. Big and quiet, Lucy was the size of a running back. She'd probably squish him.

His dark eyes were fixed on me in a manner that made me think he wished he had found me other than alive. But when he spoke, there was an unrecognizable timbre in his voice that made me nervous. It bordered on polite. But behind the politeness was a restraint I'd never heard before.

'How're ya doin', Westerlind?'

'Gotta say, I've felt better. My head feels like it's going to explode. I'm thinking of suing the helmet manufacturer.'

He was silent a moment before unleashing the anger behind the restraint. 'You know you dodged one hell of a bullet. From what we figure that slide carried you near to fifteen hundred feet. It's a fuckin' miracle you didn't suffocate or hang up on a tree. The only reason you didn't get your dumbass brains crushed in is you have such a hard head.'

Did I mention he'd started out polite? Oh well, one can dream. Before I could offer any commentary on his tirade, he shifted into the condescending voice I'd grown accustomed to. 'What the hell business did you have skiing back of Ruthie's anyhow? Did you take leave of your senses? You knew avi risk was high. Now I know you're notorious for taking chances, but skiing Ophir's in the afternoon, with the snow all set up the way it was, that's a stunt for some twenty-three-year-old idiot boarder. Not a seasoned ski patrol. What in hell were you thinking?'

The questions came rapid-fire and, to be honest, they were reasonable questions. The problem was the answers evaded me completely. I had no idea what chain of events put me out of bounds outside Ruthie's in the late afternoon when the avalanche risk was high. My memories started with being slammed by a slide and ended with being dug out while still breathing. Other than that, my brain was a vacuum of recall.

Now I'd say I'm a pretty confident woman in the larger sense, but at times Mike Neverman could level me to the proverbial little girl. As he had now. 'I . . . I don't know why I was there,' I stammered.

'Well, all I can say is you're damn lucky.' He took his hat off and stared down at the crumpled rim in his hands. 'Wish I could say the same about Warren.'

'Warren?' His name catapulted from my mouth. There was no need to ask Warren who. There was only one Warren, my longtime friend and greatest ski buddy. My next words flowed from my mouth over a tongue that hoped to make them true. 'Warren wasn't in that slide.'

The rare hint of sympathy in Neverman's face forewarned something I wouldn't want to hear. His next words confirmed it. 'You didn't know you weren't alone in your folly?'

My mind searched for Warren anywhere in the picture and couldn't find him. Bits of the slide were coming back in fractured pieces of the whole. The first boom of white. Coming to a stop on top of the snow. Being buried in the second slide. But Warren was nowhere in that memory. The real challenge now was to pose my next question without breaking down. 'Please tell me that he's OK? Please tell me he just broke his leg or something like that?'

Dark staring eyes were his only response.

'He's paralyzed. Oh, God, he's paralyzed.'

Neverman's eyes went back to the hat in his hands, his knuckles whitening as his grip tightened upon the rim. 'He's dead, Greta.'

The cruel reality of his words left me speechless. The headache throbbed in my ears, drowning out all sound except the repetitive beep of the machines. Gradually sound returned, the carts rolling down the hall, the voices carrying in from the nurses' station. Dr Larsen came back into the room, took one look at my tortured face and turned his scrub-clad body toward Neverman. 'That's enough for now. She needs to get some rest.'

My boss placed his cowboy hat back on his head, flattening the greying curls over his ears. His voice had gone schizo again, all nice and understanding. 'Yep. Like the doctor says, you get some rest, Westerlind. Come back to work when you feel like it.'

He turned and went out the door. And then he was gone, the cadence of his cowboy boots echoing down the hall, leaving me alone to contemplate my role in the death of a good friend.

# THREE

They released me the next afternoon, but not before I was walking to their satisfaction and not without Dr Larsen, who'd wanted me to stay another day for observation, giving me stern orders to lay low and 'refrain from doing anything strenuous for a week'. Easy for him to say. Sitting around wasn't anywhere in my DNA and never had been. The thought of doing nothing was as threatening to me as a jail sentence.

He wheeled me to the hospital entrance and waited beside the wheelchair until Judy came to pick me up. A wisp of a thing with dark brown hair and bright blue eyes, Judy was the first person I met when I drove into Aspen fifteen years ago in a car so packed to the gills I looked like an Okie. I had arrived in town all alone with no clue where I was going to live or how I was going to support myself. Just knew I wanted to be a part of this town. I met her in the hamburger place where she was waitressing at the time, and she took me under her wing and has been my best friend here ever since. Aside from my twin, she's the person I love and trust more than anyone in this world.

She was uncharacteristically quiet on the drive into town, silent as we wheeled along the snow-covered streets, past the Hotel Jerome and the County Courthouse and the Catholic church, all prosperous landmarks from when the town had seen its first heyday. Or silver day as you might have it. Aspen was among the most respected silver trading bases back in the 1880s when the country was on the silver standard as well as the gold. One of the richest cities west of the Mississippi, its fortune had changed drastically in 1893 when Grover Cleveland took the US off the silver standard. The end game was that the valley's population dwindled to below five hundred, a group made up basically of cattle ranchers and potato farmers.

Aspen found itself in an entirely different heyday now, the

kind that dealt with real estate and second homeowners versus precious metals, but this heyday probably wasn't any less valuable than when silver had ruled.

We continued through town along eighty-two and headed up valley toward Independence Pass. My A-frame sits about as far up eighty-two as you can go before the Winter Gate gets shut in November, closing the road off to all travel on the other side until the pass reopens at Memorial Day. It's quiet where I live and that's the way I like it. Actually, my neighbor on the other side of the highway is Kevin Costner, but he has security so it's not like I could go over and borrow an egg.

I knew part of the reason for Judy's silence was that she was irritated with me. And it wasn't only for getting myself in an avalanche. She wanted me to stay with her and Gene in their Red Mountain mansion for a couple of nights to make sure I was all right, but I'd declined. I'd already spent three days in the hospital and I just wanted to be home in my own surroundings to lick my wounds. Not the physical wounds, you know. My pain threshold is high, and I've had enough blow-ups while skiing to know the bruising of my battered body would pass. It was the psychological wounds that were troublesome, and there was no doubt in my mind that Judy knew that. She knew how incredibly close Warren and I had been. She also knew my private nature and that I'd talk about it when I was ready.

Which I still wasn't. Warren's death had been at the forefront of my mind from the moment Neverman told me about it, through the long, sleepless night that followed, until the sun cast its morning shadow on to the mountains. Later that day, Meghan and Singh and Winter had stopped to see me after work. They were the three I worked with the most, especially Singh, but I sent them packing, begging off with the headache. Warren's face and name kept resounding in my brain in a painful loop playing over and over again.

We'd been ski buddies for as long as I'd been on patrol, which would be around ten years. I met him on the slow chair ride up Bell Mountain in the early season. He'd just moved to Aspen after getting divorced and retiring from his job as a bond trader. I'd volunteered to show him around the mountain and we'd been skiing together ever since. Hard pack or powder, we'd crush it. Easy Chair to Blondie's. Northstar to Jackpot. International to Silver Queen. Anything and everything.

Over time our friendship grew, extending further than just skiing. Laughing over lunch at Bonnie's. Long hikes in the summer. Biking up to the Bells. Talking about just about anything – politics, sports, books. We were about as close as you could get without being lovers. In fact, it was better than being lovers because we knew we would never have to break up, never have to hate each other.

At least that was what I told myself when he married Zuzana.

And now he was dead and I might have something to do with it? Try as I might, I was coming up with zero reasons as to why Warren and I were skiing the backside of the mountain at three o'clock in the afternoon at a time when avalanche warnings were the terror equivalent of red.

Judy's silence persisted the last few miles up to my turnoff. Luckily the snowplow had been through earlier or I would have had to walk in to my house since her Prius wouldn't have been up to the challenge. As it was it was a rough ride down the snow-packed road with banks of snow higher than the car rising to either side of us.

She pulled to a stop in front of my A-frame on its makeshift cul-de-sac. True to the architecture of its sloped roof, not a flake of snow clung to the building, but that didn't preclude mountainous piles of the white stuff reaching up all around it. The Wagoneer was buried as well. I'd left it in its usual parking spot in town, but everyone knew the keys were always in it, so someone from patrol must have driven it home for me. The two feet of snow piled on the hood told me how much it had snowed since I'd gone into the hospital. For an instant I felt disappointed that I wouldn't be skiing the freshie in the morning. Then the memory of Warren's death settled back in, taking all glimmer off the prospect.

Judy killed the engine – though you wouldn't have known it since the engine was so quiet.

'Why did you do that?' I asked her.

'Do what?'

'Turn the car off.'

She gave me a sidelong stare. I met those piercing blue eyes with a stare of my own. Judy may have been small, but her presence was huge and she was about as determined a person as one could meet. It was a battle to overcome her once she had her mind set on something.

'Because I'm coming in with you, that's why. Did you think I was just going to leave you in the driveway without making sure you get in all right? I still can't get why you won't stay with us.'

'Look, I just want to be alone.'

She must have caught on to how serious I was, because instead of insisting as she usually would, she touched my arm and said gently, 'I'm sorry about Warren.'

I bit my lip to fight back tears and repeated myself. 'I want to be alone. You can understand.'

She nodded and turned the car back on. 'Keep your cell with you and call me if you need anything, OK?' And then she realized the folly of her words. For one, my cell was buried somewhere overlooking the Castle Creek Valley, lost in the slide. For two, my cell phone was useless up here anyway. There was no service. I did have a landline, however, and through the wonders of technology, a satellite dish for internet and television, an object about as out of harmony with the environment as you could get. Sam probably would have written me out of his will if he knew I was going to get satellite service after he was gone, but a girl can only be so alone. Even so, he was probably flipping in his grave. Hypothetically that is. He had no grave. Per his wishes, his ashes had been scattered on Richmond Ridge atop Aspen Mountain.

'You do have a phone that works in there, don't you? I mean besides that mustard monster in the kitchen.' She was referring to Sam's original phone, a rotary attached to the kitchen wall with a cord that had given up ninety-five per cent of its coil over the years.

'Yes,' I said. 'I bought a wireless to keep with me in the loft. I got tired of climbing down the stairs to answer your calls checking in on me.'

'Keep it beside you, please. I won't sleep tonight unless you promise.'

'I promise.' We kissed each other's cheek, and I got out of the car and grabbed my ski boots and remaining pole off the back seat.

'And Greta,' she said in a soft voice. 'I know how much this has to be killing you.'

'Thanks,' was the best I could do.

I shut the door and trudged up the snowy walk.

# FOUR

My sense of loss increased the moment I stepped into my house. The emptiness was profound. My eyes darted to the kitchen floor where Kayla's bowls lay untouched since I'd had her put down two weeks before. When I saw the last of the water had evaporated, tears ran down my cheeks. I'd intentionally left the water in the bowl knowing that her tongue had lapped its last drink of water from that bowl and perhaps part of her was there in the cells that remained. One of the best avalanche dogs going, she'd saved more than a couple of lives over the years, including mine, and deciding to let her go was one of the hardest things I'd ever done. But as happens so often with Goldens, her hips were shot and it was only fair to put her out of her pain.

Judy was already on me to get a new dog, but it would have been impossible to train a puppy during ski season, and besides Kayla and I had been together since I first started patrol. I wasn't ready to replace her just yet.

I hung my patrol jacket on a peg with the orange cross facing out from the black background, blessing the room. The house was freezing, as usual. Propane was expensive, so when I was out, the thermostat was set just high enough to keep the pipes from freezing. I cranked the temperature up to sixty-five and was rewarded by the sound of flames firing up in the old furnace followed by the soft flow of warm air.

Depressed or not, I was hungry. I'm like that. I can eat through practically anything. A job loss. A break-up. My mother's death. It's close to impossible to ruin my appetite. I popped open the refrigerator and stared at my lack of choices. There was a bottle of Pinot Grigio, a six-pack of Heineken, a carton of 2% milk and a hunk of parmesan cheese. Saturday, the day of the slide, was my usual day for provisioning, and for obvious reasons I hadn't made City Market. I opened a Heineken, cut off a hunk of the parmesan and matched it up with some Triscuits from the pantry. Searching to do something mindless, I turned on the television and settled into the Barcalounger.

The chair was old and beat up as hell, but it was Sam's chair and even though I had the *cojones* to put a satellite dish on his hallowed grounds, I couldn't bring myself to get rid of the tired old piece of furniture where he spent his last days. Towards the end, he didn't even get into bed at night. He just slept in the chair. If one was to call me sentimental, they'd be right. But I owed Sam big time, and if honoring his memory was one way of thanking him, then so be it.

Sam was the reason I was able to stay in Aspen. The rents here are stratospheric and always have been. That's if you can even find anything to rent. When I'd lost my housing at the end of the season years ago, and there was nothing available even close to my price range, I really feared I might have to pull the plug on the town I loved so well.

That's when I saw the ad in the *Times* for a live-in caregiver in exchange for a room. I didn't exactly see myself as a caregiver, but I was trained in first aid, so I thought why not see what that's about. Well, I gotta say, answering that ad was one of the smartest things that I've ever done in my life. Not to mention the most serendipitous.

When I pulled up for my interview, Sam was sitting on the front deck of his A-frame with the snow still piled in the shade of the trees skirting the house, an aging ski bum looking at his last powder run. Even at eighty, he was still attractive, tall and wiry with some last bits of hair clinging stubbornly to the sides of his head and clear blue eyes that had seen more than a few good times. But he'd taken a fall in his kitchen the week before and was walking with a limp after pulling his hamstring. An earlier fall, just weeks before the pulled hamstring, had resulted in a broken collarbone. He'd come to the conclusion that maybe it was better if he didn't live alone anymore.

He'd been a presence in Aspen for over fifty years, since the salad days of the sixties when, according to him, the town revolved around three major activities – skiing, partying, and sex. And he couldn't say in what order of priority. Though I suspect for him skiing won out. Most of his friends from those days were gone, either moved away or dead. He'd been self-sufficient his whole life and hated having to depend on anyone. Truth was, he didn't need a caregiver, *per se*, but someone to run errands and eat with occasionally, someone to pick him up off the floor if he fell, someone to keep him out of the nursing home. What he really needed was company and, besides, he confessed, he didn't want to die alone.

We hit it off from the start. Luckily, he loved dogs so Kayla and I set up housekeeping in the loft while Sam kept his residence downstairs in the cabin's only bedroom. And living with Sam was not only a sweet deal, it was liberating for me. For the first time since moving to Aspen, I wasn't living under the onus of searching out housing at the end of every season. The set-up worked out great for both of us. He was a private person who loved having some time of his own, which allowed for me to work all day. And days when Kayla didn't come to work with me he enjoyed having her around.

He swore the only way he'd leave the valley was in a coffin, and that held true in the end. I got up one winter morning last year and there he was in the Barcalounger, a half-finished beer in the glass that I'd brought to him the night before, his last run over. Though most his friends were gone, the turnout for his funeral was large. He was a legend. And he never had a coffin and never left the valley. His ashes on the ridge made him part of the valley forever.

When it came to his will, no one was more surprised than me that he left me the A-frame in a life estate. Well, maybe his two adult children were more surprised, but with the exception of his funeral, they had only surfaced a couple of times in the five years I lived with him. His only marriage had been short-lived and his wife had moved to Vail with the kids when they were not much more than babies, so there wasn't much relationship between them. Sam blamed this partly on himself for not being the fatherly type and partly on his ex-wife for poisoning them against him.

Either way, they now had kids of their own, and I imagine he wanted his grandkids to have some memory of the grandfather they'd never met, since it wasn't likely the estate would revert to Sam's children in their lifetime. The whole life estate thing pissed them off since the land was worth millions that they wouldn't see until I either died or moved out. Sam was sure that the second he went, they'd sell to some developer who would build a 10,000 square foot mansion on the land and slap an eight-figure price tag on it – something he didn't want to happen. He'd already seen too many changes in Aspen and wasn't going to add to them if he could help it. Guess he showed them all big time. One of the provisions of the life estate was that I didn't change the exterior of the building in any way.

His kids tried contesting the will, but it was ironclad. And so at thirty-five, I was *muy* comfortable in my ski shack and had no intention of going anywhere else well into the foreseeable future.

I ate the better part of the Triscuits with the parmesan and washed them down with the beer while watching the PBS news hour and a couple other news shows I recorded daily, my bow to the real world I'd managed thus far to avoid. I shook my head at what we had gotten ourselves into, praying the country and the planet would survive the president, thankful to be living in the bubble that was the Roaring Fork Valley. The post-avalanche headache that had plagued me on and off since the spill started coming back, so I shut the television down and climbed into the loft.

Lying on the mattress and box spring that served as my bed beneath the slanted ceiling, I propped some pillows behind my head and picked up the copy of Ovid's *Metamorphoses* that sat on the low nightstand. My latest goal was to get the college degree I'd never been able to finish back in Milwaukee, so I'd started taking classes at the local college. This semester's class was Mythology. Snuggled under the sheets, beneath a heavy wool blanket and a down-filled duvet, I picked up the book and tried to put a dent in the week's assignment, but found myself unable to read. The headache kept getting worse, making concentration difficult if not impossible. I put the book back on the nightstand and pulled the covers up to my chin.

True to my promise to Judy, my wireless phone sat on the nightstand next to a brass lamp. I turned off the lamp and closed my eyes. Warren's face appeared behind the shuttered lids, his dark hair and freckles and coffee-colored eyes. The cheek-to-cheek smile that only produced a dimple on the right side. My mind was pummeled with the unanswered question of what I had been doing on the backside of Ruthie's with Warren alongside me. Had he invited me to ski with him? Had I asked him? My initiating the run would have been unlikely. I was on duty and was supposed to stay in bounds, and besides anyone with a brain knew how dangerous it was. The riddle was painfully plaguing, almost as much as the loss of him. It had to be solved sooner or later if I was going to have any closure.

And then a tiny glimmer of memory pierced the darkness. I was shutting the door to the shed when I saw Warren slide off the Ruthie's chair. I remembered seeing him glance towards the ski area boundary and then head for it. I remembered thinking it wasn't right and shouting his name. I tried to recall more, willed myself to push the memory farther, but the hole closed up like the iris at the end of an old cartoon and the memory went black again.

The headache was getting worse, even with my eyes shut. I regretted ignoring Dr Larsen's order of no alcohol for a couple days. Could one beer really cause all this pain? I pressed my hands to my forehead in an attempt to push relief into my tormented cranium. I was feeling more peculiar than just the headache, like some kind of poison was running through my veins. Maybe Judy was right. Maybe I shouldn't have stayed home alone. Maybe I should have spent the night on Red Mountain with her and Gene.

When the headache got intolerable, I reached out for the phone and pressed Judy's number on the speed dial. The call had just gone through when a high-pitched alarm sounded, assaulting my ears and my already assaulted brain. The screeching sound was creating more pain in my head than the headache. Somewhere in the deepest recesses of my psyche I decided it was the smoke detector. But when I peeled my eyes open, there was no smoke. And there was no smell of smoke either. *Don't tell me this is all because of the damn battery*, I thought.

Putting the phone down on the bed, I made my way to the

edge of the loft and swung my legs on to the ladder, thinking to go down and change the battery or at least unplug the nuisance. My legs turned to rubber and folded beneath me the moment my feet touched the floor. And then, with terrifying clarity, I realized the noise wasn't coming from the smoke alarm at all. It was the CO detector. A wave of true terror swept over me as I knew firsthand how quickly carbon monoxide can disable. Growing increasingly confused, I thought of the phone lying on the bed ringing Judy's number and then forgot about it just as quickly.

There was no time for contemplation or decisions. I rolled on to my stomach and crawled through the kitchen like a snake. When I got to the door I reached up for the knob, but my hand was jelly and slipped away from it. I tried again with the same result. Laying on the ground, I realized my chances of survival were diminishing with each passing second. With one last Herculean effort, I pulled myself to my knees and gripped the knob with every bit of strength left in me. As the knob finally turned and the door fell open, a blast of frigid air blew over me. I crashed face first on to the deck, passing out on the icy cold of a snow pillow.

# FIVE

This time I woke up in a tent. A plastic hyperbolic chamber tent to be more precise. And with a headache as bad as the one after the avalanche. As if in some kind of warped replay, Dr Larsen was standing beside me, this time on the other side of my plastic enclosure. When he saw my eyes were open, he gave me a doctorly smile and pulled up the plastic sheet.

'Awake, eh?' he intoned in a way meant to be cheerful. He applied a thumb to my right eyelid and shone that bright light into my eye again. He nodded affirmatively and repeated the same procedure with the left. 'Well, Miss Westerlind, looks like you've dodged another bullet. Maybe I don't want to be on a plane with you after all. One more visit to ICU and we'll have to put you on the frequent flyer program.'

Finding little humor in his comment, I asked the question I was tired of asking before even posing it. 'What happened?' My last recollection was being home in the loft and the alarm sounding. Once again the events between that moment and the present were nowhere in sight.

'Your furnace must have malfunctioned. Carbon monoxide poisoning. It's a miracle you made it outside. I understand the concentrations were very high.'

Then the pieces came back slowly. Judy and Gene leaning over me. An ambulance with blaring lights. An oxygen mask pushed over my face.

A nurse parted the curtain and indicated that the doctor was needed elsewhere. 'We're going to observe you for a couple more hours and then you can leave. But it's better if you stay with someone for a night or two. CO poisoning can have some delayed effects like impaired coordination and I don't think it's a good idea to be alone.' The mismatched eyes held mine longer than necessary to inform me just how serious he was about my safety. Then he let the plastic sheet fall back in place and left me to digest what I had just learned.

I looked around the curtained cubicle and contemplated my recent run of bad luck. Within the last few days I had not only lost one of my best friends, but I'd knocked on death's door twice. The feeling was akin to being kicked in the stomach. With nothing else to do, I occupied myself watching the monitors hooked up to my body. Pulse: 55. BP 120 over 80. Guess I was going to live. The headache was getting better by the minute.

What wasn't getting better was that I was freezing. The flimsy hospital gown combined with the sorry excuse of a hospital blanket and the cool whoosh of oxygen left me chilled. I climbed from the bed and dragged my attached cords out of the tent to the small closet provided for patients' clothes and personal things. The sweatshirt I'd been wearing in the A-frame was on a hanger and I was puzzling how to get it on over the assorted medical paraphernalia when the door opened. The sweatshirt fell to the ground the moment I saw Zuzana McGovern enter the room. Her exquisite face was pinched, her nose red and raw, and her soulful blue eyes train tracks of red. It looked like she hadn't slept for a while.

'You're OK?' she asked, the remnants of a Czech accent coloring her voice.

As reprehensible as it sounds, at that moment the only thing I could do was stare at her. It was like there were no words in my brain. After all, what does one say to the widow of someone whose death you may or may not have caused? Even if you had no idea how? We stood mutely staring at each other, each suffering her separate pain. I expected her to start screaming at me, but she just stood there looking vulnerable and broken. My voice came back to me gradually.

'Zuzana. I'm . . . so . . . sorry.'

She tightened her lips and her head fell back in an effort to staunch the tears already welling in her bloodshot eyes, but the effort was for naught. Tears flooded over her golden lashes and flowed on to the flawless skin of her cheeks. She squeezed her eyes shut and reopened them, swiping at the tears with the back of her hand.

'When I heard you were back in the hospital, I just had to come see you. I couldn't wait any longer,' she said when she finally regained control. There was a long pause, her next words spilling out of her mouth like a river that had just flooded a dam. 'I have to ask you what happened? What were you and Warren doing back there?'

The sting of the avalanche came back harder than ever, the empty hollow feeling of both grief and self-blame washing over me. No one in their right mind would have been on that slope in those conditions. I had no better idea of what I was doing on the back side of Aspen Mountain now than I did when I woke up in the hospital the first time. All I had was that tiny glimpse of Warren getting off the chair. Zuzana deserved to know the truth. But what that truth was still escaped me.

'I honestly don't know what we were doing there,' I confessed. 'The only inkling I have of that afternoon is seeing Warren unloading the Ruthie's chair.' My thoughts turned to wanting to call out to him, something I chose not to share. 'I know that's no help to you, but for the life of me, I can't remember anything else. I wish I knew more, but I don't. I'm so sorry.'

And then she fell apart. At first I thought she might hit me, she looked so angry. She was shaking with her hands balled up into fists at her sides. But after a long minute, the fists loosened and she raised her hands to her face and started sobbing, her narrow shoulders heaving in a way that made me wish the carbon monoxide had finished the job the avalanche hadn't. When she finally stopped crying, she raised her blond head and tucked the loose strands of hair behind her ears. She reached for the tissues set beside the bed and blew her nose noisily.

Her voice was so quiet it was almost a whisper. 'It's just so hard to believe he's gone.' She placed a hand on her slim abdomen in her tight jeans. 'Did you know we were pregnant? He was so excited about this baby.'

Now I really wanted to die. It wasn't as if she were dropping a bombshell. Warren shared the news with me when he learned a couple of weeks before. At first he seemed apprehensive about it. His kids from his first marriage were already popping out grandkids and here he was becoming a father again. But over the last week or so, he'd seemed to grow into accepting it. I mean, it wasn't as if having another child could cramp his lifestyle in any way. Not with his kind of money.

But not even his kind of money could replace a human being and give a child a living father. Knowing all about being raised without a father made it doubly horrific for me. To think this baby might never know its father because of my recklessness was intolerable.

'You really don't remember?' she probed.

My only answer was to shake my head slowly back and forth.

'I mean, if I had some idea why he was there, I might be able to come to terms with it. Did he die because he saw some ski run he couldn't resist? Was it a mistake on his part or was making his all-important first tracks on a run more important than me and the baby? That's all I'm saying.'

Once again, I was unable to offer an answer.

She walked to the edge of the room and stood in the open door. 'If you ever do remember, you'll tell me.' It was a command, not a request, although a justifiable one.

'I promise.'

'Not knowing is almost as bad as his death.'

And then she was gone, leaving me in my misery, grief and guilt. Zuzana was the kind of woman I wanted to dislike, all soft and pretty and girly in many ways – like needing help buckling her boots and putting on her skis. In spite of her beauty and her neediness, I had warmed to her. She was clever, a great wit, and could spear you without you even knowing it – which she was prone to do from time to time – then look over with a wink and a nod. Warren loved her very much, as much as he loved skiing, which was no small statement.

The crazy thing was, they were about as unlikely a match as possible since Warren lived to ski and Zuzana tolerated it so she could lunch on the mountain in the private club and wear thousand-dollar ski outfits. She had grown up in Prague just after the fall of communism, and hadn't had a lot of material goods, which seemed to have translated to an unnatural need for nice things now. Living in a city, she had never skied, and as much as Warren loved Zuzana and encouraged her to learn, he told me she just didn't get it. She'd run through a phalanx of the best ski instructors money could buy, and couldn't advance past the easiest runs on the mountain. Skiing just wasn't in her DNA. She was so unsure of herself she always took the gondola down from the top of the hill so she wouldn't have to ski the more challenging runs at the base of the mountain.

But as poor a skier as she was, heads would turn at the beautiful blond without a helmet, her hair streaming behind her as her slim body and voluptuous bosom skied the same run over and over. As her latest ski instructor, Reese Chambers, once said, or probably said more than once, 'With a body like that, she doesn't need to ski.' In light of Warren's death, she wouldn't have to ski anymore and now I wondered if she would ever brave the slopes again.

I was dressed and had almost recovered from Zuzana's visit when Dr Larsen came in to release me. As he stood above me going over a checklist, I couldn't help but notice a sort of emerald glow in his green eye, enhanced by his green scrubs, while the brown one remained a deep chestnut color. He finished up and asked me if I had any questions.

'Not about the carbon monoxide poisoning, but I'm really bugged about this memory loss from the avalanche. I feel like a piece of my brain has gone missing.'

'That's very common in a trauma situation,' he said in an assuring voice. 'Don't sweat it. It's your subconscious trying to protect you by blocking out an unpleasant event.'

'I'm finding it even more unpleasant that I can't remember it. How long before my memory comes back?'

'Could be days. Could be weeks.' Then to my dismay he added, 'Or it could be never.'

Never. That was a reality I didn't want to face.

The disturbing idea that I may never know what happened that day dominated my consciousness as he wheeled me to the hospital entrance. Before turning me over to Judy, who was waiting at the lobby for the second time in as many days, he reminded me it wasn't a good idea to stay alone tonight. I told him I would keep his advice in mind. Looking me directly in the eye in a manner more personal than doctorly, he added, 'Please be careful, Greta.'

Snow was falling in a soft, insulating curtain as Judy and I walked across the parking lot, accumulating on our shoulders and in our hair and on our eyelashes before we even reached the car.

'You're staying with us tonight. No argument,' she stated as we climbed into the Prius.

'All right, one night,' I pretended to concede, though truth be told I was glad not to be spending the night alone in the A-frame. Not only was I taking Dr Larsen at his word, the furnace issue had me creeped out and was one I preferred to confront in the daylight.

We drove into town and turned on to the road up to Red Mountain and the homes of some of the wealthiest inhabitants of this planet. As we rose higher Aspen Mountain was directly across from us and you could see the end of the day skiers descending the lower part of the mountain. The upper half was buried in a cloud. The lingering effects of the CO left me feeling peculiar, and my heart was heavy at the loss of Warren, one memory that didn't want to recede. But just staring at that mountain was a balm, leaving me feeling that if I could just get on my boards for a couple of hours, everything would be OK.

While Judy chatted about what we would have for dinner – maybe some risotto and salmon with a good pinot noir – my eyes stayed glued to the mountain I loved so much and my thoughts turned back to the early days of my arrival.

# SIX

After Mom died, and Toby left to pursue his dream of becoming an army ranger, I was alone in the Milwaukee house. At first I was angry with my twin for deserting me, but as time passed I came to terms with it. He'd been holding off on his own life for too long while Mom was ill. It was time for him to move on. I'd held off on my life too, dropping out of college the end of my freshman year while she battled breast cancer. When she lost that battle two years later, her death left me without purpose.

Untethered and with no real direction, I took a job waitressing to both support me and to fill my days. Most of my high-school friends were away at college except for the ones who had married after high school and were already facing responsibilities that far exceeded their maturity, like having children. Waitressing was something to do, for the most part mindless, and the money was good. Most of the time the people were pretty fair.

But one January night that all turned on its head. Nothing I could do was right and all the customers could do was complain. The service was slow, the table was drafty, the food was bad. Everyone I served seemed determined to be unhappy. In retrospect I can't say I blamed them. January in Milwaukee is gray and windy and damp and bone-chillingly cold. Like twenty below cold. Milwaukee in January is a miserable place to be.

But amid all the dissatisfied customers, there was this table of three well-dressed couples who had just been in Aspen. They were talking about how charming the town was and how the snow was powder soft and how the sun came out nearly every day. That it was probably the greatest place in the country. That if winter was always like Aspen winter it would be their favorite season.

I'd skied in Wisconsin when I was a teenager and joined the

after-school ski club. And, as cold and gray and frostbite-
threatening as skiing could be in the Midwest, I'd loved it. But
when Mom got sick and couldn't work anymore, there wasn't
extra money for luxuries like skiing. I'd missed it terribly.

After dialing in to what they'd said about Aspen and how
great it was, I couldn't stop thinking about it the rest of the
night. With Mom and Toby gone there was nothing to keep
me in Milwaukee, and I really longed to experience something
more exciting in my life than the bland Midwest. I'd always
been a reader and had been enamored of far-off places in
books, places I'd never seen but only dreamed about. Though
Colorado was less than a thousand miles away, that was far
away for me. My mind was set to take on the first adventure
of my life.

When my shift ended, I took off my apron and announced
to my boss, 'I'm moving to Aspen.'

And that's how it happened. One chance encounter changed
my entire life. Just like that I picked up and left. Well, not
really just like that. I had to pack up and make arrangements
to sell the house Mom and Toby and I had shared for most
of my life. Which turned out to be so mortgaged to the gills
that there was little equity in it.

But there was some money, so the day the house sale closed,
I headed west with all my worldly goods in my car and my
savings of forty-two hundred dollars in my wallet. After
twenty-four hours of windy, icy, snow-scrubbed plains, deep-
cut canyons and slick mountain passes, my ten-year-old Corolla
chugged into the small town on the western slope of the
Rockies known as Aspen, Colorado.

It's no exaggeration when I say it felt like a dream. I was
Dorothy arriving in Oz. It was just after dawn and the sight
of Victorian buildings and miners' shacks and brick vintage
buildings rendered me awestruck. The mountains encircled the
small town like a possessive lover pouring down to her very
edge. The snow-packed streets radiated Christmas card charm
in the morning glow, a century-old courthouse and church
sidling up to the main street. If there was heaven on earth, I'd
found it. I knew then and there, I was never going back to
Milwaukee.

However, there was one little curveball I hadn't foreseen. Actually, a big curveball. As things turned out, I wasn't the first person to decide upon making a life change by moving to Aspen. Amid the millionaires and billionaires existed an entire culture just barely getting by in order to share in this little piece of heaven. Some were seasonal ski bums, some of them more hopeful, looking to make Aspen a home. Whichever the case, housing was in short supply.

It didn't take much asking around to realize that I was swimming upstream if I thought I could just land in paradise and start a life. I walked into several real estate offices in search of a place to rent, and they shook their heads and choked back laughs. There was nowhere for someone like me to live. Was my dream to die so quickly? I was totally demoralized, but when I'm demoralized I also get hungry.

I stopped for lunch in a restaurant named Little Annie's whose western-clad front suggested it might be affordable, and it almost was. Sitting at a table drumming my fingers as I waited for my meal, my mind was working on how I was going to be able to stay in this newfound paradise. And it was coming up with no answers. My hamburger and Coke arrived and the server lay them on the table in front of me. When she asked if she could get me anything else, I lost it and burst into tears. For the entire time my mother was sick, I'd never cried. Not once. I'd only cried at her funeral. But suddenly the pressure of not having a life, of not having anyone or anything, of lost hope, had broken me. Trying to make it in this place that appealed to all my dreams was like trying to make a one-nighter into a marriage. But if I didn't stay here, where was I to go? I was twenty-one with nothing and no one.

Without a word, the waitress slid into the booth beside me and put her arm around me. As embarrassing as it was, I turned my head into her shoulder and cried like a small child. When I got my act together enough to share my troubles with her, she shook her head knowingly.

'We've all been where you are in this town, trust me. I think I can help solve your problem. You said you have some money. You're not flat out.'

I nodded, blinking back miserable, embarrassed tears. 'I have around four thousand dollars.'

'No shit. You're better off than most of us who land here. And this is your lucky day because there's a bed coming available in the house where I'm living.' It just so happened she was living in a mid-sixties three-bedroom with a rent of $10,000 a month. Unbeknownst to the landlord, there were ten of them crammed into it. One of her roommates was moving in with her boyfriend and with one fewer contributor they were going to have trouble coming up with the rent money, so I was invited to make my home on the living-room couch for the rest of the season.

At first the thought of sleeping in a house with that many people was mortifying. My life thus far had been so small and insulated. I had done little other than take care of my mother, go to school and get good grades. I decided I should give it a chance. There was nothing to lose.

The waitress was Judy, and not only did she find me my first place to live, she also found me my first job. Aside from working at Little Annie's, she worked as a cocktail waitress at the Bugaboo, a hip private club that catered to three groups: the rich, the richer, and beautiful women. The woman whose place I was taking on the couch had just quit her job as coat-check girl there. She'd scored big at the 'Bug', as they called the club, and was now going to live with one of the rich patrons she'd met there. He'd made it clear he didn't want his girlfriend working as a coat checker. Which worked out fine for me. My only wish was that she would have been one of the girls sleeping in a room with a door.

Working at the Bugaboo was a real eye-opener. It didn't take long to figure out the inverse relationship between how rich a guy was, regardless of how old or unattractive, with how beautiful the woman accompanying him was. Anyhow, I worked nights at the Bug and skied during the days, taking every lesson I could so that by the end of that first season I'd become a competent skier. By the next year I was teaching skiing at the beginning levels and getting better and better myself. And while I should have been a good teacher, because I had all the skills and the teaching ability needed, I fell a little short in one category essential for teaching a sport like skiing to the uninitiated.

I didn't understand fear.

I didn't realize my lack of fear when I was young. There was nothing to test it. I liked sports well enough, and did the usual childhood things like ride bikes and play sports. But I never knew how practically fearless I was until I saw fear manifest itself in other people. I could stand at the top of the steepest run and instead of thinking what might happen if I fell, I was invigorated by the thought of conquering it instead of it conquering me. I imagine Toby and I share the same genes in that way. He's been in and out of the Middle East so many times in the past years he should be wearing robes instead of camo. But he's the same way. Instead of fearing danger, he embraces it. Only his is of an entirely different kind.

Funny, but while I wouldn't have called my mom adventurous at all while we were growing up, I now realize you can't get much braver than raising two kids on your own.

Now after spending fifteen years in Aspen, my devotion to the town was the same as Sam's had been. I thought the only way I was going to leave Aspen was post-mortem. But in the aftermath of Warren's death, my feelings had been challenged. What happened? I asked myself again and again. But the answer continued to evade me and for the very first time since driving into town all those years ago, I wondered if it might be time to move on from this place I loved so dearly.

# SEVEN

After sharing the earlier described meal of salmon and risotto with Judy and Gene, accompanied by an excellent Pinot Noir, which I declined on doctor's advice to avoid alcohol for twenty-four hours, I spent a restless night in one of their eight guest rooms. The next morning, Judy had her hot-yoga class, so Gene drove me home in his Range Rover. Gene is such a super nice guy you hardly notice he is super rich. He and Judy met at the Bugaboo when she spilled an entire tray of drinks on him, and instead of being really angry that his right side was soaked with glue-like Amaretto, he asked her for her phone number. Little had he known she did it on purpose. The rest is history.

A High Mountain Heating and Cooling van was parked along the side of the cul-de-sac, a ladder propped up against my slanted roof. Jack Johnson stood atop the ladder feeding something into the metal duct that pierced the shingled roof. Though the temperature was in the twenties, he wore shorts and the sinewy muscles of his calves flexed as he leaned his toes into the building while he worked.

'Yo, Greta, you gotta start getting your chimney cleaned a little more often,' he called down when he saw me standing at the base of the ladder. 'You should see the shit I'm pulling out of here.' He tossed down a handful of pine needles as well as a few actual pinecones. The matter landed at my feet. 'This kind of stuff can back up the flue and the next thing you know you got a one-way upload to you know where. Or download . . . depending,' he added.

'You cleaned it last winter, in case you don't remember. Just hadn't gotten around to it yet this year.' I looked down at what he had thrown at my feet. It didn't look like much. 'You telling me this was enough to put my life in danger?'

His arm disappeared into the stack. A moment later he

pulled something the size of a softball out of the chimney. 'No, but this is.'

He tossed it down to me. It was a bird's nest. Both of our eyes went skyward to the huge blue spruce that abutted the house. 'It was super windy up here on Saturday night. Must've blown free and plopped straight into your chimney. What're the odds?'

Saturday. The day of the slide. Evidently, the gods weren't favoring me that day. Or maybe they were. I was still alive. Warren wasn't.

He took a long last look down the chimney and climbed back down the ladder. 'All good now. I put a new screen on top. The old one must have come off. That's how all that junk managed to find its way in in the first place.'

'What do you mean the old one came off?'

'Wasn't here. Maybe it blew off or an animal messed with it. If you'd called me in before the season I would have caught it.' He wiped his hands on his shorts. 'Anyhow, problem solved. I'll go and fire her up to be sure.'

He went into the house while I stood outside staring up at the ancient spruce scratching the winter blue sky. I recalled sitting on a lawn chair reading with Kayla at my side last summer while an industrious gray jay built her nest, inexhaustible as she transported twigs to prepare a fine home for her eggs. After the chicks had hatched, she resumed her never-ending cycle of flying back and forth, this time transporting unfortunate worms to the ravenous beaks above. And then one day, just as the surrounding Aspens in the grove had started to turn gold, I noticed there was no more activity above. Both the mother and the chicks were gone. Just like that.

I couldn't find it in me to blame the mother jay for my near-death experience. She was a classic example of nature at work and the life cycle. Luckily it hadn't cycled for me.

Jack came out of the house rubbing his hands together in a way that indicated his task was finished. 'Working fine now,' he said. 'I put new batteries in your CO detector and all should be good.' He hesitated, his sea-green eyes flashing a bit impishly from his tan, weathered face. 'Want me to hang around a while to make sure? We could, uh, test the air with some deep breathing.'

'Jack,' I scolded. 'In your dreams.'

He gave me that smirk I used to know so well, and for a moment I was tempted. Looking at him in his shorts and blue fleece jacket, my mind travelled back to what that body looked like when the clothes were removed. Lean without an ounce of extra flesh. Every inch iron-like muscle. This was a man who could scale the Bells with two packs. Jack was my first lover in Aspen, that first season in Aspen. But Jack never quite understood that being with someone exclusively meant there wasn't room for a third party. He had long enjoyed the easy sex life that comes along with living in a resort – pretty young girls looking for fun or mature women looking for a holiday romance – and he was beyond curing on that matter. We had parted friends.

'Suit yourself, Greta,' he said with absolutely no malice. 'Don't forget, bad things come in threes. Let's see. Avalanche, CO . . .'

'Yah, well letting you stay might just be that number three,' I sniped back.

He folded up his ladder and secured it to the top of his truck. He gave me a quick slap on the bottom before driving off, leaving me alone in the snowy lane. Three white-tailed mule deer sauntered out of the woods and walked along the edge of the glade undisturbed by my presence. I watched until they blended into the trees on the other side.

I glanced back up at the spruce tree and then the chimney. A strong gust of wind rattled the tree and the fir needles moved in synch with the branches as they bowed to the wind. Seemed to me that a strong wind like that would blow a nest away from the house and not on to it.

I went into the house with Jack's words ringing in my ears. What were the odds?

# EIGHT

I slept better than I was entitled to, considering all that had come to pass of late. But it just felt so good to be back in my home. I decided not to give the furnace another thought. I knew enough of how things worked from tinkering on things with Toby as a kid. We always wanted to save Mom money, and so we could fix just about anything from the bulb that floated in a toilet to a broken garbage disposal. I understood what had caused the furnace to malfunction, and that had been solved, so there was no reason to worry about being asphyxiated in my sleep. Just as disaster didn't affect my eating, it usually didn't affect my sleep either. But since the avalanche my sleep had been spotty, and I woke frequently during the night thinking of Warren's death. I wanted so much for it to be that nightmare that you wake from in the middle of the night relieved when you realize it's only a dream. Unfortunately, this nightmare was here to stay.

I remember visiting my mother in the hospital when she was dying, when her breast cancer had metastasized to stage four and all hope was gone. Toby and I wanted to bring her home to die, to the small house with the big mortgage she had so cleverly decorated on a hairdresser's budget, but she refused. Even in death she had that Scandinavian practicality. She didn't want us to have to listen to her moan at night. For the entire week she hinged on death, Toby and I would spend the day at her side, returning home only after the drugs finally put her to sleep. I would scarf down a quick meal and hit the rack, lapsing into unconsciousness the moment my head touched the pillow. My brother didn't have the same constitution as I in that regard. He wasn't able to eat a thing, losing five pounds and barely sleeping, pacing the halls into the early morning hours until her end came.

Neither one of us was much like her. While I never doubted her love for us, she was practical to the point of boring, a demanding mother who could make us behave with a cool look. She was beautiful when we were small, with creamy skin and blond hair and the ubiquitous blue eyes of a Swede, before illness and too much sun and alcohol turned her dry and crinkled. Both Toby and I must have gotten our looks from our father, whoever he was, because while I inherited my unmanageable blond curls from my mother, my eyes are a dark brown and my skin borders on olive. The same for my twin. His thick blond hair is the color of the sun, but his eyes are black bullets.

I lay in bed trying not to think of Warren when my stomach started to growl. It dawned on me I hadn't eaten a good meal since leaving Judy's yesterday morning. Dinner last night had been the same as a couple of days prior, Triscuits and cheese, only this time I'd substituted a couple of glasses of Pinot Grigio for the Heineken. Since I wasn't ready to go back to work yet, I climbed down from the loft, got dressed and went outside to clean off the Wagoneer for a drive into town.

Though it was sunny, it had snowed during the night, and the blanket of snow burying my car had grown to nearly three feet. The car made a couple false starts and turned over on the third try. I left it running to defrost while I shoveled it out. My car was a true sixties vehicle, only rusted through in a few places. I probably should have turned her in for a newer model, but just like the Barcalounger, it was Sam's and so it was sacrosanct. Besides, it was built like a tank, able to make it down the half-mile road in all conditions, the plow in front assuring my way when deep snow made it questionable.

And anyway, I didn't want to lay out any dough for a new car. I had better uses for my money. My biggest dream was to climb Everest. Several of the guys and one of the other girls on patrol had done it, and it had become one of my quests. However, not only was the 29,029-foot peak a physical challenge, it was a financial one, costing around thirty-five thousand dollars for the bare-bones climb. Every spare penny I put aside was earmarked for the Everest trip.

It was toasty warm in the Wagoneer by the time I finished cleaning it off. Halfway down the road, I noticed the deer again, their cotton-white tails still as their lowered heads

scoured the snow for sustenance. One buck lifted his head as
the Wagoneer drove past and looked at the car with little
interest as if it were just another woodland creature, sinking
his head right back into the snow once the vehicle was past.
Part of my passion for where I live is getting close-up views
of mule deer and fox and bear and, every once in a while, a
rogue moose. The moose were the only ones to truly fear.
They were skittish and territorial and lightning quick. A moose
could turn on you and stomp you before you knew it. More
than once, I'd had to scoop my barking sixty-pound dog into
my arms and carry her inside to avoid a particularly angry
moose's ire.

Aside from the moose, with the other animals it was
live and let live. Even the bears. They just wanted to be left
alone, although I had to be scrupulous not to leave any hints
of food. Bears were notorious for breaking and entering when
they suspected sustenance on the other side of a door or
window. Kayla used to bark like she was possessed whenever
a bear approached the house, which was usually enough to
drive them off. But Kayla wasn't there anymore, meaning I
was going to have to be more vigilant.

Pushing back memories of lost humans and lost animals, I
turned on to Highway 82 and headed into town.

It's difficult to be in City Market without seeing someone
you know. Aspen is, after all, a small town despite its large
reputation. It's also a town accustomed to celebrity, so people
generally turn a blind eye when encountering the famous. I
wish I could have said the same applied to me this morning.
My fame had preceded me, my bad luck in the slide making
the front-page days prior with a half-page shot of the slide
and a photo of a smiling Warren inserted in the bottom. The
carbon monoxide incident appeared this morning, the headline
screaming at me from a stack of papers near the door. SKI
PATROLLER OVERCOME BY CARBON MONOXIDE.
Then a smaller headline beneath: ESCAPES AVALANCHE
TO NEARLY DIE AT HOME. At least three people in produce
congratulated me on being alive, deftly avoiding any mention
of Warren's death. I grabbed a bunch of bananas and navigated

my way out with my head down, hoping I could get the rest of my groceries without any more undesired recognition.

That wish was short-lived as I guided my cart into the dairy section and nearly ran into the tall, lanky body of the store's general manager, Bruff Horner. He'd been at City Market as long as I had been in town and he could be seen just about any day riding his scooter into work in just about any kind of weather from his employee housing unit on the edge of town where he lived with his family. We'd dated a few times when I first moved to Aspen, long before he met his wife and settled down. Like I said, it's a small town, especially among the worker bees, and people overlap. He was unloading a crate of milk and he stopped what he was doing upon seeing me.

'Sorry about your run of bad luck, Greta,' he said sincerely. I was surprised, because as much as I liked Bruff, he was notorious for saying something inappropriate whenever possible. Such as 'when's the baby due?' to an unfortunate woman with a larger abdomen. I tried to steer around him, but between the cart and his body, the way was blocked.

'I'm kind of in a hurry and I really don't want to talk about it right now,' I said, trying to work my way past him.

He pushed his glasses up on his nose and brushed an errant strand of gray hair from his forehead. 'Yeah, well I wouldn't buy any green bananas if I were you. These things tend to come in threes.'

What did I say about inappropriate? Or had he been talking to Jack? My torture ended when an announcement over the public address system called him to customer service. Torture came anew as I found myself wheeling down the pet-food aisle out of habit and realizing there was nothing for me to buy in that section anymore.

I was almost finished checking out at the self-service when the automatic doors behind me slid open and Joel Simpson stepped into the store. Joel was Sam's son. I'd seen him more in the two years since Sam died than in the prior five. Dealing with Joel at this point would rank with recovering from an ACL repair. I'd already been down that route and, believe me, it's slow, tedious and painful.

Joel had gotten divorced since Sam died and was living in

Vail with his mother. When he reared his head in Aspen from time to time, he nearly always went out of his way to make me miserable, like it was my fault that Sam died and left me the house in the life estate. And it wasn't like Sam had over-looked his kids entirely. He had socked away a few hundred thousand dollars in his eighty-five years and left both his son and his daughter a buck and a half. His daughter Josie, married and living in New York, had been fine with that. It hadn't been enough for Joel and he'd sued me over the property a couple of times. He'd given up after losing the second time, but my victory was bittersweet since legal fees had set my Everest trip nest egg back considerably. The last two times I'd seen him, he'd changed his tactics from trying to get me out to trying to get me to sell the place to him. And you can see how far he'd got with that.

I kept my head down in hopes he wouldn't see me, but my bad luck was determined to prevail. He called out my name, which left me no option other than to turn and acknowledge him.

'Greta,' he said in the sort of voice you hear from a cop as you're lowering the driver's side window. 'Taking a day off?'

'Joel,' I replied with equal enthusiasm. 'Yah, even patrol takes a day from time to time. Now might be the time for you to straight-line S1.' With a pitch around forty degrees, S1 is the steepest run on Aspen Mountain, I hasten to add.

'Don't ever let anyone tell you you're not funny. Cuz you are. Really.'

'Thanks. I'll call you when I decide to do stand-up so you can come and harass me.' I loaded my groceries into my canvas sack. Plastic bags are prohibited in Aspen grocery stores. That's just another one of the cutting-edge things about the town. Aspen was one of the first cities in the country to prohibit smoking in restaurants, and it's against the law to let a car idle more than a minute in town. After an ill-fated attempt to outlaw the sale of fur it only made sense that we'd attack the plastic bag. You only need to see the flotilla of them in the ocean to understand the rationale behind that. Patrons were obliged to bring their own bag to the store or shell out five cents for a paper one. And can you believe there were actually visitors who complained about paying five cents for a paper bag in a town where the average house price hovered around $3,000,000 and a day ski pass went for $180? I stuffed the last of my food into my reusable bag and slipped it on to my shoulder.

'Adios,' I said flippantly and headed for the door. He followed me out, close as an evening shadow.

'Wait, I want to talk to you about the house.' The fact that he hadn't mentioned either the avalanche or my near death by asphyxiation told me he wasn't aware of either. Which also told me he must have just arrived in town.

'What about it?' I asked, opening the car door and piling the groceries on to the back seat.

'I want to make another offer.'

This time I turned and faced him directly. He was a good-looking guy with dark curly hair and a mild cleft in his chin. There was a lot of Sam in his face, the determined mouth and stubborn brow knit over his transparent blue eyes. But the part of Sam he lacked was kindness in his eyes. His pupils were pinpricks riveted on me from above. He was also a tall man. I'm five eight and I stared back at him from the height of his shoulder. Which my gloved hand threatened to poke before its owner managed to restrain it. 'You can just forget about me leaving that house, OK? I'm not going anywhere.'

'Look, I've talked with Josie and we're willing to give you a million bucks.'

'Forget about it, Joel.' I was smoking pissed. 'Look, maybe we could have talked about this if you'd made an offer before suing my ass. Too late now. Subject closed.' I slammed the heavy door shut and pulled out of the lot.

As I drove up valley, the houses gave way to snow-covered meadows until I reached the pine-lined entrance to my road. The entire way I was wondering where Joel would ever come up with a million dollars. Then I realized he probably already had some developer lined up to buy the property off him for five times that. I let myself play around with the idea of having a million dollars. Anywhere else in the world it might be serious coinage. But in Aspen it was chump change. There was so much money in Aspen that you'd be hard-pressed to find someone who'd bend over to pick up one of the hundies that spit out of the cash station at the foot of the gondola. In Aspen a million bucks will barely buy you a one-bedroom in the local tenements and having that much money basically makes you ineligible for the subsidized employee housing.

I thought back to the housing shuffle I'd endured in the years prior to taking up residence in the A-frame with Sam. Air mattresses in basement dormitories and futons in entry halls. Often three or more to a room. Sometimes you scored with housesitting at one of the big houses in the off season, which made going back to cramped living quarters even more distasteful. I'd lasted through those years despite the inconvenience. We all did. Those of us who loved Aspen were stuck to it like flies on a glue strip, and there was no way of shaking us loose.

Selling to Joel would mean I would have to move someplace else for a million bucks to seem like a million bucks. And since I had little interest in money anyway, except to get to Everest, a million bucks held little appeal to me. Even if Joel offered me five million dollars, there was no way I was selling my home to him. And so any thought of leaving Aspen was put to rest for the time being.

Joel had gotten me so aggravated that it wasn't until I pulled on to my road that the coincidence of the bird's nest in my chimney and Joel's presence two days later occurred to me. Maybe it wasn't a coincidence after all.

It was an incredibly lonely night, my only company Ovid and his whimsical gods. We were three weeks into the winter term, and since I'd already missed a class because of my various pitfalls of the prior week, disturbing as they were, I had some catching up to do. As far as I could tell, the Greeks had it all over us when it came to violence and debauchery. Take Jupiter for example, or Zeus as the Romans called him. He was always turning himself into one animal or another so he could have his way with various women without his wife, who also happened to be his sister, catching on. One time he actually changed himself into a swan so he could screw a woman named Leda. Try wrapping your brain around that image.

What's more, Leda then went on to give birth to Helen of Troy, the most beautiful woman in the world. Jeez, you can't make this stuff up.

I fell asleep with the light on and the book on my chest and woke to the sound of something rattling below my window. I swiftly turned out the light and waited for my eyes to adjust to the dark. My heart was beating in an erratic manner that told me I was frightened. I'd been living alone in the house for two years now and had never been fearful before. Then I realized that my life had changed a lot in the last two weeks. Two weeks ago Kayla had been around to notify me of anything lurking in the dark; one week ago I'd never been in an avalanche; two days ago I'd given no thought to carbon monoxide poisoning. I was rightfully skittish. Once I could see, I pushed my face against the window. A thick snow was falling, drawing a white curtain across my yard. But through the white I could make out a dark figure moving low to the ground, skittering across the yard. It was a raccoon in retreat, its attempt to access my trash can thwarted by a bear-proof lock. This is the nature that I live in and love.

I put Ovid on the nightstand and pulled the down comforter tight around my neck. I thought of the gods and their whimsical nature and wondered if I was victim of their whimsy as of late. For the hundredth time I tried to reconstruct the afternoon of the avalanche. I remembered Neverman telling me to clean out the ski patrol shack at the top of Ruthie's. Then there was my glimpse of Warren getting off the chair. The urge to follow him. Once again, my memory remained shuttered from there no matter how hard I mentally banged the lock.

I stared at the ceiling in the dark for a long time before finally going back to sleep.

# NINE

Neverman had told me to come back to work when I was ready and the next morning I was. It had snowed all night and there was about a foot and a half of fresh snow outside, the entire world layered in white as the snow continued to fall. There was no sense spending one more day as a shut-in while the rest of my world was enjoying God's bequest. I climbed down from the loft, got dressed and took my patrol jacket off the hook for the first time in nearly a week.

When I went outside the Wagoneer looked like a long, square igloo parked at the side of the building. I dug her out, tossed my ski boots into the back and fired her up. It was still snowing as we turned on to Highway 82. As usual, this high up the valley there were no other vehicles in sight. The road had already been plowed, but a good amount of new snow had already accumulated, turning the surface into a frosted white pancake.

When I got to town, I pulled into my regular parking place at a condominium complex near the mountain. I was lucky to have the spot; the manager was a friend. Otherwise getting in from the A-frame for work would have been problematic. Paid parking was not only expensive, it was practically non-existent. At the early-morning hour, the three-block walk to the gondola from my car was as deserted as the highway had been. Aspen Mountain wouldn't open to the public for another couple of hours, but the lift was already running to shuttle staff up the hill.

With my best powder skis buried on the west side of the mountain, I went into my storage locker at the base to retrieve another pair. Our equipment is our stock in trade and we patrollers all have several pairs of skis – some all-round skis, some for icy conditions, some for powder. I grabbed my second-best pair of powder skis and climbed the stairs to the gondola. I jumped into an empty cabin, relieved to see no one else waiting to board. I really wasn't in the mood for talking. Snow had blown in through an open vent, so I brushed off the seat and settled in for the fifteen-minute ride to the top.

In the Rockies the weather can change in an instant, and the clouds parted the very moment the gondola car left the terminal, although tufts of deep metal gray looming on the horizon forewarned of another storm. The clearing sky afforded me views to the east toward Independence Pass near where I lived and west toward the airport where the valley flattens out. My eyes turned downward to the confluence of ski runs flowing down the mountain below. To me they represented an artistic sort of beauty. To my way of thinking, Aspen Mountain, sometimes called Ajax after one of the mines that operated here, is as near to skiing perfection as you can get.

The ski area encompasses a pair of ridges covering some of the best inbounds ski terrain in the country. There are expert and intermediate runs, but nothing for the beginner. For that we send skiers off to Buttermilk or Snowmass. Aspen can be a tricky mountain to ski if you don't know it. Locals have secret routes replete with powder stashes that the less informed skier might miss. If you understood the mountain, you could take run after run on only one chairlift ride, working with gravity to pull you up the side of the mountain again and again like a sailboat tacking into the wind.

Gazing down at nature's amusement park, I was struck by the irony that the slopes we so enjoyed basically existed because of the town's mining history. When silver miners seeking their fortune came to the valley in the 1880s, they denuded the mountain of trees, using the lumber to line the mine shafts below. The irony was that in doing so, they carved out perfect ski runs set smack atop a Swiss-cheese maze of underground shafts and stopes.

I was startled back to the present by an explosion, the concussion displacing the airwaves in the gondola like an extra heartbeat. Patrol was at work. An important part of our job was doing avalanche control to make the area safe for skiers, setting off bombs in areas that had accumulated snow that could slide. The explosion prompted yet another recall of the slide outside Ruthie's, and my eyes swelled with tears of frustration, both for the loss of Warren and from my ignorance of what we were doing there in the first place. More than anything in this world I wanted to know why, not knowing if the answer would put me out of this agony or make it worse.

The gondola reached the sheltered terminal at the top of the mountain and the doors slid open. I grabbed my skis from the rack and walked along the front of the Sundeck restaurant where the employees were prepping for the morning breakfast crush. The patrol hut was situated directly across from the Sundeck, a two-story building little changed from when it was built in the early years of skiing in Aspen, when super-long wooden skis ruled and spiral fractures caused by wind-milling skis attached to safety straps were as common as breaks from smacking into trees.

There were about a dozen patrollers in the hut if you didn't count Neverman, who was tuning his skis on a table in the workshop with his back to the door. I slipped past him into the main room where a fire was roaring in the old stone fireplace and the other patrollers sat on sixties-era furniture, chatting and drinking coffee. A profound silence fell over the room when everyone saw me. Meghan slipped me a sympathetic smile and came over to give me a hug. There was a momentary lull and then the others followed suit, Stu Reininger and Darren Cole giving me slaps on the shoulder, Rob Winter cuffing my gloves in a sign of solidarity. Singh was the last, wrapping his arms around me and holding me tight, his gesture nearly suffocating. Lucy, as always, kept to herself, giving me a subtle flick of her hand.

Neverman came out to see what all the fuss was about and upon seeing me went right back into the workshop, back to tuning his skis as if nothing had changed. As expected, my name was nowhere on the day's roster, which was no surprise because I hadn't alerted anyone that I was coming back. I poured myself a cup of coffee and grabbed a muffin from the perpetual stack piled on the table and plopped down on a bench to wait for my boss to come back.

The others finished what they were doing and, as if by mandate, one by one they buckled up their boots and evacuated the hut, leaving Neverman and me alone. I sat waiting while he used an iron to melt hot wax on to his skis to ensure they were just right for the day's conditions. He brushed a ski with a rag, tested the sharpness of the edge with a fingernail, and wiped his hands off on his ski pants. He turned to face me, taking in my uniform as if it were a surprise.

'Sure you're OK to work?' he asked simply.

'I'm a little banged up. Some bruises. Nothing like the time I bounced face first down Elevator Shaft.'

'I'm not talking about the slide. I'm talking about that other thing.' Even Neverman read the local papers.

'Oh, you mean the carbon monoxide?'

'That's right. How's your mental acuity?'

'No dumber than before,' I acquiesced, wondering if he would have asked one of the guys the same thing.

He took a deep breath and sized me up like a physician deciding whether or not to share the diagnosis. Finally, he shrugged and said, 'Go with Singh.'

I put on my helmet, grabbed my fanny pack filled with supplies and was out the door before he could change his mind.

Singh was just stepping into his skis. His name tag read A. Singh, but while I called Reininger Stu or Neverman Mike on occasion, no one ever called Singh anything other than Singh. I don't even know if anyone really knew Singh's first name. He'd told me once, but it was so unpronounceable I just continued calling him Singh. 'Sing with an h' he was always quick to say when asked his name.

Born in Delhi, Singh came to the US to do his graduate studies at Stanford. That was before having the bad or good luck, depending on how you viewed it, to come to Aspen on spring break his first year. It was his first time on skis, first time seeing snow for that matter, and the love affair was so immediate that all thought of becoming an engineer was shot to hell. He quit school and moved to Aspen. Eighteen years later, Singh was not only one of the most beautiful skiers on patrol, but definitely the smartest.

He was tall with dark hair and dark eyes, his creamy brown skin a nod to some European intervention into his gene pool.

It bordered on comical to see the look on some victims' faces when Singh came skiing up. I guess they didn't think of Indians as ski pros. But that look changed when he started attending to them. Maybe they thought they had an educated doctor taking care of them instead of a ski bum.

'It's me and you today if you're down with that,' I probed.

'You and I?' he replied. He could be a grammatical stickler at times. 'Westerlind, you can have my back any time.'

His response took one layer off the fog and I immediately felt lighter. We skied over to Walsh's through thigh-deep powder and started down the steep slope. As my skis parted the snow every fiber of me was alive, the crisp air fresh on my face, my muscles alternately tensed and relieved as gravity drew me toward her bosom. My turns were perfectly carved Ss, linked curves along the fall line, the weight of the snow putting natural brakes on my speed. My mind was completely in the moment, in the motion, in the snow.

All problems ceased to exist. Skiing does that to you. The marriage of body and mind against ground and gravity takes you to a higher plane, focusing all thought, commanding all concentration on the physical action, not allowing room for other concerns.

We raced around the corner to the chair lift. There was a sort of redemption in being back in my element and, for the first time in days, I felt like things might start to get better. That thought turned out to be premature.

# TEN

The morning was uneventful, or as uneventful as far as accidents in eighteen inches of new powder can be. It's totally counterintuitive, but there seem to be fewer serious accidents on deep-snow days than on other days. I think it's because the good skiers know how to handle powder and the intermediates get intimidated when their skis bog down and they can't turn. They tire out early and pack it in. Which doesn't stop them from going back to Dallas or Atlanta or wherever and raving about the fantastic powder they skied in Aspen. Which is as it should be, a win-win for all. They get bragging rights and we get the mountain to ourselves.

It's the hard-pack icy days that keep us on our toes, running loaded toboggans down the hill and empty ones back up the gondola to strategically reposition for another pick-up on the hill. Warm, sunny hard-pack days are when people get too much confidence and gain too much speed, hurting themselves when they crash into an inanimate object like a tree or an animate object like a human being. Yep. Hard-pack days are the worst for patrol. Those are the days we end up doing double duty.

But don't get me wrong, powder days have their own particular injuries, more tears and sprains than breaks. And it was a powder day, the snow falling like crazy with no indication of stopping. Singh and I decided to make the best of it until we were called into duty. This was the sexy part of the job, getting to ski powder conditions before anyone else. We did some technical work, checked some closures, marked a few rocks that were now camouflaged by snow and opened some runs that had previously been closed. But mostly we just skied, ripping down the Dumps where the gulleys between the moguls had filled completely with pristine new snow, taking shortcuts on Bell Mountain past 'shrines' like Yankee Stadium and Marilyn Monroe, and hoping the entire time our radios wouldn't spoil the fun by calling us to some emergency. We passed a couple of boarders in the woods lighting up a doobie and stopped to chastise them, stoned skiing being frowned upon, as common as it was. One of the boarders got belligerent with me, so I confiscated his lighter, and slipped it into the pocket of my inner jacket just to irritate him.

On the Ridge of Bell, we spotted a skier who ejected out of his skis after coming off a big bump. Though he'd lost both boards, the snow was so deep he'd only found one of them. The other was nowhere to be seen. Our run of free-skiing good luck over, we stopped to help him. With the gondola passing silently overhead the three of us spent the next half-hour sidestepping up and down in the area of his fall, poking into the snow with our ski poles in search of his missing ski. We were just about to bag it, meaning a ride down on a snowmobile for him, when Singh cried out, 'Got something!'

'Dude, if it's my ski, I'm buying at the end of the day,' cried the now fairly exhausted skier.

Singh extracted a ski from a mound of snow. 'Kastle, right?'

Despite his wearing a helmet and goggles, I could see the skier's face fall.

'Fuck no. Mine's Dynastar. You gotta be shitting me.'

A broad white smile cracked Singh's dark face. 'Just kidding man.' With the ski in hand, he made two swooping turns and stopped within an inch of us. He handed the ski over and said, 'Get back out there, dude. You're missing the best.'

Once the grateful skier was on his way back down the hill, we cut across the ridge to the shoulder of the mountain and swooped down on to the intermediate run at the bottom where Reininger and Winter were stationed behind ropes, waving at skiers to slow them down. Had to be the worst duty on the mountain.

'Hey assholes, how about taking your turn?' Stu Reininger called to our backs as we whooshed past them in glee.

There was no line at the gondola, a harbinger of a powder day. People line up first thing in the morning to hit the powder before it's been tracked. Then they tend to ski the higher elevations until they fold in exhaustion. Singh and I climbed into our cabin and he took off his helmet. His hairline was wet with sweat. Skiing powder was hard work. He reached into his jacket pocket and pulled out a baggie of mini Snickers.

'Lunch?' he offered.

I had a stash of my own, poached from a bowl in the ski patrol hut. I extracted my bag from my jacket pocket and displayed it to him. 'Good to go.'

Snickers were our chosen lunch on powder days. Sugar and nuts just kept us going. Quick energy that kept us light on our skis. A big lunch just bogged you down. We munched in silence, looking out upon the slopes and drinking copious amounts of water from our Camelbaks. Five minutes passed before the inevitable conversation ensued.

'How you feeling, Greta?' Singh asked, looking me steadily in the eyes, not allowing me any escape.

'I'm fine. What do you mean?'

'C'mon, Greta. You've been through some weird shit this week. You wanna talk about it?'

There's one thing I failed to mention about Singh. I'm pretty sure he's gay. Which I would say doesn't really mean anything in the larger scheme of things, but I've just always found gay men easy to talk to. I mean, now that everyone's come out and everything and everyone is in complete understanding, it's not a big thing, but I happen to think gay men have a certain sensitivity I can't describe. Every gay man I've known has always been able to draw me out of myself in ways that my female friends or straight men just aren't able to.

I played with my braid, subconsciously wrapping it around my glove as if I were trying to hide my hand.

'It's just you and me,' he urged.

My eyes threatened to well yet again. This was the most salt water I'd expended in all the time I'd been in Aspen and it was getting tiresome. 'Warren,' was all I was able to say, my voice cracking as it tripped over his name.

'He was a great guy, for sure, Greta. But he's always been a risk-taker and we all know the risks that come from this sport. I think that's the reason we love it so much. It makes us feel so alive.'

'But you know we shouldn't have been back there. Even

he would have known that snow was set up and just waiting to go.'

'Which makes me think, it must have been his idea,' Singh volunteered.

'But why? Why take the risk?' I said, re-asking the same question that had been taunting me when I wasn't able to bury it under something else. 'You know Zuzana is pregnant. Why would he take a risk like that?'

Singh's eyes grew wide. 'I didn't know his wife was pregnant. I'm sorry to hear that. How did you take it?'

'You mean how did she take his death? She's devastated of course.'

'No. I mean how did you take it when you learned she was pregnant?'

This goes back to my thing about my relationships with gay men and how we understand each other. Singh knew. He'd always known, without me ever saying a word. I was in love with Warren.

'I was happy for him,' I lied.

# ELEVEN

Once we were back up top, we racked our skis and went into the hut for a cup of coffee. It was good to see that Neverman wasn't there. It was far too beautiful a day to have it marred with his misogynistic inferences. Meghan and Cole were having a good laugh over something, bent over at the waists, reveling in some private joke, it appeared.

Meghan and I came on to patrol around the same time ten years ago, and as women we always felt we had to work twice as hard to prove ourselves. While we were both strong, capable skiers who worked out with weights to get even stronger, we were about as physically apart as two women can get. I'm five foot eight and an ectomorph who is capable of eating to my heart's content without putting on any weight, while Meghan is an endomorph, short and stocky with dense muscle. She swears every bite of chocolate goes straight to her hips. Which doesn't stop her from eating it, by the way. And while my looks evidence my Swedish heritage tempered by whoever claimed ownership over these dark eyes, Meghan is pure Anglo-Irish – frizzy red hair, freckles, green eyes, the whole package. I often get a laugh when she skies up to an injured skier with a toboggan trailing her. You can see fear on the faces of some of the men when they realize this firecracker is responsible for their safe transport down the hill.

Cole, on the other hand, looks like a ski patroller. He has blond hair, serious blue eyes with just the right amount of character etched into the corners and a nose that starts right between his brows and drops from there in a straight line. He's the type who instills confidence when he comes upon an injured skier, a sort of calm, placid guy, but tough without overdoing it. He and his wife came to Aspen straight out of school in Boulder and have a little guy five years old who is already in the process of becoming a skiing legend.

Meghan and Cole were laughing harder than ever as I walked past them on the way to the coffee pot, the laughter of one feeding on the other.

'Must be an inside joke,' I said.

'You should have seen it,' Cole guffawed, barely able to hold himself together. Since Cole's not the type given to histrionics, his laughter piqued my curiosity over what could possibly be so funny. 'These two ski bunnies in designer outfits trying to get on the lift. I've seen a lot, but this one was special.'

Meghan took over, tears of laughter literally streaming down her rosy cheeks. 'It was like they had no clue what they were doing. I have no friggin' idea how they even got to the chair without killing themselves. Anyhow, they were waiting to load and I think they thought the chair was going to stop for them and when it didn't one of them fell and pulled the other down with her. They flattened themselves out on the ground and the chair passed right over their butts before the liftie could stop it. Cole and I were dope enough to bite our tongues as we picked them up, but I gotta tell you it was hard not laughing in their faces. The entire lift line was in hysterics. I actually thought the liftie was going to piss himself.'

'Yep,' said Cole, his laughter easing off as he wiped an eye with his little finger. 'After they fired the lift up again, Meghan and I took the chair behind them, just in case something of the same flavor happened up top. Of course when they got off, they slid straight for the Mountain Club.'

Which explained a lot. Aspen Mountain Club was the private club atop Ajax where the gazillionaires went to meet, greet and eat shellfish or Kobe beef with the Elk Mountain range as a backdrop. Last time I heard they were charging about $200,000 for the privilege of being able to pay for your lunch there. Then again, boot warmers are provided as well as slippers to wear while your boots warm up. Warren was a member and I have to confess to eating there a few times as his guest, but I can truthfully say it's not a level I aspire to. I'll never forget being in the ladies' room and listening to two women speak between stalls about which plane they were taking to the 'island'. The G4 or the G5. I never did figure out what island.

Meghan and Cole were still cracking up over the snow bunnies nearly becoming doormats when Lucy, who was doing dispatch, stuck her head out the door of the dispatch room.

'Need a toboggan on Kristi.'

I looked at my partner. He was already getting up. 'Singh and I will take it,' I said, gulping down the last of my coffee. I followed Singh outside. Reininger was standing near the door after just racking his skis.

'Wassup?' he asked.

'Need a sled on Kristi,' Singh replied.

'Hate those rescues on Kristi. Have fun,' he said, brushing past us on his way into the shack.

There was a toboggan tipped up against the building and Singh grabbed it and slapped it to the ground. I checked the sled for equipment, a couple of blankets, a quick splint, pillows. We also carried the basic first-aid essentials on our bodies – bandages, straps to make tourniquets, ketamine to ease pain. Once we were sure we had everything we needed, I took the toboggan by the fixed handles in front and snow plowed on to the hill. Singh followed behind.

Kristi wasn't located far from the top, but the entry is tough and it's the kind of run even an expert skier has to be cautious about. Miss a turn and you can end up on the catwalk 700 feet below you. Well aware of this, I sidled cautiously on to the run with the sled at my back. From our high perspective, we could see the injured skier not far down the slope, in the middle of the run, a super dangerous place to be if he had taken the wrong kind of fall. Someone had set crossed skis in the snow above him to indicate an injury, and I could see Winter beside him, his skis off, his knees dug into the snow to keep from sliding downhill. Kristi is about as steep a run as there is on Aspen Mountain. You can practically reach out your arm and drop a ball and it would only bounce off the mountain a time or two. Which makes rescuing an injured skier on Kristi particularly hairy. So far I've only had to do it once, but let me tell you, it's tricky trying to basically belay 200 pounds down a thirty-something degree slope without working up some serious sweat. In fact, that's why the tobog-gans all have canvas straps trailing for the back-up patroller to use as drag. Even with that it's tough. That's why we all hate rescues on Kristi.

I angled myself towards Winter and the crossed skis in the snow just above the injured skier, moving slowly and with care. The snow was deep and soft, helpful as opposed to hard-pack snow on such a steep incline. So guiding the sled towards them should have been no problem. But just as I came over the knoll above them, the sled shifted unexpectedly and it pulled me down. It all happened so quickly that any attempt at recovery was doomed. The next thing I knew the toboggan and I were a projectile headed straight for Winter and the injured skier. Winter's goggles were up and I could see his eyes go wide. I had fallen on to my hip and was holding tight to the toboggan, trying to direct myself away from them, but gravity was pushing me in their direction. If that skier was hurt now, he was going to hurt a lot worse when I crashed into him with a hundred-pound sled behind me.

Then I went over a bump and the next thing I knew both the toboggan and I had flipped over. Somehow there had been a change in direction and the toboggan was downhill from me now, my hands in a death grip as it pulled me along on my stomach behind it. The good news was the trajectory had changed and we were no longer threatening Winter and the downed skier. The bad news was I was now in a very hairy predicament myself. I was being dragged downhill by a fast-moving sled, face forward on one of Aspen Mountain's steepest runs. If I stuck with the sled the end game was the flat catwalk below. Smacking that catwalk with the toboggan in hand meant I was looking at a broken neck at best. But if I let go of the toboggan there was a chance of it hitting a skier crossing the catwalk and you didn't need to have a medical degree to figure out what that damage might be.

My eyes darted to the right where Walsh's, the adjacent run, fed into the catwalk. There were two boarders coming up the middle of the trail. Luckily, one of them looked uphill towards Kristi and saw my dilemma. He reached out and held the other boarder back. Despite my best efforts, I was losing my hold on the toboggan. A 'God help me' flicked through my brain as the toboggan slipped free from my grasp. I watched the tobaggan rip down the hill, hitting the catwalk squarely before banging upright. It hovered like a drunk for a split second and then flipped off the catwalk and down on to the roped-off out of bounds area beyond. It bounced a couple more times before planting itself straight up in the snow below the catwalk.

My trajectory was still downhill head first, but now free of the toboggan I was able to maneuver my feet below me and dig my boots in for a self-arrest. I came to a stop just shy of the catwalk.

'I ain't never seen nothing like that,' I heard one snowboarder say to the other. And then as if nothing had happened, the two slid on past, unfazed.

'That'll teach you it's always a wise idea to look uphill, dude,' said the other.

'I guess,' his friend agreed.

I was still trying to catch my breath when Singh skied up a couple minutes later. He had retrieved both my skis and was carrying them under his arm. 'Are you all right?'

'Yah. Just a little freaked out. I don't get what happened up there. It was like the sled fell apart or something,' I admitted, more shaken than anything. Physically that is. Psychologically was another thing entirely. Ski patrollers are not supposed to fall on rescues, much less let go of a toboggan. My eyes turned upwards to the steep ski run above us, toward the skier we had come to rescue. 'What about the injury up there?'

'He's OK. It's an AFK,' he said, applying the vernacular we used for that most common of injuries – the ubiquitous ACL tears we see more than just about anything else. This was an AFK. Another fucking knee. 'Winter's utilizing a little morphine so he should be fine until we get another sled. Victim didn't see your blowout by the way and we're keeping it on the down-low. I radioed in that our toboggan came in too low off of Walsh's and we need a new sled.'

Above me I could see Meghan and Reininger joining Winter high up on the slope where I lost control. They were pulling a fresh sled, their orange crosses spreading blessings across the slope. My head pivoted downhill, towards the catwalk and the ski area boundary ropes with the valley spreading out like a stage backdrop beyond. The runaway toboggan was sticking straight up on the other side of the boundary, its yellow draped head like a tombstone in the snow.

'Neverman's gonna have my ass for this,' I said.

'Hey, Greta. No worries over Never Never. He doesn't have to know. I told you. I talked to Winter and we've got your back. No big deal. What happens on the mountain stays on the mountain, right?'

Though I shouldn't have, I felt a shudder of relief. Ski patrollers had been sent packing for a lot less. You can't be having runaway sleds, empty or otherwise, banging down a hill unguided.

I clicked back into my skis – a near miracle because I was so rattled my left leg was shaking. Singh pretended not to notice that it took me a few tries to get back into my bindings. He probably didn't want to ruffle my psyche any more than it was already ruffled. Skiing is a highly psychological sport and a damaged psyche can be as bad as or worse than having burred edges on your skis.

We cruised down to the catwalk and ducked the boundary rope to make our way down to the half-buried toboggan. It was excruciating work extricating it from the deep snow, but after some time we managed to pull it with all the supplies still attached back on to the catwalk. After sitting a while to catch our breath, we headed for the nearest chair, Singh trailing the sled behind him.

We had just leaned the sled against the liftie's hut to be transported uphill later via snowmobile when Winter and Meghan skied past the lift, dragging the toboggan with the injured skier behind them. Reininger was with them, but when he saw us he peeled off and joined us at the chair.

One of the more senior members of patrol, Stu Reininger came to Aspen straight out of high school in northern California in his only worldly possession: his van. Thirty years later he was still living in a van, his second I presume – parked in the Highlands parking lot in the winter and up the pass in the summer. Reininger didn't have much to his name besides the van and his ski gear, which had been enough for him at eighteen, but at forty-eight he'd started grousing about rich people and trust funders having it all, which told me he was re-examining his situation. He was a good-looking guy when he brushed his hair, which was thick and dark brown and grew out of his head like it was trying to defy gravity. Strong and lean with dark skin etched from years of sun at high elevation, he was also extremely bow-legged, making it easy to spot him anywhere on the hill.

'Mind a hitchhiker?' Reininger asked.

I wanted to shout 'yes'. Not only did Reininger talk nonstop, he told some of the worst jokes in the world. And I kind of wanted to ride with Singh alone so I could let off some steam about my near disaster.

'Sure, c'mon,' I said, not meaning it.

'No jokes,' Singh warned, meaning it.

This chair we were riding on was nicknamed 'the couch', with good reason. It was so slow we probably could have climbed up faster. Aside from the utter and sheer horror of screwing up so royally my first day back, I was further bothered that the slow ride meant fifteen minutes of Reininger. Not that he was a bad guy. He just made me crazy some-times. To point: he launched straight into one of his infantile jokes.

'If you're American when you go into the john, and you're American when you come out, what are you in between?'

'Please don't, Stu,' I said, dreading the punchline. Singh sat in silence.

'European.'

'I said no jokes,' Singh begged.

'That wasn't a joke. That was a riddle.'

The ride continued along those lines so that by the time we got up top, I was ready to catapult from the chair, from the dual effects of a cold headwind and Reininger blowing hot air. The moment we unloaded, I made excuses to the guys and headed to the hut for a cup of coffee.

I racked my skis and went inside. Thankfully Neverman was nowhere to be seen. The hut was basically empty except for Lucy in dispatch. I poured myself some java and sat down, cupping it in my hands. I didn't usually get so cold. I mean in my business, if you're sensitive to the cold, you'd better find some other occupation. But the shivers I was suffering were coming from some other place, from somewhere deep inside me where insecurity lives.

Some of the other patrollers came in and took seats across the room. In no mood to talk to anybody, I picked up a copy of *Ski Patrol* magazine, the chosen reading material for people working in the trade. Flipping through the pages, I randomly turned to an article on seeking therapy after experiencing a death. It detailed the story of a patrol called to an on-mountain cardiac arrest in a double-black-diamond run in Sun Valley. The patroller did everything in his power to save the guy, employed every EMT skill at his command. But he lost the battle and the skier died. Five seconds later a second patroller arrived with the paddles that would have made the difference. The deceased was a forty-five-year-old father of two, ten years younger than the patroller. The first on the scene rebuked himself for showing up without paddles in the first place and found himself in therapy for months afterwards. The gist of the article was, how much is enough? How much is the skier's own risk?

I recalled a few similar incidents in my career where decisions called the difference between life and death. A couple of heart attacks. A guy going into shock with a broken femur. A severed artery that I had to stand on to keep a guy from bleeding out. Bad as those situations were, the victims all survived.

Not so with a young woman who smacked a tree and died almost instantly of internal injuries. I'll never forget trying to break the news to her shattered boyfriend. He was standing at the base of the mountain with his snowboard in his hands trying to digest what I'd said while three other patrollers loaded what was left of his longtime girlfriend into the ambulance. Every fiber of me had wanted to lie to him about her already being dead, to keep his hope alive and foist delivery of the world's worst news on the people in the emergency room. But not wanting to give him an iota of hope to be later extinguished, I buckled down and told him the truth. I'd never seen a face drain like that. And I'm not talking about color. I'm talking about life. His face emptied of life completely. It was like someone had pulled the plug on an inner tube and let out the air though it still held its form.

My thoughts looped back around to Warren. Not that he had been far from my mind in recent days. I felt like the deflated inner-tube snowboarder at the thought of his body crushed beneath tons of snow. How much of his death was my fault and how much of it was his?

I replayed my performance earlier in the day, complete with violating the taboo of losing a sled. The patrol was rife with stories of rescues gone wrong. Of victims in runaway toboggans flipping face down. Of compound fractures in chair-lift evacuations gone bad when someone lets the rope go too soon. Of inbound slides with the same deadly results as my out of bounds one. The legends abounded and each time a new one had been added to the repertoire, I'd crossed my fingers and tossed imaginary salt over my shoulder saying 'not I'. I was meticulous and careful and thought I was immune until the avalanche. That was bad beyond bad. But losing the toboggan days later? That was a game changer.

As a woman, I knew there were situations when I had to depend upon another patroller for help, such as when the victim was too heavy to turn over or haul back up a hill. I accepted my limitations strength-wise and did my best to compensate by working that much harder, by paying that much more attention. But today's failing had nothing to do with strength. It was an utter and complete mistake and luckily the injured skier hadn't paid the ultimate price, so it could be laughed off. The way most mistakes can be laughed off – until they count.

I thought about bad luck coming in threes. An avalanche. A bird's nest. A lost sled. Hopefully my run was through.

# TWELVE

I took it easy for the rest of the day, staking poles as necessary and doing some general policing like admonishing straightliners who seemed to have confused the way to the base with America's downhill. I can't tell you how many times I've seen a racing fool nearly take out an intermediate skier in his path, in other words endangering the very people who pay my salary. The intermediates deserve to enjoy themselves without being terrified and we need them. I mean, they really pay all the bills on Aspen Mountain where there are no beginners' runs. When I ride the gondola or chair with a visiting intermediate skier, they are usually intrigued that I'm ski patrol and full of questions over how I can do my job as a woman. I can't even begin to say how many times I've been asked how much weight I can pull in a toboggan. I never answer them, but I'll answer you. Lots.

Normalcy had lulled me back into a better state of being, and I was feeling pretty good as I checked in at the shack to see about sweep. While everything patrol does is important, sweep is one of the most important daily responsibilities. Working from the top, we basically ski every inch of the terrain after the last lift has closed to make certain no luckless skier is lost in the woods or face down in thigh-deep powder or has piled into a tree.

Neverman was barking out orders on the radio, and I was glad when I heard my name called out alongside Meghan's to sweep the backside of Bell. I really liked and respected Meghan, and appreciated that our skiing styles were different. While I loved to finesse the hill, Meghan just bombed it on legs made of steel. And while I'm basically an introvert by design, Meghan's never met a person she doesn't want to chat up, which makes riding the chair with her problematic as she's practically exchanging names and phone numbers with visitors by the time we get off. Have I added she's not opposed to a free meal here and there and accepts every date she's offered?

Me, I'm more to myself, always have been. I don't like accepting things from people, like to pay for myself on a date, and have little interest in achieving the kind of wealth that surrounds me, though I must plead guilty to enjoying the perks it provides. Like living in a safe town that offers some of the best outdoor sports in the country. Access to a free museum and excellent community college and programs at the Aspen Institute such as Shakespeare and Great Books. A classical music festival and jazz festival. That's all on top of having some of the most important leaders on the planet stop in town on a regular basis and being treated the same as any other person. I must confess to having no complaint about having to rub shoulders with the wealthy in that regard.

The clouds parted as Meghan and I left the hut, sending sunlight rolling across the upper slopes like a blanket flicked across a field of cotton. The untouched layers of snow from the storm promised a joyous ride down for the two of us.

We were standing in our skis waiting for the gondola to load its last downhill passengers before starting the sweep, when Meghan burst into ribald laughter. It was her typical laugh, the kind so contagious you join in even when you don't know what the other person is laughing about. Fighting against joining in the hysteria without knowing why, I focused on the fact that it is impossible to tickle yourself. Truth? You bet. Meghan tried to stifle her laughter, but even a gloved hand over her mouth did little to stop it. She pointed a gloved hand toward two women entering the gondola terminal. A pair of ski-toting ski instructors tailed behind.

'Those are the two who ended up face down under the Ajax Express this morning,' she managed to spit out between convulsions. 'One of the funniest things I've ever seen. You had to be there.'

As my eyes followed her outstretched hand, the smile prepping to crack my face went south upon realizing that one of the women was Zuzana McGovern and the instructor carrying her skis was Reese Chambers. Warren had hand-selected Reese to teach his wife to ski, a mission that he had failed miserably.

A big guy with a big handlebar moustache and a gut to match, he'd been around since forever and was legendary for being the most patient person on the mountain.

I hadn't recognized Zuzana right off, despite the mane of blond hair blowing in the wind behind her. And then I realized why. From the day Warren introduced me to her, I had never seen her in any ski outfit that wasn't white. Fur-trimmed or garnished with medallions, down-filled or spandex stretch, she must have had two dozen white ski outfits. White was her signature.

Today she was wearing black, a shiny jacket with a quilted pattern and a wide belt at the waist barely covering a pair of snugly fit black ski pants. The ensemble was beautiful and stylish, but it was black. Her companion was dressed in some-thing equally expensive I'm sure, but it was pink and orange and I made little note of it as I had no interest in what she was wearing.

Meghan was still laughing, bent over at the waist and propped up on the grips of her poles. I jabbed her with my elbow, and her laughter dried up when she looked at me and saw the severe look on my face.

'Stop it,' I said in a tone beyond questioning. 'Did you know one of those women is Zuzana McGovern?'

Her face went serious behind her goggles and she refocused to confirm what I had just said. There was a moment of silence followed by, 'You mean Warren's wife? I'm sorry. I've never seen her in anything but white. I wonder why she's wearing black.'

And then the two of us shared an awkward silence as the answer occurred to both of us at the same time. The rich have their own way of doing things. It was her way of showing she was in mourning.

# THIRTEEN

Saturday was my night at the Bugaboo as coat-check girl, a job I'd held on Saturdays for over fifteen years. I was smart enough not to let go of the job Judy had got for me when I first arrived in Aspen. It was lucrative beyond rational. From seven in the evening until one thirty in the morning, I would smilingly accept various incarnations of deceased animals or jackets constructed of ultra-expensive man-made fibers and reciprocate with a numbered tag. Over the course of the evening hundreds of coats would pass back and forth over my counter, all redeemed for a voluntary gratuity, always at least a dollar, usually a five, and more than a fair share of tens and twenties. There was always at least one Benjamin. On a good night there could be three.

Single or hundred, I always give my best smile and most appreciative thanks as I stuff the bill into the tip jar that gets emptied several times during the evening, so my investment banker and trust-fund clients don't catch on that on Saturday nights the lowly coat-check girl is probably making more an hour than they do. But as I've alluded to before, my Bugaboo money is earmarked for a special purpose. I wish I could say it was going towards world peace or solving hunger or protecting the environment. Those are all important causes to me and throwing support their way can come later in my life. This is for the more immediate cause. My Bugaboo money goes directly into the Everest fund.

But the tab for that trip is steep – around $35,000 before airfare. And if I'm going that far, I need to throw in a few extra K for additional trekking and travel. I mean, once I'm over on that side of the world, I might as well see what it's all about. In a perfect world, my kitty would already be full and I would have booked my flight to Tibet in May. But so far my goal has eluded me.

I started the Everest fund over five years ago, back when

Sam was alive, but I'd been fickle, dipping into the funds too many times for other extracurricular trips such as snorkeling the reefs of Australia one off season and skiing in Argentina's Patagonia the next. While I'm a worker bee in a ski town where locals appear to live Spartan lives, if you ever really examine it, most of the locals here are actually far better travelled than our customers. We share a wanderlust that pushes us to ferret out new experiences as opposed to possessions, whether it's trailing a sled to the North Pole or camping in the Mojave Desert. And when we want it enough, we usually find a way to make it work. It's part of our makeup.

Unfortunately, while that bohemian lifestyle is exciting and fulfilling, it backfires on some of us with far too much frequency. Well, perhaps it backfires on the majority of us with too much frequency. I'm talking about relationships here. People who live a bohemian lifestyle get used to doing things their own way, which can be quite destructive when it comes to relationships.

Which is pretty much case in point as far as my experience in the love arena since landing in Camelot. Sure I'd been in a number of relationships, but they always ended up as tragic as King Arthur's. Take Jack, for instance, my first major squeeze in Aspen. We met as ski instructors at Snowmass and were inseparable for the first couple of months. Hit the bars, skied the Cirque, made love practically every time we found ourselves alone – a challenge in a town of shared quarters. He was about as close as I'd ever come to a keeper, but as much as he claimed to love me, he just couldn't keep himself from behaving like a deer in stud when I wasn't in earshot. As for the other men I'd passed through since, several had been contenders, but the bottom line was commitment always fell victim to complications like moving to Maui in search of the perfect wave or finding a new lover on that Himalayan backpack expedition.

As a young girl, I'd wondered why my mother didn't commit to anyone, and sometimes actually hated her for it. More than resenting not knowing who my father was, I wanted there to be a male presence at the dinner table other than my twin. And a male paycheck on top of it. My mother had plenty of boyfriends and my young self often fantasized that the ones I liked were my father. But it seemed as soon as I grew fond of them, they were gone, so after a while I learned to stop caring for them.

They all seemed to follow the same program, receiving her affections at first and then pushing off after a period of time. Not one of them ever seemed to matter much to her, and she never seemed to care when they were gone. Except for one time when I caught her sitting on the toilet crying after a guy she seemed to really care about left one night and never came back.

As much as I swore I would never be like her, at this point in my life, I found myself more like her than I ever would have thought. Not that I came close to the revolving door of men she had gone through, but my love life was a fling here and a fling there. I'd thought I was in love a couple of times, but after the initial anguish of a break-up, it wasn't long before I was on an even keel again. So far there had been no toilet-seat criers for me.

Except for Warren. Given the chance, he would have been my toilet-seat crier.

The Bugaboo was typical Saturday-night ski season packed; the music loud and mind numbing, the lasers streaming across the dance floor. The concept of time moving slowly took on a new meaning as I stared out from my three-by-six-foot double-hung domain. There was no denying the Bugaboo drew an eclectic crowd. The mix was everything from nineteen-year-olds with fake IDs to octogenarians, their pockets packed with cash and Viagra. The dance floor was undulating with breast-augmented bodies and lean sports types, rich older men and middle-aged women trying to make them. There was an abundance of good-looking young women wearing their sexiest, and trolling for the one, hopefully one with money, and men ranging in age from barely legal to seniors with that *I'm not finished yet* look in their eyes.

Then there were the couples. Married or not, straight or gay or mixed. And when I say mixed, I'm not talking interracial, I'm talking age-mixed. At the Bug, a mere ten or twenty years age difference is nothing. We're talking thirty, thirty-five, forty years and beyond. It's most often the uncle/niece kind of combo you see in the wrinkle room at the base of Ajax, but every once in a while you see a much older woman with a young stud type at the Bug. Which just tells me she must be exceedingly rich. Money is the equal-opportunity matchmaker.

Whether it's ski instructors or volunteer firemen who are members on the locals' discount, or middle-aged suburban tourists paying through the nose for the weekly membership, or the landed gentry who yawn at paying $500 for a cognac, everyone wants to be part of the scene at the Bug. Money literally hangs in the air here as thick as August humidity in Milwaukee – reassuring if you have it, irritating if you don't.

It was eleven p.m. and the line at the coat check was backed up, the club going strong with no sign of slowing. After hanging up what was possibly the world's largest and weightiest raccoon coat, the possession of an equally large male Texan wearing a Stetson, I came up for air to find myself staring into the pair of mismatched eyes I'd stared into on more than one occasion in the preceding week.

'Hello, Dr Larsen. Almost didn't recognize you out of the emergency room.'

'I might say the same for you,' he countered. His sand-colored hair was dusted with melting white and he swept the errant strands from his forehead before fixing his wire frames upon his nose. He seemed almost embarrassed to see me. Maybe it was because there was a young blond standing beside him, her skin only slightly less wrinkled than a baby's bottom, her figure so thin I wondered if they'd met at the hospital's eating-disorder clinic. Or maybe he was embarrassed to see me standing in servitude behind the half-opened door of the cloakroom. He managed a toothy smile and handed over a couple of down-filled jackets. They were still wet with snow. I shook them off and handed him a ticket.

'My daughter,' he said unconvincingly, giving the blond a nod before disappearing into the crowd.

It was nearing one o'clock and people were already queuing up to retrieve their coats. I was working as quickly as possible, deftly palming the larger paper tips into my pants pockets so as not to deter anyone's generosity by exhibiting fifties and hundreds in the tip jar. The raccoon coat had just been hefted over to the Texan and was rewarded with a twenty when Dr Larsen presented himself again. The blond was standing off to the side looking bored. He handed me his claim check and I retrieved their two coats. He smiled at me and pushed two singles into the tip jar. Guess they don't pay doctors much in Aspen.

'You're leaving early,' I teased. 'You know there's still another hour before the lights come on.'

'I live in Basalt. It's a long drive in the snow. You think a doctor can afford to live in Aspen? She isn't really my daughter,' he added, nodding in the direction of the anorexic blond. She was engaged in conversation with a far more age-appropriate guy who had approached her while her 'father' was getting her coat. 'She's the daughter of a friend from New York and I promised to show her around. She's not staying with me.'

I had no idea why he shared that with me. It sounded like he was trying to justify being with the blond. I mean, he's a good doctor and he'd been very good to me, but his personal business was none of mine. Even if I had felt a momentary glow upon his earlier appearance at my coat check.

'That, Doctor, is more information than I require,' I said.

His eyes brushed me with undue familiarity before asking straight out of left field, 'Are you working tomorrow?'

'I never work Sundays. Works out better with this shift.'

'Can I buy you lunch?' he asked.

I swear I did a double take. For one, I don't do lunch. If you go out to lunch it means you're not skiing. Going out to lunch is something to be avoided at all costs. Besides, in my mind lunch is for wimps. Lunch is mini Snickers on the gondola. For two, in case he didn't notice, it was snowing like nuclear winter outside which meant tomorrow would be a radical powder day. Making the odds less than zero to none that anyone would find me sitting in a restaurant at the noon hour.

'Only if it's on a mountain.' My words were meant to make

it clear that I would be skiing. Instead he took it as an invitation. Without intending to, I had actually given him an option. Which he jumped right on top of.

'Done,' he said. 'Where are we skiing?'

Oh my God. What had happened here? The last week had been stressful enough without having to tour guide someone I barely knew on my day off. Plus I had no idea how he skied. I had my own routine and it didn't allow for anything but steep and deep. I was going to explain to him that 'we weren't skiing', but then upon giving it further thought, he had been pretty righteous toward me at the hospital. He had practically saved my life twice and kicked Neverman out of my room when he was bullying me, so I kind of owed him. But it felt like a date and the last thing – really the last thing – on my mind was having anything to do with a man in a romantic manner or otherwise. The loss of Warren was still so fresh.

'I ski Snowmass on Sundays. But I start early. I like to be at Base Village by eight,' I said, hoping to shake him off with the early wake-up. 'I'm sure you'd rather get some sleep.'

There was a glimmer of hesitation in his eyes as he did the math. It was one a.m. which meant he wouldn't be home in Basalt eighteen miles down the road until around two, considering all the snow on the roads. Then he'd have to be up by six thirty to make Snowmass by eight, which translated to only four and a half hours' sleep. Then again, I'd forgotten I was dealing with a doctor. Sleep deprivation was in the job description.

'See you in seven hours,' he said. Interrupting her conversation with the young dude, he took the young blond by the elbow and left.

# FOURTEEN

I t was just past two in the morning when I pulled off the highway towards home. The highway had been plowed, but the service the sole other residence on the street and I employed had yet to arrive, so the road was filled with snowdrifts, the type of situation that inspires happiness in mountain girls like me and sends city people running inside to avoid the apocalypse.

The Wagoneer with its studded snow tires was up to the task of the deep snow, and I loved driving in it. There was something calming about the headlights cutting through the falling flakes, both insulating and blinding at the same time. I hadn't driven far when I realized my tires were lining up in the tracks of another vehicle, meaning someone had travelled down the road not long before me. Which seemed peculiar. My only neighbors, the Greenes, were halfway down the road and kept pretty much to themselves. They seldom went out and seldom had visitors to their log cabin.

Like Sam, Ellie and Don Greene were longtime Aspenites dating back to the sixties. But there had been a rift between them some thirty years before over land usage or water rights or electricity – Sam couldn't seem to remember which or didn't want to. He had just characterized them as impossible to deal with. I'd sort of let things ride after his death and hadn't taken the time to try and get close to them. Smiled and waved whenever I saw one of them on the road, but that was about it.

The Greenes and Sam had come to terms on plowing and phone lines, however, and after Sam died, I just continued paying his share as before, never questioning the arrangement. Story was they'd owned a popular restaurant that had been fairly successful until the landlord chased them out with ridiculously high rents in the nineties. They'd retired to their cabin and didn't stick their heads out much except to take a walk in the forest or go into town for supplies. Though the house was dark, I could tell they were home, because even at this late hour there was a mild scent of wood burning, probably the last embers of their nightly fire.

I chastised myself for not being more outgoing and starting some kind of relationship with them. After all, with Sam gone two years and only two homes on a road . . . I mean it's time to get over it, right? I promised myself to get closer to them this spring.

As I drove past their place the road angled to the right towards the A-frame, and my heart rate ticked up upon the realization that I was still driving in the ruts of someone else's tire tracks. I exercised the thought that they might be my tracks from when I left for the Bug earlier, but at the rate the snow was coming down my tracks would have been long filled. The peace of mind I'd enjoyed only minutes before ceased to exist. I toyed with turning around and going to Judy's, but then chastised myself again for being a chicken.

I followed the curve of the road until my headlights illuminated the front of the A-frame. There was no vehicle parked in front. The one that had come up the road earlier had appeared to have rounded the little cul-de-sac before tracing its route back out to eighty-two. It occurred to me that maybe Jack had swung by to check on me. Except Jack knew that I worked the Bug Saturday nights during the season and had done so for eternity. In fact, because that schedule had afforded him the flexibility to pursue some of his other interests while we were dating, he was acutely aware that I worked Saturday nights. I decided someone had driven too far up eighty-two in search of some destination and realized their mistake upon dead-ending at my place.

The porch light glowed reassuringly, the rays casting yellow on to the front porch. I turned off the engine and killed the headlights. With all the falling snow, the night stayed practically as bright as it had been with the lights on.

I got the key out from under the planter, locking the door being a new habit for me and one only acquired since the death of my dog. I missed Kayla more than words can say and for a number of reasons, especially at times like this when her barking would have been a comforting sign that all was good at home. I unlocked the door and pushed it open timidly. The entry light was on, glowing over the red-brick tile, turning the walls to a lonely yellow, and I strained to remember if I'd left it burning. In a contrived show of security to myself, I kicked off my boots and slung my parka over the hook.

And then my senses took over. The presence of another human permeated the air, echoed off the slant of the A-frame's walls. I could measure the exhaled breaths, could smell the heavy odor of work clothes, could feel skin shed in my absence. My eyes searched the entry for any evidence to confirm what I knew in my bones, that there was someone here.

Everything on the rack inside the door was in place. From where I stood, I could see past the shadowed kitchen nook into the living room beyond it, with its sofa and Sam's old Barcalounger. Both rooms were empty. Still, another presence rang out.

There was a gun in the house, something I'd abhorred but that Sam had insisted upon. Though he claimed it a necessity to ward off pesky animals, I suspected it was the human animal which caused him the most worry. The gun was stowed on a shelf in Sam's former bedroom at the far end of the house, still loaded as it had been the day he died. The door to Sam's old room was closed. As with the entry light I racked my brain trying to remember if that door had been open or not when I'd left for work. Was there someone on the other side waiting to burst out and attack me? Or upstairs in the loft waiting for me to come up so he could violate me?

My sense of unease was so overwhelming I was too afraid to check the bedroom. To stick my head up into the loft. I thought of the unlikely bird's nest in my chimney and the noise the other night that I thought was a raccoon. Maybe it hadn't been a raccoon that I'd heard at all, but something else. My heartbeat in my ears was deafening as my certainty that there was someone in my home solidified.

I decided to trust my instincts and bolt. Even if I had to sleep in my car on a downtown street, anything would be better than this. I could come back in the morning when it was light to check things out. I slipped my boots back on and took my jacket off the peg without making a sound. My hand was shaking as I put it to the knob. And then a loud creak from behind me nearly caused me to jump from my skin.

I turned my head far enough to see the door to Sam's room opening. I was right. There was someone in my home. I had to move fast. I had just pulled the door open to make my escape when a large male hand appeared over my shoulder and slammed it shut.

My survival instincts leapt into gear. Holding my ground, I jerked my elbow back hard. There was a loud *ummph* as my elbow met the invader's solar plexus, and his hand fell from the doorframe. This time I yanked the door open all the way and ran for the car.

I had one leg in the Wagoneer before recognizing a familiar voice calling my name. I turned around to see Toby folded nearly in half in the doorway, holding his side. He was wearing a T-shirt and sweats and about three days' growth of beard. The light from the entry illuminated his muscular frame.

'Greta. Greta. Stop. What the hell are you doing?'

'Toby!' I shouted, running back to give my twin a hug. We held each other for some elongated seconds and then pulled apart. 'Why didn't you tell me you were coming?'

'I didn't know myself until this morning. Ended up on an unexpected layover in Denver and one of the guys was coming up this way for a few nights. Thought I'd surprise you.' He gave his ribcage a rub. 'Man you pack a punch. You're more dangerous than the rebels.'

When I looked up at my brother's eyes, even darker brown than mine, his hair a blond mop, there is no way to explain the rush of love that flowed through me. We'd been in it together from the beginning, from a shared womb to the shared challenge of our mother, and our ties were infinitely strong. The fact that we would go months and sometimes years without seeing each other did nothing to dilute our closeness.

He had enlisted in Special Forces after Mom died, the Army Rangers, and since then he seldom told me where he was or what he was doing. There were occasional letters and texts from him, often blacked out, or calls at peculiar hours of the night. I didn't know if this secrecy was to protect me or protect him, but either way I was immensely proud of him. He'd come to visit the summer after Sam was gone and knew about the hidden key under the planter.

'You could have at least left your boots at the door to give me a heads-up,' I scolded.

'My bad,' he replied. 'By the time we pulled in your driveway I was so dog-tired I went straight for the bedroom. I hope my *compa* made it the rest of the way all right. He's staying at his folks' digs in Starwood.'

'Not bad duty,' I said, referring to the gated enclave with the airport view. 'But not as good as staying with your sister.'

We lit a fire and talked for an hour. I told him about my being caught in an avalanche and the problem with the furnace. I didn't mention anything about Warren. I wasn't ready to share that story with him yet. 'Holy shit,' he said. 'And I thought I had rough duty. Glad I didn't arrive right in time for a funeral.'

'In all seriousness, you came close.'

I noticed his head drop momentarily before he caught himself and forced himself back to wakefulness. It was clear he was having a rough time keeping his eyes open. The digital clock atop the television said it was three fifteen.

'All right, bedtime,' I said. 'I'll make you a nice breakfast in the morning.'

While Toby brushed his teeth, I went into the storage closet and got him an extra pillow and blanket. I took them into his room where a duffel bag packed with neatly folded clothing and a pair of shiny boots sat open on the floor. That was all he travelled with. There was something so solitary about it that my heart ticked an unjustified pang. I hoped he was just solitary and not lonely.

I was still staring at the bag when I remembered my ski date with Dr Larsen in less than five hours. Well, that ski date was just going to have to wait for another time. I wasn't going to miss the opportunity to be with my brother in order to spend time with someone I barely knew. Then it dawned on me I had no contact information for the good-looking doctor. In the brief exchange over the coat-check door, we had not traded phone numbers. I could try calling the hospital for his cell, but I knew from experience they never gave out the numbers of staff.

Toby came back into the room and flopped on to the bed he had been occupying when I tried to sneak out of my own house. 'Bad news,' I said. 'You'll have to cook your own breakfast. I forgot I have to meet a guy over at Snowmass tomorrow. I'll cut out early.'

'A guy?' His eyes lit up. 'Anybody special?'

'Nah. Just the doctor who keeps putting me back together. He caught me off guard and I couldn't think of a way out. All I can say is, with snow like this he better know how to ski.'

'We know that's the truth, don't we, sister? But hey, don't rush home for me. I'll be happy to sleep all day.' He climbed under the covers, closed his eyes and was dead to the world. Like that. I guess in his line of work he was able to sleep on demand. And wake up on demand too. Like when he'd heard me come in the door.

I climbed the ladder to the loft, took a deep satisfying breath and fell asleep nearly as quickly as my brother. All my skittishness, the overarching sense of danger I'd experienced these past days was gone. Toby was here. There was an Army Ranger in my house.

# FIFTEEN

Toby and I were mutual survivors of our mother. Beautiful and headstrong, she left little room for argument when we were growing up. She was a good woman and she loved us as deeply as a mother loves her children, but she was also miserly with information and affection. When I say she loved us, I know she truly did. Nearly everything she did was with our best interest in mind, from where she chose to live to how she chose to make a living. She was so beautiful she could easily have married her way out of having to work long hours on her feet styling hair. But I think she truly believed that having a full-time man in her life would detract from her devotion to us.

That did not preclude her from part-time male companionship. Over the years there was a parade of them through her life and ours. Dozens of them. Some for a single night, some for a few months. Had she lived longer, I like to imagine that she would have committed to someone after Toby and I left. But she was a Swede through and through, with an aloofness that could border on cold. She kept distance between herself and other people, including us. Not so much when we were little children. Then she was warm and I can remember her snuggling us in her bed.

Our first home was a two-bedroom apartment in Milwaukee. My mom had settled there when she was pregnant with us, an odd place I always thought since she was always quick to say how much she hated Sweden's long dark winters. But I always felt my mother was either running or hiding from something and maybe she thought that Wisconsin was a good place to take shelter.

In our early years, Toby and I shared a bed and a bedroom and a series of babysitters. As we moved into adolescence, I think my mother decided it probably wasn't such a good idea for Toby and me to be sleeping together and somehow she scraped up the money for the down payment on a house. It was a small three-bedroom ranch in a solidly middle-class neighborhood. We all shared one bath, but it was luxury compared to the cramped apartment. We each had a room of our own and, better yet, there was a fenced backyard where we could build snowmen in the winter and spray each other with the hose on those hot Midwest summer days that hung on your skin like a wet shirt.

Then as we neared our teenage years, hugs became briefer, kisses were perfunctory, conversations limited. And our mother started drinking. It was almost like some internal signal went off, telling her that we were capable of taking care of ourselves so she could indulge in behaviors that would never have been acceptable were we still toddlers.

There was a series of men. Lots of them. They went through our house like there was a revolving door. Sometimes I felt like she was making up for the absence of them when we were small. Even though she'd had periodic boyfriends then, it was nothing like this. She was born somewhere in the north of Sweden, and I knew the Swedes had open attitudes about sex, but all in all it was embarrassing to have a revolving door of men in our quiet neighborhood. When I would ask her about her childhood in Sweden, she would never say more than it was her home and the winters were long and exhaustingly dark. Every once in a while she would make a reference to her parents and maybe a cousin or two, but from what I figured, her childhood had held some trauma she didn't want to share.

As a kid, I used to fantasize about a father somewhere, that maybe one of the stragglers she brought home was really my dad. There were so many though, that after a while they all started to blur together. But there are two that stick out in my memory. The first was named Bart and he was big and round with a round laugh as well and was probably one of the nicest men you could meet. He owned a plumbing company that he worked himself and sometimes when he came to see my mom he'd drive over in the truck. He'd bring candy and flowers for my mom and little gifts for Toby and me. Like CDs or six packs of Coke or huge bags of potato chips. He even took us all to a Brewers game. Though he clearly adored our mother, it was almost as if his kindness was a turnoff to her and she treated him horribly. It seemed the nicer he was to her, the less she wanted to do with him until one morning he got into his truck and drove off – never to be seen again.

The other man was memorable for an entirely different reason and not a good one. His name was Terry and he was tall and super good looking. He was something supposedly important in the financial world, and replaced the plumber's truck with a late-model BMW. I could tell my mom liked him a lot, and I thought, well, maybe this is the one.

He'd been seeing my mom for about a month when one night I heard them come in about midnight. I could tell they were drunk by the volume of their conversation. There was loud laughter as they went into the bedroom, a routine I had grown accustomed to for most of my adolescent life.

I had just turned twelve and was dealing with having one of my first periods, the cramps curling me up in a ball on my bed. When it grew quiet in my mother's bedroom, I was grateful so I could try to go back to sleep.

I had just dozed off again when I heard my bedroom door open. At first I thought it was my mom checking on me, because I had told her earlier how painful my cramps were. But then I quickly realized that would be highly unusual as my mom was hardly the type to come in and kiss me good-night. I heard the door shut and before I could assess the situation, there was a male figure atop me. I was lying on my stomach and his hand had circled round my face to cover my mouth. I was fighting him, but he was so much stronger, there was little I could do. He lifted my nightgown and put his filthy hand on my growing nubs of breasts. Then he was pulling down my panties. Not only was I terrified, but there was misplaced embarrassment because I was wearing a Kotex. I tried fighting harder, but he was so much bigger. Unable to scream, I lashed out a hand and knocked over my bedside lamp. It crashed to the ground, but that didn't stop him. I could feel what I realized was a male erection pressing at me from behind.

And then in an instant, the overhead light came on and he was off me, picked up from behind by my brother and flung to the floor. Toby wasn't big at the time – at twelve his growth spurt would come later – but his strength was fury fueled. And then I saw he was holding a butcher's knife. He brandished the knife in Terry's face and said, 'You get your fucking ass out of here now. And if you ever set foot in this house again, I'll cut your balls off while you're sleeping.'

Terry was up and out the door in seconds, grabbing his pants on the way. I was crying and Toby sat down on the bed next to me and rubbed my back. 'It's OK,' he kept repeating.

When I finally calmed down, the two of us went to my mother's room to check on her. She was passed out on the bed with her mouth wide open. We decided not to tell her what happened.

And when she hadn't heard from him for days and realized he wasn't coming back, she was the saddest I'd ever seen her. He was her toilet-seat crier.

It was then I stopped fantasizing about ever having a father.

Who needed a father figure when you had a brother to protect you?

# SIXTEEN

M orning came far too quickly, especially in light of sitting up with my brother until after three in the morning. When I cracked open the curtain hanging over the small window in the loft, the sky was turning over from black to gray. Though it was dawning clear for the first time in a week, the sun would not crack Independence for another good hour. I lay under the covers half wanting to go back to sleep, but knowing that if I slept in I'd miss the freshest crisp powder going under clear skies.

Nothing beats making tracks with the sun delineating every bit of the path. Skiing in snowstorms is great, because it keeps the wimps at home or in the cafeteria. But you need to know how to ski those conditions, which means skiing next to the trees for visibility. Even a seasoned skier knows how disorienting it can be skiing in a wide-open space without anything to anchor your eyes. Sometimes you literally can't tell up from down. But that wasn't going to be a problem today. The clear sky this morning told me the visibility would be limitless.

Then there was that other reason I had to get out of bed: my ski date with Dr Duane Larsen. At eight o'clock in Snowmass. I needed to move my tail in order to get to the Base Village on time.

Regretting more than ever having made a commitment that meant sharing prime powder time with a stranger, I threw on my only non-patrol outfit, a rust-colored parka with matching ski pants, purchased at the local thrift store before the start of the season a couple of years ago with the original tags still in place. That's another thing about Aspen. The richest rich think nothing of buying expensive ski clothes they know they'll never wear, and when this prophesy is self-fulfilled they don't even bother to take the unused clothes to consignment where they might recoup some of their wasted dollars. They either pass the goods on to the help or take them into the Thrift Shop of Aspen, Aspen's equivalent of the Salvation Army.

I happened upon my $2500 ski ensemble (according to the tags) through a system that I've worked for years. One of my good friends is the housekeeper at one of the highest perches on Red Mountain, Judy and Gene's neighborhood, where prices start in the seven figures and go up to the mid eights. Sarah always lobs in a call when she sees the lady of the house packing up the previous season's clothes to 'give away to charity'. Her boss and I happen to be the same size, so when she saw the untouched Bogner ensemble going into one of the black garbage bags for delivery to the Thrift Shop she called me right away. I was stationed in the store waiting when the Range Rover pulled up with its bags of unworn winter wear. I walked away with the outfit one hundred dollars later after talking the Thrift Shop volunteer down twenty-five bucks.

Before leaving for Snowmass, I stuck my head into the bedroom to check on my brother. He groaned something and turned his face into the pillow. A minute later he was dead to the world again. I figured he'd rather take care of his own mess than have me wake him for breakfast. As for me, breakfast today would be eaten on route in the form of a power bar and a cup of coffee – half milk – in my to-go cup.

It took over ten minutes to shovel out the Wagoneer, but after years of having cars that lived outside, I was used to it. There were some tricks that every local worth their ski pass knew. One of them was to never leave the windshield wipers flush on the windshield. Pointing them skyward before turning in for the night saves about five minutes of waiting for them to thaw from the glass.

I hit the road just in time to make my eight o'clock rendezvous. The roads were snow covered and there was little traffic on the thirty-minute drive. Just as in Aspen, I have a secret parking spot in Snowmass, a living bequest from a compound fracture extracted off the Face of Bell years ago. I left my car in the empty driveway of the two-week-a-year resident and pushed back anticipation about having a ski date with a practical stranger. I clicked into my boards and slid on down to the gondola.

He was standing there waiting for me, sending all my dreams of busting down extreme terrain directly to hell. For one, he didn't even have powder boards, but some old version of K2s that looked like they dated back to the era of the Maher brothers. Second, he was wearing a one-piece ski suit, probably bought the same era he bought the skis. Now, I'm probably the least fashion-conscious person on the planet, but really, might he have worn something from this century? If I were prone to embarrassment, this would certainly have taken it over the top. His only concession to modern-day skiing was that he was wearing a helmet, but given his profession, it made sense that he would protect his head.

'Hey there,' he called out upon spotting me, waving a pair of ski poles that most likely predated the skis. 'My wake-up call sure did come around quick. Ready for a big day?'

Well, I had been before seeing him. May I repeat, I'm not one to care about appearances, but ability is an entirely different creature. There's something everyone should know about dedicated skiers. We can never get enough. Ever. Summer is just a season to be endured until the first snowfall. The super addicted of us head to South America or New Zealand in the southern hemisphere when the days grow too long in the north. It's the same psyche as the surfers who search out endless summer, only the polar opposite – if you can stand the pun. We search out endless snow. And the holy grail to a skier is untracked powder. The deeper the better. It's the heroin of skiers. Make that nicotine, since I understand nicotine's even more addictive.

I've seen couples break up and people walk away from primo jobs over being able to make those first tracks. Even parenthood didn't stop the most committed skiers from skiing with their babies on their backs until the powers that be banned it. And it's my understanding the Skico took a lot of grief for it. As the saying goes, there are no friends on powder days.

I gave the body builder in his tired ski suit the once over, wishing he'd opted for the gym, cursing myself out for accepting his invitation to spend the day together. The Cirque was going to be heaven, the Headwall even better, and I wouldn't be there. If I were a cruel person, I would have taken him to those runs to shake him off, but I don't have a cruel bone in my body. Besides, taking him down challenging runs like those would most likely entail re-assuming my day job as rescuer. I reminded myself of how good he had been to me in the hospital and decided to offer the day up.

'Howdy,' I greeted him, a little stuck for words, trying not to feel like a teenager with a geeky friend you didn't want your other friends to see. 'Head for the gondola?' I said, anxious to move away from the base where I was likely to see a few familiar faces. I led him to the gondola that services the beginner and intermediate slopes. The line was short, the less passionate skiers sleeping in until the slopes were groomed. The hardcore skiers had already queued up at the six-pack chair back at the plaza, and headed to the good terrain.

We shared the gondola car with a family of four who were entirely engaged in planning their route from the top, so Duane and I sat across from each other and made small talk during the sixteen-minute ride. His goggles were raised and he wasn't wearing his glasses. His mismatched eyes stared at me from under a fringe of curly lashes, the brown one unreadable, the green one inviting with a blue-green ring delineating the iris from the stark white of his eyeball. It was as if the two eyes belonged to two different individuals.

Without any prompting, he gave me a thumbnail sketch of himself, telling me he was raised in the east and went to Harvard medical school after getting his undergrad at Cornell. That during his residency in Cleveland, he met a nurse who became his wife. How after getting a divorce and wanting a total life change, he'd taken the ER position in Aspen just a few months ago. I almost felt like he was laying out his CV for approval.

'So why aren't you living in Aspen?' I probed.

'Are you kidding? I'm still in shock at the price of real estate. The hospital offers some employee housing, but I found a rental in Basalt. In good weather the drive is less than a half-hour, better than what I was dealing with in Cleveland.

A lot prettier too. Luckily it's furnished. I couldn't begin to think about furnishing a place with all the time I'm spending at the hospital. They're short-handed, you know?'

'Well, I do know that housing is problematic when it comes to hiring people, that's for sure.'

Then, completely off topic, he said, 'I wasn't kidding when I said my date last night was the daughter of friends. I told them I'd look out for her while she was visiting Aspen.'

I shrugged off his explanation, not sure if that was some kind of come-on. 'No need to explain if she wasn't. Age presents no limitations here if you haven't noticed.' I couldn't have cared less about his romantic inclinations. My heart slid down the west side of Ajax under tons of snow last Sunday. And likeable as I found the attractive doctor, that attraction had turned entirely sideways upon seeing him in the one-piece. OK, maybe I do care about appearances. I just hadn't realized it.

It was difficult not to draw a mental comparison between him and Warren who wore low-profile ski clothes but executed high-profile turns. In my mind, it was Warren sitting across from me, but then again, were Warren with me, I can guarantee we wouldn't have been on the Elk Camp gondola cutting across the mountain to intermediate turf.

Had Warren not died in that avalanche, he would have been here at Snowmass with me, and right now he and I would have been riding the Poma lift to the top of the Cirque and the highest lift-served terrain in Colorado. It would be Warren leading the way down the Headwall into the glades, moving gracefully yet powerfully through the trees. Warren was without a doubt one of the best skiers I ever had the pleasure of taking turns with outside the pros.

After that we would have skied Upper Ladder and acres of untouched terrain, floating through virgin fields of powder, coasting between the trees in the glades. No one would have been there except the two of us, and when we jumped on to the next chair we would high-five each other and rejoice in the wonder of the day, in the wonder of being alive in such a beautiful place, completely grateful to be a part of it.

When the last lift closed, after having been fueled all day

by Snickers and power bars, we would ski down to Base
Village on Gumby legs for an après ski. The only thing that
would mar the day would be Zuzana waiting in the bar with
her ski instructor, drinking a glass of white wine, composed
in her perfect beauty, white ski pants and white-fur trimmed
jacket, not a hair out of place after doing loops all day on
the green terrain. Frankly, I was always surprised that Reese
didn't fall into a coma out of boredom. Then again, he couldn't
afford to.

Zuzana would smile and he would give her a huge hug and
tell her what a great day it had been. And she would say, 'I'm
so happy for you, sweetheart.' Keeping a smile on my face
then was the hardest part of the day.

'Are you all right?' The doctor had stopped talking and was
scrutinizing me in a manner suggestive of his profession. My
eyes had turned teary revisiting the notion that Warren and I
would never ski together again. My stomach actually lurched
at the thought of spending a day on the slopes with the man
seated across from me. His very presence felt so wrong in
light of Warren's death.

'Oh, yeah. Just an eyelash in my eye.' I lowered my goggles
to avoid any further eye contact.

'Covering up those beautiful brown eyes. I think it's pretty
rare to see a blond with brown eyes. You know brown eyes
aren't as light sensitive as lighter eyes?'

'I've never really given it a thought.'

'Let's see, with a last name like Westerlind, you should
have blue eyes. I'm assuming your mother must be the dark
one. Am I right?'

'No. My mother was Westerlind. Pure Swede. I don't know
anything about my father.'

That shut him up for the rest of the way and we rode without
talking further, while the family of four did their part in keeping
the noise level up. As we passed over the gentle groomed
slopes below, my eyes focused on the rugged terrain in the
distance, a backdrop so vast and overwhelming that it almost
felt we were looking at a stage.

We got out of the gondola at the terminal and took another
chair higher up on the mountain, looking out over the jagged

peaks of the Elk mountain range. From the chair we could see the expert inbounds cliff-studded terrain to our right. Someone had already ducked the boundary ropes to cut a pair of perfect Ss in the out of bounds terrain before skiing back inbounds to safety. I was grateful I wasn't ski patrol on duty at Snowmass today. The poachers would be testing the limits of their ski passes.

When we got off the lift, Dr Larsen skied over to the trail map, oblivious to the giggles of some teenagers who were too cool for their own good. 'To be honest this is my first skiing since I got here,' he said, staring out over the rope that marked the edge of the ski area. 'These views are breathtaking.'

'I never get tired of them,' I said honestly.

He scrutinized the trail map, turning his head first one way and then the other, as if he were examining a museum piece. 'Just blues over here?' he asked. 'Isn't blue intermediate?'

'Thought we'd start out easy. There's a little blackage in the glades if you feel up for it later,' I ventured. Before I had a chance to add anything else, his skis slipped off the ledge where we were standing and he started sliding downhill backwards, his body rotating back and forth as he fought against physics and gravity to turn himself around. Helpless to do anything other than watch, I held my breath as he sailed across the run into a pile of virgin snow on the other side, and landed unceremoniously on his butt. It was hard not to laugh, much less cringe at the reality that the day was going to be far worse than I'd imagined. I skied over to where he was working to pull himself out of the deep snow.

'You OK?' I asked, getting ready to take off my skis to help him.

'I'm fine. No, leave your skis on,' he commanded. After some effort, he managed to get himself upright and brushed the snow from the one-piece suit. 'That'll wake you up.'

'Look, maybe I got you in a bit over your head,' I lamented, watching my perfect day go all to hell. 'Just follow me and take it slow. We'll do something easier from here.'

He slid unsteadily back on to the groomed slope and followed me as I started making wide gentle turns, the type I'd employed during my years as a beginning ski instructor when my students would follow like a row of penguins. After executing a half-dozen of the controlled turns, I looked back to see how he was doing. He had stopped and was standing uphill from me on trembling legs. *Oh God, he's terrified,* I thought.

'Just take wide turns,' I encouraged him, preparing to side-step back up the hill to help. Without warning, his skis pivoted downhill and he shot right past me. I took off in pursuit, praying he'd be able to stop without hurting himself. Most of the area was groomed, making it easy to pick up speed, and he was quickly out of sight. Chasing after him, I broke all the rules I lecture skiers on regularly, like skiing without making any turns and not skiing too fast, in hopes of catching him. Occasionally, he would come into my sightline and then disappear behind a rolling bank. It wasn't until we were halfway down the run that I realized he wasn't out of control, but was actually skiing, and with a good deal of finesse I might add. He had been gaming me all along.

He was waiting at the bottom when I did a hockey stop behind him. 'That was a nice warm-up,' he said. 'Now, let's go ski.'

What do they say about not judging a book by its cover? I guess it's never too late to learn. It turned out that Dr Duane Larsen was not only a good doctor, but a damn good skier as well. When he said he had grown up in the east, he failed to mention that it had been Vermont and that his family had owned a small ski lodge in Stratton.

'So what's with all the old gear?' I asked after we settled on to another chairlift, this one servicing the more challenging terrain. 'Those skis have to be collectors' items.'

'They're not *that* old. I bought them in the nineties, just before starting med school. That was the last time I skied before moving here. They are shaped, you know?'

I looked at his skis resting on the footrest. 'Yah. Probably the first year of shaped skis.'

He ignored my slight. 'Anyhow, wasn't really much time for skiing in my life after starting school. You know, internship, residency, fellowship in the Midwest. That kept me busy for around twenty years. Besides, my parents got old and sold the lodge. They're gone now,' he said, bowing his head briefly. Then he bounced back up. 'Hey, these skis've only got about twenty days on them and I am vehemently against waste. Besides, I never put a whole lot of stock in having the "latest" equipment.' He used his fingers to put 'latest' in quotation marks.

'Well let me give you directions to the Thrift Shop, so you can at least get some ski clothes that don't make you look like you belong in the dinosaur museum here.'

'Dinosaur museum? There were dinosaurs here?'

'Yep. This whole area was a big watering hole for Mastodons. Of course, no one knew how big until some contractor was digging a new reservoir and saw a big bone sticking out of the earth. He stopped to investigate and realized it might be something important. They ended up digging up dozens of Mastodons. Just imagine if he just kept going and plowed all those bones back under the surface. Probably never would have known they were there.'

'I bet there are a lot of buried bones around here that no one knows about,' he said.

We skied expert terrain the rest of the morning, the double black diamonds of the Cirque and the Headwall. While he wasn't as strong as I am in the deepest snow, he qualified as competitive. Unlike Warren, however, he was tired by early afternoon and, being a physician, he recognized that most ski accidents happen because of fatigue. Contrary to my custom, we stopped for lunch.

He filled his tray with an edible from just about every food group in the cafeteria line, and I opted for a turkey chili. He insisted on paying, and we carried the trays to a table near the window with a view of skiers heading towards the lift. It was obvious he had been ravenous. The moment we sat down he started eating and didn't come up for air until he was halfway through his tuna melt and sweet potato fries.

He put the sandwich down and took a huge drink of water. 'I've been meaning to ask you how you've been feeling after your CO incident. Any after-effects?'

'I don't think so,' I said. 'I mean, I felt a little strange for a couple of days, but nothing too serious. Why do you ask?'

'You mean for what other reason than being an MD? None really. Just doing a little follow-up. You know a lot of people suffer memory loss, not to mention poor coordination after CO poisoning. Anything like that happen to you?'

I started to shake my head and then thought of losing the sled on Kristi. I pushed back a pang of anxiety.

'What about the avalanche? You getting any memory of that back?'

I started to shake my head no again when a new image came to me. I was standing at the shed watching Warren get off the Ruthie's chair. I'd called out, but he hadn't heard me. My heart dropped as I watched him ski over to the boundary. I heard myself calling 'Wait' as I skied towards him. And then the memory stopped, once again pushed to its edge. I looked up at the doctor and said, 'Wow. I just remembered a little more. I think I was trying to stop him from going out of bounds.'

His smile was like a mother's caress, soft but not overwhelming. 'Sometimes memory starts coming back when you're relaxed,' he said.

We took it easy for the rest of the afternoon and skied less challenging terrain, and I could tell he was struggling on the final run back to Base Village. But all in all, it had been a great day. For both of us. His car was parked at the intercept lot on Highway 82, so I offered him a ride down so he wouldn't have to wait for the shuttle. He made a sound that could only be described as a chuckle when he saw the Wagoneer.

'And you're picking on my skis?'

'Beggars can't be choosers. Besides, this thing is a tank in the snow. At risk of sounding like someone's grandfather, they don't make them like this anymore.'

'They sure don't. We had one in Stratton. But it rusted out after twenty years of salt back east. If it'd been here, it'd still be running.'

We rode in exhausted silence down the road to the highway, the January sky still deep blue, framed against the white

of the surrounding mountains. We pulled into the intercept lot
and I asked him where he'd parked. He looked a little embarrassed and then directed me to the far row of cars. We stopped
in front of a steel-gray Porsche SUV.

'How's it in the snow?'

'Not as good as the Wagoneer,' he confessed.

# SEVENTEEN

The day had gone so unexpectedly pleasantly that I'd almost forgotten I had a hungry soldier in the house. Toby had always been a huge eater, and so I stopped at City Market on my way home to stock up on supplies. I lucked into a rare space in the parking lot and was climbing out of the car when a down-clad man in a black watch cap trailing a cameraman behind him came up and stuck a microphone in my face. The cap was pulled low on his forehead, his round cheeks pink with cold, a thick brown moustache curling over his upper lip.

'Hi there,' he greeted me in a sing-song of forced friendliness. 'We're making a documentary about Ted Bundy and we're wondering if you could answer some questions for us?'

'Sorry, but I'm in a hurry,' I said, shutting the door for emphasis.

'It wouldn't take long. We're looking for stories about him. Were you around when Ted Bundy escaped from the County Courthouse building?'

'Look, I'm not sensitive about age, but I was about three when Bundy made his appearance here in Aspen. And I was in Milwaukee, Wisconsin, thank you. But this car was probably around. Too bad you can't interview it.' The interviewer's eye slid from the Wagoneer to give me a better look. Considering the age of my vehicle, he must have assumed his interviewee would have been older.

He laughed. 'Never hurts to ask,' he said. He signaled to his cameraman that I was a no-go. I watched them move on to their next victim, an older woman with time-weathered skin getting out of a Jeep. She was deep in conversation with them as I went into the store.

Wheeling my cart down the aisles, I thought about the story I could have shared with them about the serial murderer, and I would have had I not been in a hurry to get home to my brother. Nearly everybody in town had a Ted Bundy story and I was no exception even though I wasn't here at the time. It wasn't my story, it was Sam's, but it was a real hair-raiser.

You see, serial killer Ted Bundy had made his first appearance in Aspen in 1975 when he abducted a twenty-three-year-old nurse from the hallway of a resort hotel in Snowmass. The woman had left her fiancé in the room to go retrieve something from her car and was never seen again. Alive, that is. Her naked body showed up the next spring. His next victim was a young woman in Vail. Same thing. Disappeared not to be seen again except as a corpse.

Of course women disappearing makes everyone a bit skittish, and Ted had already left a trail of victims behind him in Utah. The women who went missing were all young women with long dark hair parted down the middle, which could have described half the female population of Aspen at the time. Sam told me that following the nurse's disappearance, the whole town was so on edge, girls were afraid to go anywhere without companions, some of them even dubious of their own boyfriends.

Bundy was finally arrested in Utah and tried for the murder of a young Utah woman, and the whole town took a deep breath. But there was no body in Utah, so it was impossible to pin a murder charge on him. Not so in Aspen. Caryn Eileen Campbell's body had turned up, the twenty-three-year-old nurse who disappeared in Snowmass. Her corpse was tied to Bundy from hair fibers found in his car, and he was extradited to Colorado to face charges for her murder.

Now a slick guy like Bundy didn't get as far as he had gotten without having some high-performing brain cells, however evil they were. Insisting on representing himself, he asked to use the library in the vintage 1880s courthouse on Main Street. One day when the deputy guarding him turned his back, Ted jumped out a window and stripped off the black and red lumberjack shirt he wore to a less obvious blue shirt underneath. A witness saw the whole thing, but nonetheless, Bundy disappeared into the mountains for five days. Sam told me the whole town was on its ear. Even guys were afraid. The sheriff put a road block on the only road out of town in

the winter and refused to take it down long after everyone was
sure Bundy had fled.

This is where Sam comes into the story. At the time, he
was living with another ski bum just on the edge of town. In
those days no one thought a thing about leaving their keys
in the cars, so when a cold and hungry Ted Bundy came upon
their driveway, he thought he'd found the mother lode. He
stole Sam's car. Since the road block prevented him from
escaping the valley, he drove into town, in search of what, no
one was ever sure. For some reason he was weaving. Hunger?
Trying to keep his head low? No one knows, but luckily Aspen
was a smaller town at the time. An Aspen cop pulled him over,
ready to lecture Sam about driving after a few drinks too many.
Sam said in those days the cops would just give you a lecture
and let you walk home. When the cop approached the car, Ted
grabbed a pair of sunglasses from the dashboard and kept his
head low. The cop walked up to the car, and what does he see
but an unshaven man cowering behind the wheel. 'Hi Ted,'
was all he said.

That could have led to a happy ending, but unfortunately
the cagey murderer went on to escape the Glenwood Spring
jail a few months later out of a heat duct. He made his way
down to Florida where he murdered three more women in a
sorority house. The sicko bit one of the women on the ass and
it was his dental impressions that eventually sent him to the
electric chair.

I shivered and not because I was in the frozen section.
Reliving Sam's story and the thought that that kind of evil
could be present in a place as beautiful as Aspen was as
frightening as things got.

I loaded up big time from the protein section with two large
T-bones, and then headed to produce for potatoes and spinach.
Back out in the parking lot the documenter and his cameraman
were interviewing yet another victim, Martha Binyon, a local
who had been an Aspen teenager in those days. She would
remember Sam's Ted Bundy story well. I graced Martha with
a wink and a nod and fired up the Wagoneer.

She was pointing at my car as I drove away.

# EIGHTEEN

Toby was sitting in the Barcalounger watching television when I walked in, a Heineken perched on the table beside him. He was wearing a sweater and jeans, his stocking feet crossed at the ankles in a picture of ultimate relaxation. A pair of damp boots at the door testified to a walk some time earlier. The History Channel was playing, a program about trench warfare on the screen. He muted the volume when he saw me.

'War is such a fucking waste,' he said. 'Did you know that over twenty million men died in World War One? Of disease if they weren't blown to pieces?'

'If war's so bad, and I agree, then why do you do it for a living?'

'Because man has been a predatory creature since the beginning of time and somebody's got to play the good guy.'

He got up and took his anger into the bathroom. I put the groceries down on the kitchen counter next to several empty beer cans. No judgment to be passed here. I just hoped the fresh six-pack I'd bought would be enough to get us through the night. When he came back, he left the TV muted and perched himself on a bar stool at the counter that divided the kitchen and living area and served as my table. He watched me unload the groceries.

'How was your day?' I asked.

'Best one I've had in a long time. Didn't get up until after noon, fixed up some of your eggs, and then I went out and hiked for a while. Jeez, it's beautiful here, but it's sure fucking cold!'

'Not when you get used to it. Besides, there's no humidity so it doesn't go to your bones the way it did in Milwaukee.' I stopped unloading groceries and unloaded a smile on my brother. 'Sorry to be so late. Time sort of got away from me.'

'Yeah? How'd the date go?'

'It wasn't a date,' I said emphatically. 'Though it did go better than I thought it would.' My mind flashed to floating through the powder of the Headwall with Duane Larsen in my periphery. As heartless as it may sound, Warren's loss had been muted for that period of time by the foot of fresh snow. I went back to unloading the groceries. Toby's eyes rested on the overpriced steaks I'd bought.

'I'm sorry you went to all that trouble,' he said, 'but I'm really not in the mood for meat.'

'All right,' I said, mentally putting the steaks into the freezer. It would take me forever to eat all that beef. 'Since when don't you eat meat? And you are in the mood for what?'

'Since I've seen a lot of what I've seen I'm not into red meat. You know what? I'm really craving sushi. Let's go into town. I'll take you out.'

My brother eating sushi. That was a first.

Thirty minutes later, after a hot shower and a change of clothes, I was riding beside Toby on our way into town. Toby was driving despite having consumed nearly a six-pack of beer. He wanted to drive and I let him. Which didn't particularly bother me. I figured the danger of him driving after a few beers was nothing compared to the danger he faced from incoming weaponry.

'Can't tell you how good it feels to be behind the wheel and not worry about the road blowing up,' he said as if reading my mind. He followed the headlights' path down the road toward the Greenes' cabin, the lights burning bright from within, smoke curling from the chimney, the air scented with the familiar smell of burning wood. The way the house was lit up made it seem like the perfect place for an elderly couple to cocoon. 'They friendly?' he asked, giving the cabin a nod.

'I wouldn't say they're unfriendly. We're just not close. Sam was never too keen on them.'

'Well you really should strike up a friendship. I hate to think of you all secluded at the end of this road.'

'You're putting me on,' I said, actually laughing out loud. 'You're driving around a hostile country in armored vehicles being shot at by people who would love to send you to the far end of eternity, and you're worried about me being alone in what is probably the safest town in the country?' Then I thought about Ted Bundy. Weird stuff can happen anywhere I guess. 'I forgot to ask you how long you're staying.'

'Gotta shove off zero six hundred hours tomorrow.'

'So soon? But you just got here.' The disappointment in my voice was hard to cover.

'I know. But just got my marching orders a couple of hours ago. You know, duty calls.'

I knew all about duty, but it didn't keep my heart from aching at the thought my brother was leaving already. It had been nice to have someone else around for a while, even if it was only a couple of days. My house would feel lonely without Toby.

Town was crowded, the streets packed with seasonal traffic and tourists out in search of a meal. After parking in my secret spot, we walked over to the best sushi place in town. It was stratospherically expensive, but was well worth it, and besides Toby was buying. I'm not sure what his pay grade was, but I figured he couldn't have too many expenses since he was fed, housed and clothed by the government. The restaurant was jammed and there was a waiting list about as long as the gondola line on a powder day, but I knew the manager, Jimmy Finkle, and he somehow squeezed us in. In fact, he gave us a prime booth that was probably reserved for some hedge-fund manager. But the hedge-fund manager hadn't brought Jimmy Finkle down Aspen Mountain in a sled after a torn Achilles tendon, so he was SOL.

'You sure?' I asked Jimmy as he lay the menus down in front of us.

'Nothing too good for you, Greta. Not compared to what you do for all of us.'

'Wow, sister. You are quite the hero,' Toby said after Jimmy had taken his leave.

'All in a day's work,' I said, turning my eyes toward the menu.

A waiter came over and we ordered beers and a couple of handrolls to start. I drank nearly half my beer in one gulp.

The long day of skiing had left me thirsty. Skiing does that to me, leaves me with the kind of thirst that takes more than water to quench. Toby had slowed down and sipped at his beer. Evidently he had quenched his thirst back at the A-frame.

Sitting across from my brother, it would be hard to not appreciate how good looking he was, his chiseled jaw dusted with a couple of days' blond stubble, his dark eyes intense in a tired face, his thick blond hair mussed in a stylish manner. I must have been staring at him so hard, I missed him visually dissecting me at the same time.

'What's eating you?' he asked.

'Nothing,' I fibbed. 'Why you asking me that?'

'You just don't seem yourself. You don't seem like you're happy.'

'Huh? Of course I'm happy. How can I help but be happy? Look at my life. Where I live. What I do.'

'Don't lie to me,' he countered. 'Maybe we haven't seen each other for a while, but last time I visited here you radiated happiness. That "joy de viver" or whatever it's called. Your obstinate way of just daring someone to try and take you down. I'm not seeing it, Grets.'

'It's been a rough month,' I admitted. 'Having to put down Kayla. The avalanche. The carbon monoxide thing.'

'Is that all?' he pressed.

'Is that all? That's a lot to have happen in a short period of time.' He stared at me unblinking and I knew he had me. After sharing our first ten years together in the same bedroom and the next ten in the same house, more or less looking after our mother in drunkenness or sickness, my brother knew me better than anyone. 'Someone very special to me died in that avalanche last week.'

'See, I knew it. I knew it. What kind of special?'

'Special-special.'

'A lover?'

'No,' I huffed. 'He was married. He was just a great guy and a ski buddy and he shouldn't be dead.'

I recalled the snow encasing my body in an icy cast. My inability to move a muscle. Neverman's face peeking at me through the snow. 'And I have no idea why he was there.' My eyes teared up and I fought against crying. Toby handed me a handkerchief and I dabbed it against my eyes, grateful for the privacy of the booth. I almost never cried and the fact that I was near tears again bothered me. 'In fact, as things figure I might be responsible for his death.'

'What?'

I told him what had happened that day, of not remembering much of anything except the white wall of snow bearing down on me.

'Wow, sis. That really sucks. I'm really sorry to hear about it. So you were in love with him?'

'I told you, no. He was just a friend. A close friend.'

'Right.' He let it drop without pushing any further. 'What about the guy you skied with today? Any possibilities there?'

'Absolutely not,' I shot back. Though the day had been a pleasant break from perseverating over the loss of Warren, it didn't make him any less dead. 'What's with the sudden interest in my love life?'

'Actually, because I'm thinking of getting married.'

'You are?' A pang of possessive jealousy shot through me. If my twin were to get married, he'd be a couple, and he'd be closer to her than to me. I forced myself to let go of that thought.

'Yep. Met her in Afghanistan. She reminds me of you with her fearlessness. She's special ops too. Well, was. Was in a vehicle that hit a mine and lost her right leg. She was lucky though. She got hit just below the knee.'

I didn't see how losing a leg was lucky, above or below the knee.

'She lose her leg before or after you met her?'

'After. But it doesn't change a thing.'

When the initial shock of his announcement passed, I found myself gracing my brother with a smile. A bit forced maybe, but who was I to infringe on his happiness? Then I realized the forced smile was the same forced smile I used to sprout while having drinks with Warren and Zuzana at the end of the ski day.

I studied my brother's face and saw in it a new dimension, an underlying sense of belonging I'd never seen before.

I probed him about the woman he was thinking of marrying and he shared some more information about her, that her name was Fenicia and she was black. That took me by surprise at first, even more than the missing leg. I mean, we were raised in a working-class community where that kind of mixing was frowned upon. Not that I was ever in that camp, but it came from so far out of nowhere, I must have appeared astonished at first.

He took a picture from his wallet and handed it to me. I suppose I was surprised that he didn't have the picture on his phone, but then I realized his phone probably didn't always work in combat. He kept the hard copy picture with him always. She was a beautiful brown woman with even features and hair divided into neat rows of braids close to her head. I found it unusual that her eyes were green and gave Toby a puzzled look. 'Her mother was gang-raped by a bunch of crackers. She doesn't know who her father is either. Something we have in common.'

I cupped my hand over my brother's paw resting on the table and squeezed it. 'I'm so happy for you,' I said.

Before we could say anything more, I became aware of another person approaching the table. Thinking it was the waiter, I looked up and was taken aback to see Zuzana standing over us. You could say she was dressed in widow's black if a low-cut black leather dress and black fringed cowboy boots qualified. Her pregnancy was not yet visible in the tight sheath of a dress, but the press of her cleavage into the V of the dress sure was, making her look more like a cougar than a grieving widow. Her eyes were glued to my hand resting atop my brother's.

'I didn't know you were dating anyone, Greta.'

The comment would have been uncalled for in any case, certainly nothing you would say to two people sitting together in a restaurant when you only know one half of the duo. 'This is no date, he's my brother,' was the best I could manage. 'I'm sure I've told you guys about my Army Ranger brother, Toby.' Too late, I realized the error of my wording since one half of the 'guys' was no longer around to be counted.

'Yes, you sure did,' she said, smiling at Toby with the sort of bewitching smile that I assume makes men do a lot of the nasty things they do. The sort of smile I couldn't pull off even for free airfare to Nepal. My brother smiled back in a way that made me question his commitment to his one-legged bride-to-be. Zuzana had that kind of effect on men. She'd met Warren at an art gallery opening in the mall not even a year ago and, well, we all know the end result of that meeting.

Then as quickly as the smile came on it faded and she turned her attention back to me. 'We really need to talk about something regarding Warren. Are you free for lunch tomorrow?'

Her melted smile had morphed into a needy look that owned her face, her eyes those of an orphaned child on a street corner begging for sustenance. As much as I didn't want to sit alone through a lunch with Zuzana, it just so happened that Monday was my other day off, and she knew it since Warren and I skied most Mondays. Not to mention I was still feeling somehow responsible for Warren's death, which left me indebted to his widow. I swallowed the 'no' that wanted to come out of my mouth and told her I'd be happy to have lunch with her.

'I'll make reservations at the Jerome then.' She turned her face towards my brother and the smile grew back. 'Nice to meet you, Toby. It's reassuring to know we have people out there like you protecting our country.'

As if it was her country. Her Czech accent lingered behind her as she crossed the room to rejoin a table of women friends. I resented that she had seen fit to go out to dinner so soon after her husband's death. Or maybe my resentment had more to do with the way she was dressed. Zuzana's clothes always bordered on flamboyant, so she was within her rights to dress the same way she always had, but with her husband dead it seemed in bad taste. I told myself to stop being judgmental.

'What was that?' Toby asked, his eyes riveted to her leather-clad bottom until it was settled back in her seat.

'Warren's widow. And don't go there. She's pregnant,' I said, choking on the words. It also hurt that there would be a piece of Warren on this planet that had nothing to do with me. 'Besides, you're engaged.'

'Yeah, but I'm not married yet,' he said, only half kidding as he turned back to his sushi.

The rest of the meal was uneventful except for the check. I thought Toby was going to pop a blood vessel when he saw the total.

'Three hundred and thirty dollars and twenty-two cents. What the fuck is this? I didn't think you could spend that much on fish.'

'That's Aspen for you. And that's before tip,' I added – insult to injury. I pulled out my wallet and threw my credit card on the table. 'We'll split.'

Toby pushed my card back at me and reached into his pocket for his wallet. 'No, sis. This is mine.' He put his card in the folder and the server swooped it up before he could even lay it back down on the table. I looked back to the mobbed bar area. Evidently there were people waiting for the table.

Back at the A-frame, Toby raided the refrigerator for another beer and plopped himself into the Barca. 'This thing is really comfortable,' he said. 'I'll have to think about getting me one.'

'That mean you're thinking of leaving the army?' I pressed.

'Don't think I'll ever leave the army. But I'm actually noodling on getting out of Special Forces. You know, Fenicia will have to be Stateside.' I held my breath, not wanting to risk saying one word that might change his mind about taking himself out of that hellhole. 'Then again, as nice as it is being here with you in the mountains, in this oasis from evil, there's something about my job that keeps me going back. After fifteen years, I think I'd die of boredom if I went back to civvy life.'

Words I didn't really want to hear. Naturally, I worried about him being in such a dangerous place, but kept it parked somewhere in the back of my mind so it wouldn't ruin my waking hours. Toby was so important to me I didn't know what I'd do if anything ever happened to him. A sick part of me hoped he'd lose a leg too, below the knee, so he'd be relegated to a desk job like his soon-to-be wife. That was the only thing other than the final battle that would stop him from chasing adventure. He was an action junkie. Just like me. It was clearly in our DNA. Only the kinds of action we chose were worlds apart.

# NINETEEN

I was in the loft, trying to do my reading for the next day's Mythology class after a few glasses of wine, nodding in and out as Circe turned Ulysses' men into pigs. I was dozing with the book parked on my chest when the sound of howling woke me with a start. I was used to howls from animals in the night, especially coyotes, but this howl wasn't coming from outside. It was coming from inside the house. From downstairs. It didn't take much to figure out where the ungodly sound originated. It was coming from my brother.

I scrambled down the stairs and flung open the door to Sam's former room. Toby's eyes were closed, but he was thrashing about in the bed, the sheets and blankets thrown to the side, his muscled body taut and lean in his boxer shorts. His convulsive movements reminded me of playing dodge ball as a child, standing against a wall trying not to get hit. He was shouting something that didn't make any sense. Then I realized he was screaming in Arabic.

'Toby!' I yelled. 'Toby!'

His eyes sprang open. He glared at me standing in the open door as if I had just interrupted him in a private act. 'What?'

'You were having a bad dream. You were howling like a banshee. And shouting gibberish.'

'I was?' He sat up and rubbed his eyes and I could tell he was revisiting what nightmare had prompted the outburst. 'Oh, yeah. I was having a bad dream. I was working out in the camp gym and some guy wearing Arab robes came in with an AK forty-seven and opened up on us.'

'Oh my God, that's horrible,' I said. 'Could something like that really happen?'

'Already did,' he said, laying back down in the bed and pulling the blankets back to his chin. 'Nighty-night, sis,' he said, closing his eyes. It wasn't long before he was snoring.

I climbed back into the loft, wide awake now, and looked

out the window to the bright night, the whole of my yard and driveway lit by a full moon. The deciduous trees like the Aspens were bare of course, but the pine branches sported a frosting of snow so thick it was a wonder it hadn't fallen to the ground. I studied the tranquil scene and thought about my brother. The idea of him committing to Fenicia was growing on me. Maybe having some nieces and nephews, so our minuscule family wasn't just him and me.

Then I thought about him working in an arena so close to death. I wondered how he could think of getting married and having kids. Would his wife move to some base in the US where she didn't have to worry about being shot? A place Toby might come home to some day sooner or later? Then I thought about the terrorist shooting up the gym. Mom never really taught us to be religious, but I did believe in a higher power and found myself praying that nothing bad would happen to Toby. Right now, he was the person I loved most in this world.

I woke at five a.m. to make him breakfast. I wasn't about to let my only sibling leave hungry. He had showered and dressed and was clean-shaven for the first time since he'd arrived. His packed duffel bag waited at the door. Just seeing it made me lonely.

'Hi Grets,' he said, greeting me with a brotherly kiss. 'You didn't have to get up.'

'Right. Like I'm not going to get up to say goodbye to the brother I only see every blue moon or so.' I recalled how he had howled in his sleep. It had happened again a couple of hours later, but the second time I hadn't bothered to check on him. 'How'd you sleep?'

'Like a rock. Must be the elevation.'

'I thought Afghanistan was high.'

'It is now that you mention it.'

I made coffee and gave him a mug. I didn't even bother to ask how he took it. A soldier would take it black, of course. There probably wasn't a lot of milk in the Afghan mountains unless you wanted it from a goat. I scrambled some eggs and toasted him an English muffin. Bays from the refrigerated section. I knew they were his favorite. He ate like a soldier, head down, no talking. When he came up for air, I resumed conversation.

'So what now?'

He looked at his watch. It was a thick, tough-looking model. A soldier's watch. 'Garrett's picking me up in fifteen. Back to the Springs where we'll catch transport back overseas.'

Overseas. He made it sound like a vacation. 'Will you be married the next time I see you?'

'Hope so. I really do. She's amazing. When I'm with her, it's like something indescribable. Gives meaning to life. But makes me feel out of control too, like the most out of control I've ever been. It's a good out of control though. Not like out of control trying to herd Mom's boyfriends out the door.' He laughed, but it was an ironic laugh. 'That was a bad out of control. This out of control is like driving as fast as you can in a good car – like there are no speed limits in sight. But there's another person sharing the controls with you.'

'Please, y'all are going make me vomit,' I said, imitating a southern dialect. 'Was that supposed to be poetic?'

'As close as I come.' A pair of headlights appeared down the road and stopped in front of the A-frame. He gave me a big hug, picked up his duffel bag, and headed out the door. 'Love you, sis,' were his last words. As I watched the red tail lights recede, they reminded me of an animal peering out from the brush.

A vacuum of loss fell over me, and I pushed it back with a second cup of coffee. Then I did what I always do when I'm feeling poorly. I put on my ski gear. I may have had that lunch date with Zuzana, but that wasn't until one o'clock and I wasn't going to let the day be entirely ruined.

I was on the bucket the minute it started.

# TWENTY

I sat in the lobby of the Jerome trying not to squirm out of my seat. The hotel was the *grande dame* of Aspen, one of the few places in town that retained much of its vintage character from the mining days. The furniture was heavy, the sofas velvet-fringed, and a grandfather clock ticked out the time. It was one of my favorite venues in town, and I should have been able to appreciate the grandeur of my surroundings, but for the fact that I was going to be dining with Zuzana McGovern when that clock struck one.

Even after having skied and going home to shower this morning, I made a point of arriving early. Though I don't know why I'd bothered. Zuzana was usually late. Both my mind and my stomach were churning as I sat among the casually dressed clientele talking or texting on their smart phones. The longer I sat, the more unwound I became. Why had Zuzana invited me to lunch? What exactly was it all about?

She made her entrance fifteen minutes after the appointed hour, nothing outside the ordinary. Dressed all in beige, she was a monochromatic vision of style. Beige slacks and sweater and jacket. Even beige leather boots. I was sure her ensemble was as expensive as it looked comfortable. I was wearing my second-hand black cashmere turtleneck gleaned from the Thrift Shop last winter and one of my better pairs of jeans.

Her eyes scanned the room for important people before she floated over to me. 'I'm so sorry to be late,' she said not very quietly. 'I had a call from the mortuary in Glenwood just as I was walking out the door. There were some last-minute questions about the service.'

I let the comment drop, a none-too-subtle shot across the bow that pre-warned me of the direction the lunch might take. Warren's service was scheduled two days from now, an event I dreaded more than I can say. Without waiting for my reaction to her announcement, she turned and walked into the dining room, leaving me to follow behind her like a humble servant. The hostess seated us in a corner booth, enabling both of us to look out across the room. The clientele was typical of winter. Half were local bankers or real-estate agents looking for the golden calf and half were tourists taking a day off from skiing.

We looked at the menus and placed our order quickly, pumpkin soup for me, chicken noodle for her. Two green salads. Zuzana ordered a glass of wine, something I found peculiar in light of her pregnancy though from what I knew a glass or two is within reasonable limits. But at lunch? I stuck with water.

The waiter brought out Zuzana's Chardonnay followed by the two bowls of soup. She sipped at her wine and stared at me over the rim of her glass with cool blue eyes set in porcelain skin, her lashes dusted blond. 'You know Warren and I considered you among our closest friends,' she opened.

The hackles that climbed my back made me wonder if this was how Toby felt when he was in an ambush. My intuition had told me that lunch was going to be unpleasant, but it hadn't me prepared for just how unpleasant. My friendship with Warren dated back ten years pre-Zuzana, so where did this 'our' come from? Her use of 'our' was sort of like men saying 'we're' pregnant these days. I've never quite figured out the other half of the 'we' in that equation. Did that mean my father, whoever he was, the guy who disappeared, was pregnant with Toby and me too at the same time as my mother? That would be quite the trick.

'So I hate to bring you back to that day,' she continued, 'but I'm sure you can understand how disturbed I am. I just can't get it out of my mind, trying to figure out what the two of you were doing out of bounds together. I'm going to stop beating around the bush and ask you straight out. Were you having an affair with my husband?'

The question was so unanticipated it would have blown me off my chair had we not been sitting in a booth. Even so, I was having trouble staying upright, the blood draining from my face like it had been plunged into ice. In a few sentences I had gone from being one of 'our' closest friends to a conniving mistress. Though the question didn't merit a response, my resounding

*NO* drew looks from around the room, and I should have let it rest at that. I owed her no explanations. But the question was eating at me, so after a count of five I asked, 'Where in hell did that come from?'

'I don't know . . .' she started to say. Then she stopped herself. 'Yes, I do know. Since no one seems to know what the two of you were doing there, I have to wonder if you two were having some kind of rendezvous that went wrong.'

My soup spoon fell from my hand and clattered loudly against the bowl. The heads that had turned at my forceful response turned again. Well, maybe the spoon didn't just fall. Perhaps it was thrown down a little. It was a challenge not to shout out the five-letter word banging the sides of my skull. The one that starts with a B. But somehow I maintained my cool. 'What would give you an idea like that?'

'These,' she said. She pulled a manila envelope from her purse and threw it on the table in front of me. Inside was a stack of photographs. I leafed through them and recognized them as Warren and me in the pre-Zuzana years. There was a shot of us at the top of the Highland Bowl on a clear day and another at the top of Walsh's waiting for tandem paraglides. There was a photo of us sitting at the top of West Maroon Pass on the hike to Crested Butte and of a moonlight ski up Buttermilk. Warren and I always seemed to end up together somewhere at the top. The photos were all innocent, each taken by some unremembered third party. There was nothing incriminating in any of them. 'I found them in his desk.'

'Zuzana,' I said, staring her directly in the eye. 'I have no idea why he was keeping these pictures other than as memories of good times.' I studied the photo in my hand. We were straddling our bikes at the top of Independence Pass, sweaty and gritty after the tortuous ride, our helmets off, his hair stuck to his head with sweat, my hair whipping in the wind. He was wearing the smile of achievement while I looked at him with what was clearly adoration. Was I that transparent? Evidently. I re-examined the other photos and saw some variation of that look on my face in all of them. The thought that he had intentionally saved these pictures from the dozens taken of the two of us over the years made me sadder than I already was.

You see, the truth was that I *was* having an affair with Warren. Unfortunately it was only in my mind. I lay the pictures back on the table. 'Look,' I said. 'I want to make it perfectly clear that I was not sleeping with your husband and never have. The only physical contact I ever had with Warren was giving him a hand up. And vice versa.'

She pushed the pictures toward me. 'These are yours. Keep them.'

Any protest I may have offered died as a local realtor, a tall redhead with a facelift that basically left her teeth barred, came over to the booth. Edna Blood was renowned for sweetening her deals by buying her clients Range Rovers after their closings. As if someone who can afford a fifty-million-dollar house needs another car. She'd been part of a group who'd tried to do a land grab on Sam's property while he was alive, starting at mere pennies and offering him everything from a place in Honolulu to a trip to the moon by the time they were done.

Her eyes glossed over me and glued themselves on Zuzana. I scooped up the pictures and stuffed them into my backpack. Edna Blood sat down uninvited and started offering up condolences to the widow. This segued into a question if she intended to stay all alone in that huge Starwood house, a thinly veiled attempt to solicit business.

'Well I won't be totally alone,' Zuzana said, her chameleon face finding the silver-lining-in-a-tragedy kind of look. 'We were pregnant.'

'Congratulations,' the realtor gushed, toning it down appropriately after realizing the congratulations were bittersweet. She continued a tête-à-tête with Zuzana while I quietly ate my soup. The pumpkin turned bitter in my mouth and suddenly I wanted nothing more than to be out of there. Edna Blood got up and said something consoling before taking her leave, and it was just Zuzana and me once again. I wanted the realtor back. I wanted out of there so much more than bad it was sick.

Deciding I'd filled my obligation to Zuzana, I made a show of looking at my watch. 'Hey, I really hate to do this, but I just remembered I have to be somewhere.' Anywhere but here. 'I hope you don't mind.'

Her face turned entirely kind. 'I've upset you. Of course, I don't mind, but before you go, can I just ask you one more thing?'

I nodded to keep the resounding *Yes, I mind* from exploding out of my mouth. Anything, anything to be out of there. Exercising the utmost patience, I asked, 'What is it, Zuzana?'

'There's this part of me that wonders if this pregnancy didn't upset you. And that maybe . . . just maybe . . .' She didn't finish her statement, but the words hung in the air, their ugliness slowly taking shape in my brain, congealing like grease floating on the top of last night's cold dishwater. And then she articulated it. 'Only you didn't die.'

That was it. I couldn't hold myself back. The words catapulted from my mouth. 'You bitch. I may not remember everything that happened on that mountain, but I remember some. What I saw was Warren going out of bounds before me. And I'm pretty sure I went to stop him. My memory may be coming back slowly, but it is coming back and when it does, you'll be the first to know.' I stood up and threw a twenty on the table which actually wouldn't have come close to covering my half of the meal, but that was all I had on me and I was in no mood to wait for a credit card transaction. 'I'll see you at the service.'

Her face, which had at first registered shock at the revelation of my partial recovery of my memory, turned to plain ugliness as she said, 'I'd rather you didn't come.'

I wanted to gasp. To shout how dare she cheat me of the chance to send Warren off to wherever. Then again, that wasn't nearly as bad as accusing me of attempted murder-suicide. By banning me from Warren's service, she was emancipating me from worse pain. I left the room feeling liberated. I had suspected lunch was going to be unpleasant, though I'd had no idea how much so. One good thing had come from the lunch, though. Zuzana's actions had absolved me of my guilt. My grief and misery had morphed into anger, which felt a whole lot better than guilt.

I should have thanked her.

# TWENTY-ONE

My anger kept intensifying as I walked along the streets, and I was so spitting-fire mad by the time I climbed into the Wagoneer, I was probably a danger behind the wheel. The good news was I was no longer the simpering put-upon wimp I'd been since Warren's death. That dog had taken its tail out from between its legs. I was myself again. An angry self, but myself. And although anger sure isn't the finest emotion, it ranks far above guilty in my world. The anger stayed with me the entire way home. The nerve of Warren's widow, implying that her husband was dead because of some misfiring of my impulses.

The anger grew worse as the afternoon passed. I circled the living room thinking 'how dare she' to 'what a bitch' that she would deny me access to the funeral. I tried to calm myself – I'm good at deflecting negative energy – but all logic was overruled in this case by my unchecked emotions.

The saving grace was that it was Monday and I had Mythology class at four o'clock. I contemplated skipping class altogether, but I'd already missed last week's class because of the avalanche and getting my degree was important to me. I wasn't going to let Zuzana ruin that. Besides, I needed something to knock my brain back into its normal groove. This confrontation with Warren's widow had put me into an alien mental state. The only time I've felt my blood pressure rise is coming upon a ski accident or tossing off one of the charges we use for avalanche mitigation. Right now I felt if I didn't have some kind of distraction my head might explode.

I grabbed my books and headed out the door.

I'd started back to college after Sam died, taking one class a semester. I'd done some community college while Mom was alive, but it was tough both time-wise and financially. At the time my goal was getting a degree in finance. We were always so on the edge of bankruptcy in my youth that I thought the only thing a person should want to do is make a lot of money. So to me finance said it all. I was going to make sure our family was financially secure.

Then Mom died and life changed. I bailed from Milwaukee, came to the mountains, and my eyes opened up. Money can't buy the peaks with the setting sun cresting over them or the pure blue sky at noon or waking up after a major snow and taking your first crisp breath of morning air. It can't buy the feeling you have floating down the mountain both conquering or working with gravity. It can't buy the feeling you have when you're beholden to no one other than yourself or when working feels the same as not working. And in all truth, there hasn't been one minute of regret about moving here instead of getting a degree.

But there was this part of me that wanted to better myself. I loved my job and the folks I skied with, but the reality was that at thirty-five my brain was hungry. So another goal I was acting on was getting my degree. God knows what I was going to do with it when I got it, but for the time being attending classes filled a need to expand my horizons. Who knows, maybe I'd end up teaching some day. Or going on to law school. Take history, for example.

But at this stage of the game, I found myself intrigued by the story of our world, how we kept screwing things up over and over and somehow recovering before doing it all over again. In other words history. If you understand what's gone before, you have a better chance of understanding what's happening now. Or misunderstanding what's happening now.

Now I know Mythology isn't exactly history, but Greek culture sure is. Besides, there were no openings in American History that semester.

I got to class late on purpose, not wanting to share the perils of Pauline with any of my classmates and especially not with the professor, Timothy Dale. Tim and I had a dating encounter during my first semester a couple years ago, and while the relationship ended on a positive note, he occasionally acted like he still had some skin in my game. Courtesy of the local paper, he would already have been informed about the avalanche and my near miss with carbon monoxide poisoning, and I was in no mood to answer the questions I knew would be forthcoming.

He was putting an outline on the board with his back to the class when I snuck into the room. Rail thin with an intense lean face, he wore his hair in a gray ponytail swept back from a receding hairline. And though he was pretty far along in the second half of the game, you'd never guess it. Even as the marker swept across the board, he exuded a sense of suppressed energy. He'd stopped skiing for what he called 'safety' reasons, but he was a distance runner in the summer and snowshoed the back country in the winter. His not being a skier was one of the reasons we weren't really compatible. That and the fact he was the controlling type and I wasn't the type to be controlled.

The room was nearly full. It was early in the semester and interest remained high. His class was the typical mix you found at the community college, half young age-appropriate people working towards degrees, the other half north of fifty, most of them older women expanding their horizons or looking for a positive way to kill time. I couldn't be sure which. The older people audited the classes, which meant they didn't take the tests and they didn't write papers. But they always did the week's readings, unlike some of us taking the class for credit like yours truly this particular week.

My attempt to slip in unnoticed was an exercise in futility. My celebrity of the past week had preceded me and all heads turned at my entrance, including that of Tim Dale who had the visual acuity of a fly.

'Ms Westerlind, we are truly glad to see you in one piece,' he said, returning to his work on the board, putting into words what the rest of the class must have been thinking. The room more or less broke out into a flurry of congratulations on my being alive, on my good luck to have survived two so very close calls. No one made mention of Warren. They didn't have to. He was there in the room with us. Tim Dale finished his outline and turned around to face the room.

'And now since we've noted how Greta has avoided having her thread prematurely cut by the fates, let's see what's happened to those less fortunate at escaping the wrath of the gods.'

The board behind him held an outline of the Titan family tree. It was more of the same lunacy that Ovid was throwing us. At the top of the tree was Cronus, who ate all his children at birth so they couldn't grow up to usurp him. Number two on the board was his wife Gaia who threw him the ultimate curve and hid Zeus from him. Uh-oh. We all know who won that battle in the end. Thank God he hadn't outlined Zeus's progeny. I don't know if the semester was long enough for that outline.

Professor Tim erased the Titan family tree and moved on to the story of Heracles, who, as it turned out, was one of Zeus's many sons. Big surprise there. Tim pointed out Heracles' name had been changed to Hercules when the Romans hijacked Greek culture, as had Zeus changed to Jupiter and Hera to Juno. 'The Romans so worshipped the greatness of the Greeks, that the better educated Romans spoke Greek rather than Latin. And we all know that the Romans were only good for two things. What are they, class?'

'Wars and sewers,' the upper ten per cent called out.

Anyhow, over the course of the evening's class, Heracles was conceived when Zeus seduced Alcmene by disguising himself as her husband. Hera was so pissed about Heracles being spawned by Zeus's seed that later in his life she inflicted him with a madness that caused him to kill his wife and children. So what do you do when you've committed such a despicable act?

'You go to the Oracle at Delphi. Kind of like going to confession,' said Tim Dale, crinkling his nose in a manner that told us he found the entire concept of confession absurd. 'The oracle told him he would have to report to his arch enemy, King Eurystheus, who assigned him to twelve labors to exonerate him from his crime.' The nose crinkled again. 'You see, purgatory hadn't been invented yet, so Heracles had to do his penance on earth.'

Tim walked us through one of the more creative of the labors, cleaning out a stable that hadn't been cleaned for thirty years, a daunting and unpleasant chore to be certain. But

Heracles rose to the occasion, changing the course of a couple of rivers to flush all that shit out. And you think we live in creative times.

More mythological notes. At one point Hera was tricked into nursing baby Heracles and her milk was so strong he spat it out and invented the Milky Way. Hera often punished Zeus's girlfriends by turning them into animals or causing them to explode into flame.

For some reason, this led me to think of my lunch with Zuzana McGovern at the Jerome this afternoon. Given the choice between dealing with her and Hera, I'd take Hera any time.

When class ended three hours later, I deftly slipped out the door before Professor Dale could corner me to ask me any questions. I grabbed a copy of the local paper on my way out of the building and tucked it under my arm. Snow was coming down harder than ever and everything was blanketed in white, including my car. I tossed the newspaper and my backpack on to the front seat before brushing it off.

The windows were fogged up when I climbed into the car, so I turned on the defrost. Switching on the interior light to read while waiting for the windows to clear, I was jolted upright in my seat upon seeing the photo of a young woman gracing the front page. The copy underneath said she had not taken her flight as scheduled on Sunday and no one had been able to locate her since. Looking back at the picture, there was no doubt in my mind who the missing person was. It was the young woman who had been at the Bugaboo with Dr Duane Larsen on Saturday night.

# TWENTY-TWO

read the article squinting under the Wagoneer's dim interior light. According to the girl's roommate at the Snowflake Inn, Kim Woods hadn't made it back on Saturday night. Which her friend didn't find terribly odd in and of itself. She just assumed Kim had hooked up with someone. But when she hadn't returned by the time they were supposed to leave for the airport on Sunday, she called the police as well as Kim's parents. It hadn't taken her parents long to push the panic button and now the missing girl was front-page news. Further down in the article Dr Duane made his appearance. He told police he had dropped Kim off at her hotel before making his way back to his down-valley home. The article went on to explain that he was a family friend and felt absolutely horrible that she had gone missing.

I put the paper down, beyond weirded out that I had spent my entire Sunday with the guy who was perhaps the last person to see Kim Woods before she disappeared. My fertile brain started scrolling through options that didn't involve Duane Larsen. The young blond found a guy and ran off. Unlikely. She'd left the Bugaboo around one a.m. and since town shuts up tight as a drum at two that didn't give her a lot of time to make a new friend. Unless it was the guy she was talking to in the Bugaboo before she and the doctor left. Or maybe she'd decided to go for a late-night walk, made a drunken mistake and wandered off to parts unknown. Not impossible. There were plenty of places to wander off the beaten path and fall victim to cold and wilderness. Her lodge was one of the last old-fashioned ones on the edge of town. It was also walking distance to the river.

My heart skipped, thinking of the banks of the Castle Creek and how steep and slippery they could be. There had been a sad story the year before of a young New Zealander who up and disappeared. There had been all kinds of talk of foul play until his body turned up at the base of the Maroon Creek bridge a week after the alarm was sounded. It was determined he had somehow stepped over the edge of the bridge in a snowstorm.

I'd been on the volunteer search party, but wasn't there when his body was recovered. Instead I was with his parents when the bad news was delivered. They had flown from New Zealand to help in the search, and it was utter heartbreak to watch the couple clinging to each other with all hope gone, trying to digest the loss of their only child.

Could something so bizarre have happened to young Kim?

I pulled from the college lot on to eighty-two and headed into town with thoughts of both Kim Woods and Duane Larsen occupying my mind. OK, I barely knew the guy, but something about him was compelling. Don't get me wrong, there was still a huge block of sadness left by Warren's death, but much as it seemed premature, my day with Duane had created a wedge towards moving that block along. And while the loss of Warren hurt, the stark reality was that Warren wasn't mine, never had been and, thus, wasn't mine to lose. He was a great ski, bike and hike buddy who had been killed in a bizarre, inexplicable ski accident leaving behind a widow and an unborn child. His death was a true tragedy that may have belonged to me, but he didn't.

So now, I was admitting to myself that maybe subconsciously, I had been thinking things could go someplace with Dr Duane. He ticked all the boxes. His looks for one, his comely face and strong jaw, those lovely mismatched eyes behind the wire rims, his calm manner. The fact that he not only had a regular job, but it was one that helped people. He was cute, he was fit, he had a career and a life. He lived here, he was available, and he could ski. In truth, though I hadn't wanted to admit it to myself, somewhere in the recesses of my mind maybe I was thinking there were possibilities with him. With forty looming in the not-too-distant future, it might be time to think about where the rest of my life might be going. Right now it was a one-wheeled cart on a one-wheeled street. Don't get me wrong, I had a great life, and you would literally have to crane me out of this valley. But

I'd reached the age where you might give up some things for the right person. Had I actually been flirting with the idea that Duane Larsen could be a right person? A guy who now turns out to be the last person to see a missing girl?

When I reached town, I headed straight to City Market. I may have been weirded out about Duane Larsen and Kim Woods, but that didn't stop me from being hungry. It takes more than utter disaster to ruin my appetite. I parked and went inside.

The store was its usual seasonal packed chaos and I had to squeeze past a group of Argentines in the entrance who were clearly oblivious to the existence of people in the northern hemisphere. I went straight to the sushi counter at the back of the store and picked up a tuna roll and a sashimi package, my mind churning in multiple circles as I went through the self-pay.

The Bundy guy and his cameraman were outside the store again looking for fresh victims. As far as I could see, they had hit the mother lode. They were interviewing a long-time local who was not only a hotshot skier, but a local journalist. I remember he'd had his own Ted Bundy story in the paper a few years ago. He'd been around ten years old the day Ted jumped out the courthouse window. And like all little boys, his imagination had filled up with possibilities. So when he came home one day and reported that he had ridden his bike past Ted Bundy wearing lederhosen, no one believed him. Later, it was learned the house of a local Austrian guy had been broken into during Bundy's disappearance and his lederhosen stolen. The apologies from adults had flown like the river filled with snowmelt.

I brushed the snow off the windshield and climbed into the car. MISSING GIRL screamed at me from the front seat. I picked up the newspaper and threw it into the back seat.

I pulled up in front of my home with stories of Ted Bundy filling my mind, of how all the local girls had been terrified and how no one had gone anywhere by themselves the entire time he was unaccounted for. Though my solitude meant the world to me, I got out of the car thinking of how truly isolated I was. Maybe it was the resurrected Bundy stories, maybe it

was the missing girl, but suddenly the idea of getting a new
dog didn't seem such a bad idea.

I'd eaten my carryout sushi dinner and was in the loft reading
the next week's Mythology assignment. Zeus had just impregn-
ated Danae in the golden shower of all time when the landline
rang. I picked up the cordless phone next to me. It's hard to
say whether I was more freaked out or excited to hear his
voice.

'Hi. Duane Larsen here.' He sounded nervous, like a nerdy
high-school junior building up confidence to ask the most
popular girl to the prom. There was vulnerability present in
his voice that had not been there before. An unfamiliar trill
of excitement ran up my spine.

'Dr Larsen,' I lobbed back, putting the realm of conversation
in his hands, trying to sound flippant, as if I had no knowledge
that he was the last person to see a girl who went missing in
the early hours of the morning.

'I don't know if you've read the paper or not.' He left it
dangling. I had no option but to pick it up.

'Uh, yeah, I did. I saw about your friend's daughter. That's
terrible,' I added swiftly, stuck for better words.

'You don't know the half of it.' And without any further
mention of the missing girl, he said, 'I could really use a friend
right now. Could you meet for a bite?'

It was eight o'clock and I was dressed in my pajamas. Well,
the oversize T-shirt I sleep in. My grocery-store sushi was just
making its way along my digestive tract. The last thing on my
mind was more food.

'Sure,' I said.

'You like sushi?'

'Love it.'

# TWENTY-THREE

was on my way into town for my second sushi meal of the night, and my third in two days, questioning the wisdom of a rendezvous with a man who was the last person to see a young girl before she went missing. But my curiosity was in full thrust and I figured there could be no danger in meeting him in a public place. Not wanting to put Jimmy Finkle at risk of aggravating his well-heeled clientele again, I told Duane to meet me at the second most popular sushi place in town, a place half as expensive as where Toby and I had dined the night before.

He wasn't there when I arrived, so I took a seat at the sushi bar thinking that was safer than a table. He walked through the curtained door five minutes later, brushing snow off his jacket and hair in the entry. He saw me watching him and smiled. My smile back was manufactured. After all, there was no way of knowing for sure if he was a good guy or a predator.

'Hello, Doctor,' I said, holding out my hand as he sat down in order to avoid any intimate gesture such as a hug. He took my hand and held it a bit too long, one green eye, one brown, intent upon mine. He looked rattled.

'Greta, I'm so glad you came. You're looking at a guy who could really use an ear.' A Johnny-on-the-spot waiter appeared to take a drink order and we both ordered a beer. The waiter disappeared and with the first round of business taken care of, he proceeded to the second. 'So you read about Kimmy disappearing?'

The intimate use of the girl's name threw me a little. The paper had referred to her as Kim. 'It just defies imagination,' he continued. 'I dropped her off in front of the Snowflake and watched her climb up the stairs. What happened from there is a total mystery. Her roommate said she never came inside.' He bowed his head in frustration and a thatch of hair fell across his forehead. He brushed it back with his hand. 'You can't know how responsible I feel. I've known Kimmy since she was born. Her father was my college roommate at Cornell. I was an usher at her parents' wedding.'

He paused to sip his beer. It looked like he was having trouble swallowing. Nerves, I decided. He continued his story. 'Dave and Nancy flew in this morning and spent the day with the police. I just left them at their hotel. They didn't want to eat anything. They're completely distraught.'

'I would guess so. But what about you? What are they saying to you?' I asked frankly, wanting to spit the question into open air as quickly as possible.

'Dave and Nancy?'

'Them too. But I'm talking about the police.'

His face turned incredulous that I would even pose the question, like he'd just been summoned to testify against his best friend. 'You mean, because I dropped her off? They asked what we were doing together and I explained that I'm like an uncle to her. She'd asked me to take her and her friend to the Bugaboo because she read in *People* about all the celebrities there. But her friend decided not to come at the last minute. I guess she'd strained a muscle skiing and wanted to stay in the room and watch TV.

'Anyhow, she found her celebrities. She pointed a couple of them out to me, one guy she said was a famous rapper. She was excited about that.

'When I told her it was time to leave, Kimmy wanted to stay, but I told her she had to take a ride home from me. I didn't want her walking home alone in the cold with her hotel on the edge of town like that. Dave and Nancy told me the police asked a couple of leading questions about me and they set them straight right away. They know how much I love that kid. This is as upsetting to me as it is to them.'

'Maybe there's some explanation,' I offered lamely. 'Maybe she met a guy or something and will turn up.'

'I don't know. I have a bad feeling. When I left Dave and Nancy at their hotel I felt so bad I didn't know what to do. That's why I called you. I didn't want to be alone after leaving them. I didn't want this sick feeling to gel any thicker than it already has.'

One of the sushi chefs leaned over and asked in broken English if we wanted to order. Duane turned towards me and asked, 'How hungry are you?'

'Medium?' Actually, I wasn't hungry at all, but I'm always good once food is put in front of me. Especially good food. He turned back to the sushi chef and to my utter astonishment started speaking in Japanese. They went back and forth a couple of times before the chef smiled and began to work on a fish, his knife rapidly rendering it into perfect slices.

'Were you just speaking Japanese?' I asked, realizing the absurdity of the question the moment it left my mouth.

'Bad Japanese, I'm sure. But I like to sharpen my tongue once in a while. Studied for a semester in Kyoto.'

The chef laid a tray of sashimi on the ledge of the sushi bar. Duane picked up his chopsticks and began deftly sliding pieces into his mouth. I noticed he ate without any compunction, his appetite unaffected by being on the cutting edge of a disaster. Like mine. I ate too, my appetite healthy for someone who had already eaten dinner.

After demolishing half the tray, he put his chopsticks down and turned to me, his eyes luminous in the low overhead lights. They were warm enough to melt me. 'If you don't mind, I'd just rather not talk about Kimmy anymore. There's nothing I can do other than what David and Nancy are doing. And that's wait. Who knows, maybe she'll turn up tomorrow. She did have a small wild streak,' he added.

One would hope she'd turn up, but to me it wasn't looking good.

He played with his chopsticks for a minute and looked at me, putting on his professional face, probing my face with doctorly concern. 'And how are you holding up? I mean after your two near misses?'

'You asked me that the other day. And like I told you before, I feel fine. Physically anyhow.' Without giving it proper thought, I blurted out, 'Mentally is a whole other story. I'm having trouble with the widow.'

'What kind of trouble?'

'She's got it in her head that I was having an affair with Warren and we were out of bounds for some kind of sexual tryst.'

'Were you?'

'Was I what?'

'Having an affair with him.'

'Only in my mind.' Had I actually said that? I sure wanted to grab those words out of the air and shove them back in my mouth. But they had already gone to wherever sound goes when it brainlessly slips out of the hole you eat with. I hurried to clarify. 'I might have had feelings for Warren, but it was totally one-sided and he never knew. It was never a topic of conversation and it never went anywhere except in my imagination.'

I couldn't believe I was confiding in this relative stranger like this. I mean, all said, it wasn't like we were long-time buddies. I'd known him for less than a week. But there was something about him that was reassuring, a steadiness, an even keel. And he was safe to talk to. He didn't know Zuzana or any other of the town's players. It was a kind of safety net to have an unprejudiced third party to bounce things off. 'If I could just remember, I could explain everything to her. There had to be a reason we were there. There had to be.'

'Now I have a sense for what you're going through. You know, the feeling something bad has happened and it's somehow your fault.'

'I don't think that Warren's death was in any way my fault. In fact, now I think I may have followed him out of bounds.'

'You're getting more memory back?'

'Pieces. But each time they appear the time line goes farther.'

'Well,' he said. 'Remember how you got more memory back when you were relaxed after skiing?'

I nodded yes.

'Then I suggest you relax more.'

The rest of the meal passed amicably, and I think both of us were able to escape the pressures of circumstances beyond our control for the time being. We shared a little sake, but not too much, because we were both driving. I ate too much, kind of like the way early humans used to gorge until they were ready to explode since they could never be sure when or where the next meal might come from. He continued to blow me away with his command of Japanese as he went back and forth with the chef and then several other members of the staff. He would say something and they would laugh and nod, and I was starting to feel privileged just being with him. I'm usually not that kind of person at all. Maybe it was the sake. Or maybe it was him. All I know is I was feeling the best I had since Kayla's death – not to mention Warren's.

After he paid the check, he insisted on walking me to my car. Which cracked me up since I'm a girl who can ski downhill with a 200-pound man behind me in a sled, carry seventy pounds on my back, throw a stick of dynamite thirty yards. I would dare anyone to mess with me. Plus the last thing in the world anyone needs to worry about is being attacked on the streets of Aspen, probably one of the safest places in the world. But I accepted his offer because I think we both wanted to prolong the moment.

It was still snowing lightly, the gentle fluff that floats so very slowly it almost seems suspended in the air. The night was crisp and still and the streets silent as we walked side by side to the edge of town where I'd parked. There was a half-inch of new snow on the windows and the two of us brushed it off together with gloved hands.

The door opened with a heavy metallic squeal, and I climbed into the driver's seat. Then I rolled down the window, extending my time with him just that little bit. 'I really enjoyed myself tonight,' I said. 'You gave me a vacation from my brain.'

'Me too,' he said. His arms were propped on the doorframe and his head was close to mine, his eyes intent behind his glasses. He leaned in through the open window and gave me a light kiss on the lips. I pulled away, more from surprise than anything else. He backed off and stood up straight, looking embarrassed.

'Well, goodnight,' I said, trying to recover.

'Goodnight.'

I rolled up the window and started the car. Let me correct that: I tried to start the car. When I turned the key in the ignition nothing happened. Not even a click. A 'please tell me this isn't happening' feeling swept over me. I swore softly and tried again.

He stood beside the car in the falling snow looking at me curiously. A glance at the dashboard explained the problem. The old-fashioned knob for the lights was pulled out all the way. I had left the lights on. I rolled the window back down.

'I don't suppose you have a jump?' I asked sheepishly.

# TWENTY-FOUR

'It's a good thing I walked you to your car,' he said, the beams of his SUV bouncing back at us on the empty road. 'You would have been stuck.'

'Oh, I could have called triple A,' I said, already thinking about how I was going to have to cross-country ski into town in the morning and get them to come start the car before it got a ticket. 'You don't own a fifty-year-old car without having triple A.'

'As a matter of fact, I've been meaning to ask you where you got your car. I think it's older than my skis.'

'I inherited it from a good friend.'

'Isn't that nice,' he said.

We were coming up on to my turnoff and I pointed it out to him. He made the left turn and drove slowly down the narrow unplowed road. The Greenes' house was lit and he asked me, 'Here?'

'Nope. I'm another quarter mile down the road.'

'Neighborhood's getting crowded,' he said. The lit house receded behind us as we were absorbed in dark once again. We pulled up in front of my house. The A-frame was etched in darkness against the falling white. In my hurry to leave I'd forgotten to leave a light on.

'Used to be a lot of little A-frames back east,' he said, admiring my home through the windshield. 'How'd you get this?'

'I inherited it from a good friend.'

'Same friend as the car?' I nodded. 'That was some friend.'

I gave another nod, kind of rendered speechless. I put my hand on the doorknob but didn't pull on it at first, once again wanting to draw out the evening. Finally I opened the door and climbed out. The snow came nearly to my knees. When I turned to say goodnight, he asked, 'Can I walk you to the door?'

'You don't think I can make it fifteen feet by myself?'

'That snow looks pretty deep.'

'My life is deep snow.'

He turned face forward and gazed out into the woods. 'Could be wild animals out there. You might need protection.'

Now my mama didn't raise no idiots. His offer to walk me to the door of my mountain cabin could only lead to one thing. As far as I could tell the only wild animal in the vicinity was the one sitting inside the car. But he was being a gentleman about it, keeping his distance, leaving the decision to me. I looked at his silhouette in the darkened car, the way his glasses sat on the mild slope of his nose, his head of sandy hair. He was looking at me in a way that went straight to my southern hemisphere without passing go. Putting my dog down, the loss of Warren, my worry about Toby had all built up inside me like a radiator ready to explode. It needed a little release.

'As a matter of fact, I think I see a bear out there,' I said.

He broke into a slow smile, the sides of his mouth turning upward and creasing a dimple into his left cheek. He killed the lights and the engine and came around to where I stood, taking my arm gently and escorting me up the snow-covered walk to my door. I bent down and retrieved the key from beneath the planter.

'That's a great hiding place,' he said, his smile owning his face. 'No burglar would think to look there.'

'I don't even know why I bother to lock it.' I opened the door and reached inside to turn on the light.

'Don't,' he said, taking my hand and leading me into my home. The door clicked shut behind us. Standing in the dark, he reached up and put a hand to my face, stroking my cheek and down my jaw. His hands were the smooth soft hands of a doctor, unlike mine that were more like those of a tradesman. His hand dropped and found mine and he put it to his lips, kissing the back and then turning it over to kiss the palm. One by one he took my fingers into his mouth, sucking in such a manner that I could feel the groove of his tongue. In the dark, the gesture was beyond erotic and my heart started beating harder, my pulse throbbing in my ears as he took my thumb into his mouth. He did the same to my other hand. The intimacy of the action made me squirm.

'I want to do this very slowly,' he said. 'I want to savor every moment of making love to you. I want to lick every inch of you, Greta.'

It's been said the sound of one's own name is the sweetest sound to be heard, and in this case I would certainly make an argument for it. In fact, they could feature me on a testimonial. The way my name had rolled off his tongue made me delirious with happiness that Greta was my name, wrapping my name around me in a manner that made me feel like crying out, 'Yes, I'm Greta. I'm Greta.'

He pressed his body up against mine teasingly, and since he was only slightly taller than me, our parts matched up nicely through our clothes and it wasn't difficult to ascertain his immediate interest in me. He held my face in his hands and finally kissed me on the lips, gently at first and then with increasing intensity.

He took his lips from mine and pressed them next to my ear, whispering as if there were other people around who might hear what he had to say. 'I'm your doctor. I had to undress you when they brought you in the day of the avalanche. Pulled off your parka and all those layers you were wearing.' He put his hand to my chest over my turtleneck. 'I've seen your perfect breasts. Not too large, not too small, and the perfect pink nipples.' He touched a finger to my nipple over the cloth and it hardened to his touch. He pulled my turtleneck over my head and undid my bra, dropping both items of clothing to the floor.

'I've seen that long waist and that flat stomach.' His hands moved along my torso and down my body to my jeans. 'I've seen those thigh muscles and that firm ass.' He undid my zipper with an expert hand and slid off my jeans. They puddled around my boots and socks. I was wearing a cotton thong and he slid a hand beneath it. 'This is the only part of you I haven't seen,' he whispered. 'That wasn't my department. Until now.'

He slipped my thong down my legs, stroking my skin in a way that made me fight not to scream in excitement. His hand returned to the flesh between my legs where he sighed out loud at the discovery of how my body was acknowledging his advances. I tried not to jump out of my skin.

There was no denying, I was reacting to this man in a manner I'd never known before. I've had more than a few lovers and some short-lived relationships, but no one had ever made me respond the way I was responding at that moment, like I just wanted to fuck and be fucked like nothing else I'd ever known.

And we were just getting started.

He pressed his still-clothed body against my naked one, our mouths locked together as we inched along the wall, my pants still around my ankles, until we reached the open bedroom door at the far end of the room. As if guided by instinct he walked me backwards until the backs of my thighs touched the bed. He lowered me on to it and went down on his knees and removed my boots and socks, my jeans and the thong from around my ankles. He parted my legs and his tongue teased me briefly with what was to come. Then he proceeded to make good his promise to lick every inch of my body.

I was ready to scream with desire when he finished, lying on my back on the bed wanting him more than anything. I could hear him taking off his clothes in the dark, feel him as he stretched out beside me. I reached out to stroke his skin, touch his smooth muscles, feel the hair on the back of his thighs.

'Greta.' He was whispering my sweet, sweet name again and it was a glorious sound. I have never liked my name so much as at that moment. 'I've wanted to make love to you since I first met you. Wondered how it would feel to be inside you, to please you as much as I knew you'd please me.'

'Dr Larsen,' I begged, the first words out of my mouth since we'd breached the front door. 'I know you wanted to do this slowly, but could we please get on with the procedure.'

And there in Sam's old bedroom and on Toby's unwashed sheets he put himself into me, and I was Leda and he was the swan and he made sweet, sweet love to me until I cried aloud with happiness. Three times.

# TWENTY-FIVE

Dawn was just finding its way through the cracks in the shuttered bedroom window when I awakened. He was sleeping soundly beside me, the smooth muscles of his chest rising and falling as he took each barely perceptible breath. In the morning light I could finally see his body and I pulled the blanket back to get a better look.

His skin was a smooth olive and his chest and his legs covered with hair a shade darker than his head. I liked that. There was something so masculine about hair. I checked out his body. It was lean and masculine as I would have guessed, his biceps smooth and rounded, his stomach flat, the body of a man who works out with weights. I gazed down to the dark triangle where his legs met and where the object that had been the source of my pleasure in the night lay curled in grateful exhaustion like a sleeping animal. I bent down to kiss it.

My attention turned to his face. I hadn't noticed before how long his eyelashes were or the tiny mole next to his left ear or the small scar on his chin. He was so beautiful. There is no way to explain my feelings at that moment. How grateful I was to be alive. I felt I had discovered some vast secret that rendered me nearly godlike, that the planet and I were one.

He must have sensed me hovering over him, because his eyes slowly opened, one green, one brown in the dark lashes. The way he smiled at me brushed the length of my body. He reached out a hand to touch my face.

And then the expression on his face changed quickly, all the languid beauty gone, replaced by a frantic look.

'Oh, God, where's my phone? I have to check with David and Nancy.' He leapt from the bed, picked up his pants and began rummaging through the pockets.

'Maybe you left it in the car,' I offered, my balloon deflated as the hope of a bliss-filled dawn retreated to parts unknown, even as the soreness between my legs reminded me of the ecstasy of the night before.

He was pulling on his pants and the thick gray turtleneck he'd worn the night before. 'I have to go get it.'

'Your phone won't work here, but I have a landline. It's in the kitchen.'

He rushed to the kitchen, picked up the old rotary phone and dialed, which told me they were really close friends since he knew their number by heart. An eternity passed before I heard him say, 'Dave. Any news?'

There was a dead silence, the kind that screams with bad energy as it drains all air from the room. I had gotten out of bed and was putting on my clothes when I heard him say, 'Where are you?' I finished dressing and went into the kitchen where he stood ashen, still talking on the phone. 'I'll be right down.' He put the phone back on the hook, its mustard cord touching the floor, stretched beyond eternity. His eyes were filled with pain and disbelief.

'They found a body off Castle Creek,' he said in a trembling voice. 'Blond woman. They think it might be Kimmy. Dave and Nancy are going over to identify . . .' His words trailed off and then started up again. 'I told them I'd meet them at the hospital.' And then as if some force reminded him of the night before, of being together in the restaurant, of my dead Wagoneer, of the otherworldly experience that followed, he wrapped his arms around me and gave me a meaningful kiss. 'I'm so sorry,' he said. 'I thought we'd be making love this morning.'

The clouds had cleared and though the sky was still dim, it was going to be a beautiful sunny day. We cleaned off his car in the still early-morning air. He'd left his phone in the drinks holder, so naturally the battery was dead, its life sucked out by the cold. We rode into town together in near silence, his face a mitt of disbelief. Occasionally he would reach his gloved hand over to pat mine, but it was clear his mind was with his friends and their daughter. If I hadn't been through a similar experience a week prior I might have found his behavior odd, but I had, so I didn't.

He dropped me at my car. 'I'm sorry I can't stay around to help,' he said. He sounded like he meant it, but we both knew the best course for him to take now.

'Don't be ridiculous. Your friends need you. I've got triple A.'

He drove off without another word. I felt desolate on his behalf, imagining having to try and bring consolation to a couple who have lost their daughter, especially under such bizarre circumstances, especially after he was the one who dropped her off at her hotel before she went missing.

I waited until his car was out of sight before calling for a jump.

# TWENTY-SIX

What else to say? I spent the next hour in a mixed euphoria, my head so in the clouds from the night before I barely noticed my frozen feet in the numbing early-morning cold, my head weighed down in pain for Duane and his friends. Once triple A arrived and the Wagoneer was up and running, I drove to my usual parking spot and headed into work. Luckily my locker had a change of clothes as I had just thrown last night's clothes back on to ride into town with Duane. I hadn't showered before we left and probably reeked of sex, but I didn't care. I had no desire to wash him off me. Not yet.

The gondola had just started running and I climbed into one of the cabins alone, looking forward to reliving the night before in my head on the way up to the patrol hut. As luck would have it, Singh hopped in as the gondola car rounded the bull wheel, followed by Neverman and then Reininger, Meghan and Winter, filling the car to capacity and pushing asunder any thought of mentally relishing the night before, of replaying each delicious moment of his hands upon my body, not to mention his tongue.

Which actually may have been a good thing. For while I was totally absorbed in my own newly realized happiness, there was no forgetting the urgent nature of the activity that Duane was immersed in at the moment. There was probably no room for me in his mind, nor would I want there to be, not while he was with his dearest friends identifying the body of their daughter. In my private ecstasy, his personal pain had been selfishly pushed to the back of my brain.

So instead of playing my personal soft-core porn in my head or worrying about Duane and his friends, I dialed into my patrol mates as Neverman gave his blow-by-blow of the day's activities. As the gondola moved higher up the mountain the fresh snow-covered slopes glistened like granulated sugar in the morning sun. I listened as Neverman assigned early-morning clearing work and who was going to do avi control.

Aspen Mountain inbounds is relatively safe as far as western ski resorts are concerned, unlike Snowmass that has a lot of inbounds terrain that has to be roped off to prevent skiers from getting into life-threatening slides. Every once in a while a rope-ducking skier defies fate and bites it and the whole Skico catches shit. *That's why the ropes are there, people, get it?*

When it comes to snow conditions, one should never be lulled into a false sense of security. While Aspen Mountain has no huge uncharted territory, it still has aspects that collect enough snow to be dangerous. The odd thing about avalanches or slides is they often take place in some of the most innocuous-looking terrain. It's being lulled into a false sense of security that's the most dangerous.

Conditions have to be perfect, for the avalanche that is. Super-steep slopes aren't usually a problem because when the snow gets too deep or unstable, gravity brings it down. And of course mild grades don't slide because of the inertia. It's those mundane pitches in between you have to watch out for, the friendly-looking rolling slopes that accumulate snow over the weeks with melt/freeze cycles in between, basically turning the surface of the snow into a roller board just waiting for enough accumulation until, whomp, tons of snow go sliding like a sunbather off a greased raft.

We did most of our avi work on Aspen Mountain on sweet-looking slopes that could turn deadly. But those slopes never turned deadly because patrol made sure they didn't, dynamiting the snow loose before it took on ideas of its own.

Anyhow, Winter and Reininger were trash talking some woman while Singh faked being interested. Meghan raised her goggles on her helmet and rolled her eyes at me. We were more or less accustomed to listening to conversations that most women would find offensive. While the talk bugged Meghan, it never bothered me. I considered it valuable insight into the male mind. I mean, we could put a governor on their conversations, but we couldn't put a governor on their minds. I've always considered better understanding of the male psyche good ammunition.

So, Meghan was sitting across from me and it occurred to me she was dissecting me in the knowing way of a fellow woman. Aside from the fact that I probably reeked, was she able to intuit that I had spent the night before having the best sex I'd had in years? Maybe in my entire life? Then it occurred to me that her dissection might have more to do with my physical wellbeing than my romantic.

'Everything OK, girlfriend?' she asked. She was barely younger than me, but sometimes I think she thinks of me as from an entirely different generation.

'Beyond OK,' I replied, suppressing a smile. 'Why you ask?'

'You look tired.'

She'd hit that nail straight on. Maybe Duane and I had slept for about four hours. Between the two of us. It was only fitting that I looked a little rough around the edges.

'Had to get up extra early,' I used as an explanation. 'Left the Wagoneer's lights on while I was out to dinner last night and had to come back into town this morning for a jump.'

'That's a bummer,' Reininger piped in unsolicited. He'd obviously been listening. 'How'd you get home?'

Suddenly all conversation had stopped and five pairs of eyes were on me. 'I got a ride from a friend.'

'Who's the friend?' he teased.

Before I could even attempt an elusive answer, Neverman was on me. He clearly had no interest in who I was with. His interest lay outside that.

'You left your lights on?' he probed. 'How in hell could you walk away from that monster without turning off the lights? The light that thing throws off could illuminate an operating theatre.'

'Nice military reference.' Reininger to Neverman.

'I don't know. I guess I was in a hurry.' Me.

'In a hurry for a little poontang?' Reininger. I would have smacked him on the head if he weren't wearing a helmet.

Neverman was not to be put off. He had little interest in why I was in a hurry last night. His interest lay in my overlooking such a detail as remembering to turn off my lights. Something that would have had me a little concerned too, had the payoff not been so divine. 'No really, Westerlind. That's so unlike you. Just like letting a sled go is unlike you. Just like being on the west side of Ruthie's is unlike you.'

His mention of the lost toboggan made me draw a deep breath. As far as I knew, he had no knowledge of that slip-up. It was pin-drop silent in the gondola as everyone's focus on me intensified, either concerned for me or embarrassed for me. Meghan, Singh: concern. The others: embarrassment. Except for Neverman, whose nearly black eyes were riveted on me, awaiting comment. When I didn't say anything, he added, 'And not remembering why.'

I've never been one to wear my feelings on my sleeve. In fact, if I weren't ski patrol, I could have been a crack litigator. People can say shit to me and it rolls off me like frozen peas off the counter. But everything about the slide bugged me, still bugged me. Put me in the corner like a raccoon trapped in the garage. Duane might be in the picture now, but Warren was still dead.

Normally, I wouldn't have let him bait me, but the avalanche was still sensitive territory. Wanting to blunt Neverman's attack, I shared the following with everyone in the gondola. 'Yeah. Well guess what? My memory is coming back and according to my doctor I should be about to give you one hundo per cent of what happened in a few days. If I don't get stressed out,' I added for Reininger's benefit.

There was momentary silence and then Meghan said, 'Wow, aren't you afraid?'

'Afraid of what?' I might have felt anxious to get my memory back, but I sure didn't feel afraid.

'Afraid of remembering you're secretly in love with Neverman?'

The ensuing laughter broke the tension, and discussion for the rest of the way up dealt with the day's responsibilities.

# TWENTY-SEVEN

That night I sat in front of the television, stuffing potato chips into my mouth and drinking Heineken. I'd tried reading the Metamorphoses, but my mind was too otherwise occupied to concentrate. So I'd turned to mindless TV to keep me awake past my normal bedtime of ten, thinking of Duane's three o'clock text that afternoon. *WITH DAVE AND NANCY. CAN'T LEAVE THEM. WILL CALL LATER.* Even though I couldn't begin to imagine how horrid it must have been to be sharing something so final as the death of a young woman with her parents, that sick, self-absorbed side of me was happy beyond belief he'd texted. And while I understood all too well the pain of loss, my meeting with the girl had been brief and I had no emotional investment in her. I reread the text at least a dozen times. *WILL CALL LATER.* Coddling the phone in my hand like a teenage girl waiting to be asked to the prom, I hoped he remembered there was no cell service at the A-frame. That he had to use the landline number. I flicked through the limited channels of the old-fashioned big box TV, grateful for its mind-numbing company.

I was watching a *Gilligan's Island* rerun on Nickelodeon when the phone rang. My heart nearly jumped from my chest.

'Hey.'

I heyed back at him, trying not to let him know I was over the moon at the sound of his voice.

'Sorry for not calling earlier. I've had one hell of a day as I'm sure you can imagine.' His voice held a world of hurt in it. It no longer held the promise of a caress. 'I hope I didn't wake you.'

'Nope. I'm watching *Gilligan's Island*. I want to improve my mind.'

His laugh relieved a little of the pressure. 'You're kidding, right?'

'Wish I was. It was the only thing I could find and I wasn't ready for bed.' *Because I was waiting up for this call.* 'How are your friends doing?'

'It's so bad, Greta.' There it was again. My name. My beautiful name. 'You can't even begin to imagine. They found her at the bottom of Castle Creek Bridge. So the big question is how did she end up there? Was she running from something or someone or was it some kind of freak accident?' I could hear him suck in air in preparation for his next words. 'From what the coroner says, she died from a broken neck. She guesses it happened when she hit the ground. She said Kimmy's death was immediate and from what I saw I would concur.'

'Her poor parents,' was the best I could muster. I pictured the young blond watching Duane drive away and then heading back out to the clubs for last call. Did some asshole get her into his car and she jumped out at the bridge? I couldn't help but think of how Ted Bundy had removed the door handles on the passenger side of his Volkswagen so his victims couldn't escape. The very personification of evil.

'Didn't anyone see anything?'

'The cops are asking around, but so far nothing. A couple who live down near the creek found her when they went out on cross-country skis this morning.'

I thought of how busy that two-lane bridge was during the day and how traffic trickled down to nothing late at night. I thought of how the young New Zealander had stepped off a similar bridge and fallen to his death. Could her death have been a similar accident? A growing nausea rose inside me. How did a young woman head up to her hotel room one night and end up face down in Castle Creek days later?

The way Duane's voice choked told me he was holding back tears. 'I feel so guilty. I should have seen her to the door. It could have made all the difference.'

'Don't do that to yourself. No one walks anyone to the door in Aspen unless . . .' I stopped short of ending the sentence: *unless they want to get into their pants.* 'Things like that just don't happen here. Well, not since Ted Bundy, anyway.'

Having no further comfort to offer, I remained silent, waiting for him to direct what course the conversation would take. My connection to him felt so strong, it was like we were holding hands through the telephone line. And then he said the exact words I had been mentally trying to draw from his mouth. 'Would it be OK if I came up to see you?'

'Of course,' I replied gently.

I turned off the television and went back to Ovid, trying to concentrate on Icarus flying too close to the sun with the words dancing off the page. A half-hour later the dead silence outside was broken by the muffled sound of his car on the snow-covered road. I closed the book and waited for him in the open doorway.

More snow was predicted overnight, but for the time being the night was crisp and so clear the stars were a mix of nonpareils in a dark chocolate sky. Duane's SUV stopped in front of the walkway. He didn't move from behind the wheel, sitting immobile looking out over the headlights' beams into the woods, the illuminated Aspen trees white jail bars imprisoning the secrets within. From out of nowhere, two mule deer appeared in the headlights, slipping from the trees into the clearing and disappearing on the other side. He rested his head on the steering wheel for a poignant moment and then with what looked like a great deal of effort, he turned off the car.

My feet armed against the cold by my shearling slippers, I walked without a jacket to the driver's side of the car. His head turned towards me and his brown and green eyes held as pathetic an appeal as I'd ever seen. It was I who finally opened the car door, who reached in to take his arm.

As if in a trance, he let me lead him up the walk and into the house. The fire I had built in my Hamilton stove had burnt down to almost nothing, but the living room remained warmed by the glowing embers. I walked him over to the Barcalounger with the intent of making him as comfortable as possible. He pulled me into the chair with him, the two of us a snug fit. It was my turn to touch him, and I ran comforting fingers across his face and along his jawbone.

He turned his eyes on me, the rim of the green one a shade darker than the foamy sea within, and a tear fell on to his cheek. I took his glasses off and wiped the tear back with a fingertip, and then as if the action of wiping the tear away had opened floodgates, he began to cry. 'You should have seen her,' he sobbed. 'I've known her since she was a little girl.' I held his head to my chest and stroked his sleek hair. We were crushed together, but neither of us cared. His sobs tapered off until they were the sorrow equivalent of a dry heave.

'Pardon my outburst,' he said, letting out a sigh. 'I needed to do that. Thank you for being here.' He didn't appear embarrassed he had cried. Slowly regaining his composure, he snuggled his head into my armpit and after a while fell asleep.

We stayed like that, he in a dead slumber, me nodding in and out of sleep until two in the morning when he woke up to use the bathroom. It was cold in the room by then, and even in the dark I could see the snow falling outside the high windows. When he came back from the john, we climbed the ladder into the loft together, pulling my down comforter over our heads to escape the chill.

He reached out to me, and I stopped his hand, bidding him to lay still. This time it was my turn to make love to him.

# TWENTY-EIGHT

We left in separate cars the next morning after brushing off the copious piles of snow that had accumulated since his arrival the night before. Luckily the plow had been through, so the road was clear. I followed behind him, basking in the aftermath of yet more lovemaking in the morning – his needy, mine gleeful. We followed with eggs and toast and coffee. It was the typical morning of two lovers if you left out the death. Was I selfish to enjoy it?

Our paths separated as we reached town. He drove on to check on his friends and the arrangements for transporting the girl's body. Afterwards he would go to work at the hospital. Following my usual routine, I parked and waded through the knee-deep snow to the gondola.

There were a lot of employees uploading, so there were six of us in the bucket again, thwarting my plans for a solitary ride filled with private musings. Neverman was his usual officious self, his salt and pepper curls shaking as he decided who would detonate charges on which aspects to ensure the safety of the day skiers. The snow report said eighteen inches overnight and avalanche risk was high. Certainly some of the steeper slopes still holding snow would need blasting. Elevator Shaft and Silver Rush, and the runs that fed into the slopes directly above the town would need blasting as well. He listed off a couple other places with challenging descents.

'What about Traynor's?' I heard Singh suggest. Traynor's is the extreme terrain on Aspen Mountain just above town, seldom open and difficult to monitor during usual conditions.

'Not opening Traynor's. Not enough people on patrol to deal with Traynor's in snow like this. Nope. Biggest priority today is clearing off the megaton of snow hanging over Kleenex Corner.'

Kleenex Corner is the point nine-tenths of skiers have to

pass to get to the base of the mountain. A innocuous-looking catwalk run located directly beneath cliffs and a rocky outcropping, it is exactly the sort of place skiers would never suspect the possible danger of tons of snow ready to let loose on their unsuspecting heads. In fact, the primary concern of most skiers on Kleenex Corner is avoiding other skiers.

As Singh and Neverman continued discussing where to bomb, my mind drifted back to the night before. I was even more in awe of the doctor than I had been before. His physical appearance. His kindness and his concern for his friends. His ability as a lover. In all my life I'd never experienced anything like the way Dr Duane Larsen made love. My heart started throbbing at the very thought of him. Having him inside me was like coming home for the first time. It was all I could do to suppress a moan seated among my coworkers on the gondola. That's how good it had been.

'Are you with us, Westerlind?' Neverman's voice brought me out of the bedroom and back to the gondola.

'Sorry,' I said. 'I must have drifted.'

'Well you better not drift on that ridge over Kleenex,' he cautioned. 'I know we're used to these pep talks every morning and it's "yah, yah, yah, same old, same old". But we've had a shitbox of snow in the last week and me, well, I'm not quite sure what to expect here. That's why I want you and Singh to grab your gear and get on it right away.'

His voice held a peculiar stress that was alien to me. 'Why don't you chill, Mike?' I asked my sometime nemesis. 'I don't know when I've seen you so worked up.'

'Yeah, try paying attention to these conditions. Maybe you're still punch drunk from banging your head. Sorry,' he said quickly, trying to eat his last words, but they hit square where they were intended. But even as he sucker punched me, the skies were clouding up again, the sun disappearing behind a thunderhead of blue-black. Snow began falling again. 'Good for us, bad for us,' he added, looking up.

And then he rotated his head back at Kleenex Corner and picked up his radio. 'Ski patrol requesting late open to east side Ajax until we finish avi control.' Singh and I gave each other the eye. Aspen Mountain was the crown jewel of the ski company and closing half the mountain for whatever reason could be financially painful. Then again, safety was foremost and dollars always took a back seat to safety. It appeared more than a few bucks would be lost this morning.

We neared the top of the mountain, each of us immersed in his or her own thoughts. I'm sure most everyone else in the bucket was thinking of the tasks ahead of us this morning. Although I should have been thinking along the same lines, my thoughts couldn't stay off Duane Larsen.

Singh, Reininger and I were slogging through the accumulations over Kleenex Corner. Neverman wasn't exaggerating when he said the ridge was a mess. I hadn't been up there all season and just negotiating our way through the heavy powder told us the snow was unstable. Reininger stopped to dig a pit and called Singh and me over. 'Look,' he said, pointing to where the snow had crusted in the warm weather earlier in the season. 'It's a good goddam we closed this side of the mountain or we might have been looking at some human pancakes later today.'

We were each carrying one bomb. We outsource the bombs as well as fuses and blasting caps and assemble them ourselves before we go out to do avi work. We didn't do explosives on Ajax often, and although we were all experienced, there was always some danger involved, so I was feeling some tension. Believe me, as we lined up to do our work, my mind was totally focused, all thoughts of Duane Larsen relegated to the back-burner.

The protocol was to light the fuse with a spitter and then toss the bomb into the selected area. We were lined up at equal distances on the ridge. Reininger was up highest and he went first. He sparked his fuse and tossed his bomb. It landed in the snow over Kleenex Corner and exploded ninety seconds later sending a first wave of snow to the trail below.

Singh was next. He lit his bomb and tossed it into the deeper snow further down the ridge. The ensuing explosion caused a greater slide than the first, sending ever more snow down the mountain.

It was my turn. I was situated at a lower, more critical point where the snow accumulation could be most threatening to skiers below. I lit the fuse and tossed the bomb at the desired area. But before it could even hit the ground, the explosive detonated with a boom. The ensuing shock waves sent me sailing backwards on to my butt and knocked the snow off all the surrounding trees. A minute later, a massive slide let loose beneath us, sending the last of the snow down to the trail.

I pulled myself upright. Singh was nowhere to be seen. I sidestepped up to where he'd been standing as quickly as I could. My heart nearly stopped when I saw him lying in the snow. Then it started back up as he moved, shook off the snow and got to his feet. Thank God he was OK.

Reininger came skiing up. You could tell by his body language that he was angry. 'What the fuck was that, Greta? Didn't you check the fuse? You could have killed us.'

'Jesus, Greta,' Singh said, looking at me in a way unfamiliar to me. Then he didn't say anything else.

I was so flustered I didn't know what to do. I could feel Neverman's eyes boring a hole in the back of my head from the patrol shack at the top of the mountain. And rightfully so. I had endangered the lives of those around me. For the first time I started thinking maybe there really was something wrong with me.

To say the rest of the day went poorly would be an understatement. The near miss with the explosives left me completely shaken. Like a lifeguard who has been rescued from a pool and relocated to the shallow end, I was relegated to speed control on the lower part of the mountain once we'd cleared it to open. I was reeling in self-doubt after nearly taking Singh's life in an accident I didn't quite understand myself. I most certainly would have been dead and the others injured, at best, if I'd held on to that explosive a second longer. No longer able to find the place for pleasurable memories of the night before, my brain was taxed with how I could have made such a mistake. As with the avalanche, there were no available answers.

At the end of the day, just before sweep, Neverman pulled me aside in the hut. 'Look, Greta,' he said, putting me on notice by using my first name. 'I know you've been through a lot of shit in the last couple weeks, but we gotta be honest here. Losing control of a toboggan is bad enough, but almost blowing yourself and your fellow patrollers up is too much. I've been giving you the benefit of the doubt, but today was just one too many. I want you to take some time off.'

'Time off? But, Mike,' I said, frantically treading to keep my job afloat, 'I have no idea what happened today. It was freakish, but I can guarantee you it won't happen again.'

'That's right, it won't,' he said and I realized that was his final word on the subject. Never one to whine, I knew my case was beyond begging, so I went to my locker, took off my uniform jacket and walked away, unsure of what to do next.

# TWENTY-NINE

I t was getting dark as I neared home. For the first time in what felt like weeks, it wasn't snowing as I passed the Greenes' house. As usual, it looked warm and inviting, glowing warm within, grey smoke curling from the chimney. While my road always represented peace and tranquility to me, this night it felt not only lonely but foreboding. I supposed it was my reaction to all the things that had taken place in the preceding weeks. So much in such a short period of time. My suspension from work was just another layer of shit in an already dense cake.

The only thing lightening the load was the existence of Duane. He had texted me early in the morning, manna from heaven that read: *GRETA, SO GLAD YOU'RE YOU. SPECIAL DOESN'T BEGIN TO DESCRIBE YOU.* I hadn't picked up the text until after the incident with the bomb, but it sure helped to assuage some of the mixed emotions I was having about my dubious performance at work in recent days. Maybe Neverman was right. Maybe my noggin was a bit screwed up from the avalanche and the carbon monoxide.

There hadn't been another text from Duane since the early morning, but I had no doubt he'd call me later. He felt like a sure thing, like a familiar pair of old socks that I could slide right on. Or right into. Or him into me. I assumed his day had been more insufferable than mine, burdened with thoughts of his friends and their daughter while dealing with dozens of torn ligaments, broken wrists, sprained backs, banged heads. The ER had probably been humming all day.

Caught up in my own emotional tizzy, more than anything I longed to hear his voice. *Needed* to hear it. He was the light at the end of my tunnel. I wanted him to be with me to take the edge off my pain as I had taken the edge off his, to take my mind off the thought of doing great harm to Neverman.

I let myself into the A-frame, popped a beer open and

plopped down in the Barcalounger. I sat in front of the blank television screen waiting for the phone to ring, willing it to ring. A popular song started playing in my head about a woman putting on a dress so her boyfriend could take if off. Suddenly that seemed like a very good idea.

I only had one dress, but it was cute and sexy, purchased for a wedding a couple of years ago. It was cut away at the shoulders and the midriff was a thin transparent sheath and the skirt reached to my knees with a slit up the side. Black, of course.

I changed into my sexiest underwear and put on the dress and went back to the Barcalounger to wait for his call. I waited and waited and waited. One beer turned to two turned to three as the clock marched past seven and eight and ten and eleven.

By midnight, the six-pack was gone and so was I. Realizing he wasn't going to call, I peeled off the dress, donned my sweats and climbed up to the loft. I'm not usually a big drinker, so I was unsteady making my way to my bed. I crawled across the floor and flopped on to the mattress. The only good thing to be said about being drunk was that it helped my unemployed, unloved self fall directly asleep.

The sound of a car coming down the road woke me. The clock's digital readout glowed three a.m. I sat up in bed, my ears primed in the darkness. My heart gave a hopeful thump that it was Duane coming to see me after all. I hoped he remembered the key under the planter. I crawled on hands and knees to the small upper window at the front of the loft hoping to see his Porsche come round the bend, my heart trilling in anticipation. I could see the glow of headlights painting the road from behind the trees.

And then the road went black.

I stared out the window into the dark, wondering what this meant. Maybe his car had died. Maybe he wanted to surprise me. And then gradually, another less attractive thought occurred to me. Maybe it wasn't him. The sky was clear, but it was a moonless night, and even the snow seemed washed in black, making it difficult to see anything other than the darkness out of my window.

I climbed down the stairs and waited. Five minutes passed

in silence. I was beginning to wonder if I'd imagined the whole thing when there was the sound of someone or something on my front deck. The snow muffled the footsteps, but the creak of loose boards told me it was real. Fear having sobered me up, I pressed an ear to the door and listened. The voices were low, but I could tell there were two of them, because it was clear that one person was answering the other. And then there was a loud *shhh* and all talking ceased.

Minutes more of excruciating silence. And then the void of sound was replaced by a scraping coming from the east side of the building. Had I not heard the voices I would have thought it was an animal foraging for food. I had no idea who was out there or why. What I did know was it didn't bode well for me.

Fear is a disabling thing. But, being the sort of person who can stand at the top of a run with a drop-off of ten stories, give or take, a run that would unnerve most skiers not to mention ordinary people, where a mistake can mean sure injury, I've found myself rather insensitive to fear. I've jumped out of airplanes or off cliffs with chutes, and aside from the initial adrenaline rush, the moment I'm floating earthward I'm as calm as if I were sitting at home in front of the fire reading a book. I've hiked treacherous trails, biked rim trails with fifty-foot drop-offs, rafted down whitewater rapids rated as five with insides as untroubled as if I were walking a garden path.

But the fear taking hold of me now was unlike any I'd ever known. I could only conjure up one time that even came close. It was the time I climbed Capital Peak with Jack, back when I thought he was my true love. Capital has a notorious knife's edge that has to be crossed in order to summit the 14,000 foot peak. Fear had to be conquered in order to navigate a section of the climb where there was no foothold other than on the side of the actual knife's edge. If a hand slipped or a foot failed, the plunge meant certain death.

Jack had taught me basic climbing skills and convinced me that I'd have no problem on this most challenging of peaks. And true to his word, summiting hadn't bothered me at all. But when we started back down and it came time to go back across the knife's edge, I was gripped with a lethal fear that rendered me frozen halfway in. It was as if my precarious position suddenly dawned on me, that I was a rag doll poised over razor-sharp cliffs below. My mouth went so dry it extended to my lungs where the sacs stuck like collapsed gum bubbles with each breath. I was paralyzed with fear. I started fantasizing a helicopter rescue and wondered how long it would take.

Jack was in the lead and was nearly across the knife's edge when he turned to check on me. What he saw told him I was in big trouble.

'Greta, c'mon,' he prompted.

'I'm afraid,' I howled. 'I don't think I can get back across.'

Now Jack had always been a calm guy, fairly immune to panic, seldom one to lose his cool. But it was clear that the sight of his girlfriend frozen on a cliff side like a horse refusing to be led past fire had taken him unawares.

'You can do it,' he shouted over the wind.

'No I can't. I'm afraid.'

'You can't be afraid. You'll freeze.'

'It's too late,' I called back. 'I'm already frozen.'

He acted oblivious to the fact that I was near a meltdown, my heart pounding so I was near fainting and I was frightened beyond rational thought. In my mind, there was no way I was going to cross that knife's edge again. I wondered if they might be able to air lift me off the peak and wondered how long I could last while Jack went down for help. I stood there a trembling mess, fighting back tears. And then Jack did what I thought at the time was the most insensitive thing imaginable. Instead of trying to coddle or persuade me into action, he turned back to crossing the dangerous stretch, moving as gracefully as a tightrope walker on a sidewalk. When he had safely made it to the turf at the other end, he stretched and sat down on the ground with his back to me.

I was furious. Somehow, I'd had the notion that he was going to save me. I came to realize the only one who could save me in this instance was me. If I did nothing, my body might be frozen on that precipice into perpetuity. My anger transformed my fear and the survival instinct kicked in. I mentally shut my eyes to the danger and imagined the ridge

was in the middle of a park, not out in the open with a bottomless drop to either side. It was completely negotiable. I coolly
set out hand after foot, hand after foot until I reached Jack
sitting on the other side.

His ears must have been primed for me, because the moment
my foot touched safe ground, he jumped up and hugged me
in a manner he never had before, and it occurred to me that
he was nearly as frightened for me as I was. Knowing there
was no way to help me across the ridge, turning his back was
the only psychology he knew. And it had worked. He had
taught me there are times when one has to completely depend
upon oneself. I had taken control.

But this situation was different. It was the outsider who had
the control and I was a cornered animal pinned down inside
my home. I listened to the muted scraping, barely drawing
breath as if the rush of air in and out of my lungs might make
the invaders aware of my presence. My only consolation was
that whoever was outside couldn't see me in the dark. I focused
on what could be taking place out on the deck in the snow as
the scraping sound became louder.

My mind kept looping around to Ted Bundy and all the
women he had murdered. I thought of Kimmy Woods dead at
the foot of the Castle Creek Bridge. I thought of sounds I'd
heard in the night recently. There was something evil out there
and it was after me. My heart was beating harder than peddling
up the Smuggler Road on a thirty-pound mountain bike, and
I was sweating a cold sweat that soaked my armpits and glued
my hair to my brow. Visions of torture ran through my head,
being tied up and dismembered and left until someone like
Judy came looking for me. Unlike the night when I feared
Toby was an intruder, there was no backing away from the
situation. This time there was no escape. I had a front door
and rear windows, but I was unsure where the intruders lurked.
And since the windows on the side of the house faced skyward,
there was no way for me to see what was happening on the
outside of my house.

I needed to call for help. My cell, of course, was useless
and I'd left the cordless phone up in the loft next to the bed.
But the old-fashioned rotary was hanging on the wall in the

kitchen, its ancient cord brushing the floor. I moved through the inky night into the kitchen and reached for the phone. I could dial 911 and not even have to talk. They would pinpoint my location by the phone number. I picked up the phone and any worry about making noise talking was immediately put to rest. The line was deader than my Wagoneer had been two nights prior.

My fear was reeling out of control, rendering me useless to act. Someone wanted to do me harm, of that I was sure. But *why* remained the big question. My heart was pounding two beats for each of its usual ones, the blood pooling in my ears. My mouth was like a paper towel.

And then I remembered Sam's rifle on the top shelf in the bedroom closet where it had lain untouched since he died. Before he got ill, Sam was a dedicated hunter and aside from his dozen pairs of skis, his Remington was his prize possession. I'm no fan of guns, and while I make allowances for hunters, I have no idea how anyone can really take pleasure in shooting another living creature for sport. But Sam had insisted I learn to shoot, in case a wild animal threatened, and he took me to the clearing several times for target practice. He'd taught me how to load and clean the rifle at the same time. One of his last bits of advice was you never know when a weapon can come in handy. Now his words seemed prophetic.

The scratching had grown stronger as I stole into Sam's former bedroom. The night was so dark that the bedroom window was as ebony as if there were no window at all. I moved along the wall until my hand found the closet.

The doors were bi-folds and I cringed as they squeaked open. The storage shelf was high, and upon reaching up the only thing my hand met was some old blankets, carefully folded by Sam and untouched ever since. I cursed myself for not leaving the rifle closer and tiptoed back into the living room. I carried one of the chairs from the kitchen counter into the bedroom, careful not to make any noise. Once up on the chair, I had no trouble locating the rifle and was glad it had been left loaded.

I felt in the dark for the safety and slid it off. Now that I was armed, I understood for the first time the power of a gun.

Crouching in the corner on the bedroom floor, I waited with the Remington pointed at the door. My heart rate had slowed and my breathing had returned to normal. Taking action had dulled the raw fear to something more manageable. I had changed my position from being a victim to being more in control.

The scratching stopped and the newfound silence was unnerving. Knowing whoever it was still lurked outside my home, I decided to use the element of surprise and take action. I stole to the front door and looked out the side panel to make sure no one was on the front porch. I turned the knob to open the door, but it wouldn't budge. I tried again, but it was stuck. Something was locking me in.

It was then I smelled smoke. I gave the door another pull and it still wouldn't open. I looked around in the dark for a tool. My ski boots were sitting at the door. I put one on and kicked the handle with all the thrust I could summon. The knob gave way.

The door fell open and I stepped outside waving the rifle. There was a slice of wood laying on the deck, knocked to the ground from where it had been wedged into the door frame making it impossible to open the door. I fired an angry round into the air, and the noise reverberated across the surrounding mountains. I fired off a second shot. A moment later I could make out motion along the Aspens at the edge of the clearing. Feeling emboldened, I considered giving chase but smoke coming from the side of the A-frame commanded my more immediate attention.

As soon as I rounded the structure, I understood what the scraping had been. Whoever it was had been scraping snow off my foundation to make a platform for building a fire. I clomped off the deck with a ski boot on one foot and my other foot bare. The light from the fire illuminated the side of the A-frame, and I could see the snow had been cleared from beneath the rafters that supported the roof. Wood had been piled up in the open space and was already burning strong, the flames teasing the subfloor of my home. I grabbed an armful of snow and threw it on to the conflagration. The fire sizzled and hissed in protest. Using both hands as shovels, I started scooping snow on to the flames until the fire slowly died out and the night turned black again.

I stood in the dark, breathing hard and sweating from the effort to save my house. The sound of an engine starting round the bend broke the silence, but this time no lights illuminated the road. The vehicle retreated without ever revealing itself, leaving me standing in the snow next to my A-frame in total shock. I could make out a bulky shape in the snow. I picked it up. It was a half-filled gasoline canister. Shivers ran the length of my spine at the realization that I had stopped the culprits in the midst of the act.

At this point it became clear to me that someone wanted me out of the house, either by burning me down or burning me up. My demise seemed to be the clearer goal since if they wanted to burn down my house, they would have done it while I was out. My first impulse was to jump into the Wagoneer and drive into town to the police. But what if the culprits were waiting in ambush further down the road? I thought of going to the Greenes for help and ruled that idea out too. The couple was old, and I didn't want to endanger them.

I clomped back into the house and took the ski boot off the one foot, massaged my other frozen foot with my hand. I was pissed enough that my fear had retreated. I jerry-rigged the door shut with some wire and decided the best move would be to sit up the rest of the night. Spinning the Barca in the direction of the door, I sat down with the Remington in my lap and waited. I stayed that way for much of the night in the cold, afraid to start a fire with its soothing but distracting noise. All my senses needed to remain on alert.

I did my best to remain vigilant, but my eyelids grew stone heavy after a while and, despite my best efforts to protect myself, I fell sound asleep.

# THIRTY

Maybe it was the beer, maybe it was the draining trauma of the fire, maybe it was the sheer exhaustion of the night's events, but by the time the morning light fractured my eyes it was already eight o'clock. I shook myself awake, seated in the Barcalounger with the rifle across my lap, and thought over what had transpired in the early hours of the morning. At first, I wanted it to be some weird dream, but the Remington in my lap was no dream. I went to the splintered door, pulled on my shearling boots and went outside to investigate. The crisp air pinched my face as I trudged through the knee-deep snow to the side of the house. Sure enough the evidence was still there, the heap of shoveled snow, the gasoline canister, the black stain of burnt wood on the rafters. I put the gasoline canister on the deck and went back inside.

After dressing, I grabbed a quick cup of coffee, went out and fired up the Wagoneer. As I rounded the bend to the Greenes' house, I saw Don out front shoveling snow. He was wearing what was possibly the world's oldest wool jacket and an equally old wool cap that covered his ears. He waved and I slowed the car. He walked down his driveway to the road at a slow, deliberate pace. His thick face was red with cold, his blue eyes bright beneath the sagging lids. We hadn't spoken in a while, but he seemed not to notice. I leaned over and rolled the passenger-side window down.

'Heard a few shots last night,' he said, matter of fact. 'Figured you were scaring some animal off.'

'Only the human kind,' I said, giving the gas can a nod. 'There was someone messing around outside. I think they were trying to either burn my place down or burn me out. Did you see anyone come down the road around three in the morning?'

'At three in the morning they would have had to drive over me for me to notice. But this is most unsettling. You have any idea why someone would want to burn up your place?'

'Your guess is as good as mine.'

He squinted and his gray brows came down low over his eyes at the same time a picture of enlightenment came over his face. We were both thinking along the same lines. We both knew of one person who had a vested interest in me not living in that A-frame anymore. Or living anywhere for that matter. But he didn't say the name and I didn't offer it.

I asked about Ellie and he informed me that she was recovering from her hip surgery quite well. I hadn't even known she had a bad hip, that's what a bad neighbor I was. I drove off, reminding myself to talk to the Greenes more often.

When I got into town I headed directly for the courthouse where the sheriff's offices were located. My house was far enough up eighty-two to put me outside the Aspen city limits, but I still was in Pitkin County. Sheriff Dan Nichols was standing in the hallway drinking coffee and talking to one of the clerks when I came huffing down the hall carrying the half-filled gas canister in my right hand. I'd known Dan for quite a while, since about when I first came to town. My first encounter with him was when he was a deputy and I'd hit a deer on Owl Creek Road racing to an interview for a ski instructor job.

I'd been so near to hysterical when he pulled up, feeling so bad about the animal laying at the side of the road, that I'd not even noticed the crushed front end of my Toyota. But he'd calmed me down and reassured me that it wasn't my fault, that I was lucky it was the deer and not me. My second encounter with Dan was a week later, when I was driving my battered Toyota down the same road doing sixty in a thirty-five, late for my first day of work. He'd given me a pass with a raised eyebrow, and instead of writing me up he asked me on a date. He was a good-looking guy back then, about thirty or forty pounds leaner, and I figured a date sure beat the hell out of a ticket. We went out a few times before I had to tell him I wasn't interested in anything besides friendship. And that's how it's worked out to the present day though, truth be told, I still think he wouldn't mind otherwise.

'Greta!' He doffed his cowboy hat to reveal a large shaved head rising like a balloon over his double or triple chin. He gave me a friendly smile. 'What're you doing in civvies? I hear it's epic out there after this last storm.' His eyes drifted down to the canister. 'If you're here for gas, you're in the wrong place.'

'Somebody tried to toast me last night. And not with champagne,' I said, putting the canister on the ground in front of him.

His face took on the appropriate expression for an officer of the law learning one of his constituents was in harm's way. 'Want to tell me about it?'

We sat in his office with the door shut while I relayed the series of events that had taken place at my home during the night. When I'd finished, he nodded. 'Anyone have a beef with you? Bounced check? Scorned lover?'

'I've got a widow mad at me, but she's not going to burn down my house. I just can't stop thinking of Joel Simpson, Sam's son. He's got a lot to benefit by me not being around.'

'Ha! The son of Sam. Never thought about it this way.'

'Stop it, Dan. This is serious. Someone tried to burn down my house. With me in it.'

'Greta, I am taking it seriously. Believe me. If Joel's still in town I'll find him and talk to him. See what he was up to last night.'

There was a knock at the door and one of Dan's deputies stuck her head around the door. 'Need to talk to you for a minute,' she said. He excused himself and left the room. I took advantage of his absence to check my phone. My heart sped up when I saw Duane had texted me at 6:39 a.m. while I was asleep in the Barca. *SORRY FOR NOT CALLING LAST NIGHT. HOSPITAL EMERGENCY. DO YOU HAVE TIME FOR A COFFEE BEFORE WORK?*

My fingers couldn't move fast enough. *NO WORK TODAY. COFFEE WHERE?*

His response came right back. *HOSPITAL CAFETERIA.*

Mine. *TWENTY MINUTES.*

His. *CAN'T WAIT.*

I was grinning inwardly when Dan came back into his office. Dan didn't return to his desk, but rather remained standing in the open doorway with his hand on the knob. 'OK, Greta. We'll get on this. In the meantime, you given any thought to staying somewhere else tonight?'

The image of Duane Larsen filled my brain. He'd never asked me to come home with him, but then again I'd never given him the opportunity. 'Maybe,' I replied.

'Well, if you've got somewhere else to stay I think that's a good idea. I'll station a deputy at the entrance to your road in case whoever it is comes back. But I rather doubt they will now that you're on to them.'

I got up to go, anxious to get to the hospital to meet my coffee date, the thought of someone trying to kill me now a sorry second priority. Dan seemed anxious for me to go too, which was unusual. He generally extended our visits with a little harmless flirtation. But he was all business and I was getting the impression he was as ready for me to be on my way as I was.

'Sorry to give you the bum's rush,' he apologized. 'Gotta suspect in the Kim Woods murder. We're holding a little powwow before the arrest.'

'You got somebody?' My first thought was how relieved Duane would be to learn that someone was going to be held accountable for Kimmy's death. 'That's good work!'

'Yep. Think we've got him cold. Her blood in his car, her blood in his house.'

'Congrats,' I said, now more anxious to get to the hospital so I could deliver the news to Duane myself. 'Can't wait to read about it in the paper.'

He walked me down the hall, and I could tell how distracted he was. But, true to form, he always threw in that little flirtation. 'Seeing anyone special these days?' he asked.

'As a matter of fact I am,' I teased. 'I'm meeting him for a cup of coffee in a few.'

'Does he have a name?' he pried.

'As a matter of fact he does,' I replied. I opened the courthouse door and walked past him with a big smile on my face.

Duane and I were huddled in the corner of the hospital cafeteria over two cups of coffee, holding hands. He was staring at me so intently it almost made me feel naked, but in a good way.

'I was really hoping to see you last night, but then the other ER doctor had a car accident in the canyon on his way to the hospital. He was in pretty bad shape when they brought him in, ruptured spleen among other things. I ended up tending to him instead of him relieving me. There was no one else to cover, so I was here all night. Luckily, we were busy so it didn't give me time to think about much else. Not Kimmy. Or you,' he added. 'We were so busy my mind was totally on work. I'm sorry. I hope I didn't disappoint you.'

I was barely hearing his words, my attention focused on the feel of his hands upon mine, questioning how this moment could be so sublime despite an attempt on my life and the loss of my job, temporary or not. Was it possible my soulmate had finally appeared, my *raison d'être*? I wasn't much of a romantic, but there was no denying something special was happening between us.

He bent his head down and pressed his lips to my palm, causing me to think I may never wash that hand again. Or at least for the rest of the day. I put my hand to his cheek and stroked it and watched his mismatched eyes light up behind the wire frames. It's both elevating and humbling to feel you can create a response like that in another person. I think that was the best moment I've ever felt in my life when not skiing.

I was preparing to tell him about the suspect in Kim's murder, pleased to carry the news that they might know who was responsible, when Dan Nichols and two deputies walked into the cafeteria. My first thought was Dan had found the arsonist who had attempted to burn me out, thinking it odd that he knew where to find me. Then I started wondering how he knew I was here. His eyes widened when he saw me sitting with Duane, and an eerie feeling came over me. He approached the table with a look unlike any I'd ever seen on his face, like a doctor about to deliver a fatal diagnosis.

'Long time, Sheriff,' I said. Turning to Duane, I added, 'I was just going to tell you. There's a suspect in Kimmy's murder.'

There was an uneasy silence, the eerie feeling bloating like a dead cow three days on a prairie.

'Greta, I'd like you to leave,' said the sheriff.

'But . . .' I looked at his face and then back at Duane's. Duane looked puzzled. 'I'm not going anywhere,' I said, taking Duane's hand and holding it hard.

'Suit yourself.' Dan turned towards my newfound love and in a most controlled voice he said, 'Duane Larson, we are here to arrest you for the murder of Kimmy Woods. You have the right to remain silent. What you do say . . .'

My ears screamed 'NO' in denial. I jumped in before he could finish giving Duane his rights, my voice shrill and anxious. 'Are you crazy? There's no way he would have killed that girl. She's his friend's daughter.'

'Greta, I'm going to ask you again to leave,' Dan said without looking at me. 'I want you to get out of this room. Now.'

'No!' I cried defiantly.

Then I looked at Duane's face. While he had turned as pale as the snow on the windowsill behind him, his face remained closed and calm. He stood and offered his wrists. 'Greta. Do as he says. This is a big mistake, but you're not helping things by making a scene.'

'No,' I cried, reaching across the table. 'You're not taking him.'

Then one of the deputies, a woman, took my arm firmly in her hand and held me back. The sheriff finished reading Duane his rights, and I watched in mute anguish as they led him out the door.

# THIRTY-ONE

What does one do when it has been suggested that your newly discovered soulmate could be responsible for the death of a young woman who just happened to be the daughter of his close friends? And actually, 'responsible' is a euphemism. The cold fact of the matter was the police were saying that my newfound lover might have *murdered* that young woman. Can't get much more responsible than that.

I'd watched in numb disbelief as they escorted my hand-cuffed lover from the cafeteria to a waiting squad car, my mind reeling as though it was the day of nine-eleven all over again. My mind flashed to that day that was carved in the memory of anyone who wasn't senile or dead drunk. I'd gotten up early that morning to give my mother some breakfast and turned on the TV. The twin towers were already gone. She died later that week.

As I watched through the cafeteria window, they loaded him into the squad car while excited voices all around me informed newcomers carrying breakfast trays about the arrest that had just taken place. I wanted to tell them they had it all wrong, wished I could chase after the police car to tell them again they had made a big mistake. I wanted to let Duane know I was there for him no matter what and everything would be all right. That it was folly that anyone like him could possibly commit such a heinous act.

But instead I sat immobilized, unable to move, back on the knife's edge of Capital Peak. When the police car drove off, I could see Duane's sandy head in the back seat. Afterwards I dragged myself out to the parking lot and sat in the Wagoneer for a solid ten minutes, thinking about how euphorically happy I'd been not a half-hour before. I thought of his kindness and gentleness and the tender way he made love to me. Certainly a man like him couldn't possibly be capable of such a horrible violation of life. He was a doctor. He saved lives. I felt certain that a grave error had been made.

Then slowly the veil of rabid love started to lift. Wheels started turning in my brain, examining the situation from a less emotional standpoint. I reviewed each of my encounters with him outside the hospital. His appearance at the Bugaboo with the young blond. His clown-like skiing and his ancient ski gear followed by his expert performance at the sport. Speaking fluent Japanese to the chefs at the sushi bar. The way he made love in the dark. The way he had memorized every inch of my body even though I was an emergency room patient. His ability to make love to me while his friend's daughter was missing. A new paradigm clicked in, one I didn't want to face. Duane was charming and well-versed at many things, but he was a chameleon. And when you're dealing with a chameleon, you can't really be certain what lies beneath the skin. Maybe he had two differing sides just as he had two different eyes.

The thought set me spinning. Everything good had turned bad. My world had turned upside down. I was in a blinding blizzard and couldn't find up. The sky was the ground and the earth was celestial space. The object of my affection had not only been snatched from me, he was possibly a murderer. I was unemployed. Someone was trying to kill me. My lot was worse than Job's, the only thing missing the festering boils. I was Europa turned into a cow by Zeus.

With the world melting down around me, I looked inside myself for something to ease the pain. Many people take pills. I turn to the one constant in my life. Skiing.

I drove the Wagoneer into town and double-parked in front of Gondola Plaza, not caring if I got a ticket. Like an addict in need of a fix, I stormed into the patrol room for my gear. Singh and Reininger were there and I turned my head from Singh's sympathetic looks, ignored Reininger's lame attempts to make me smile. I just stared back at him like the moron he was. I knew they knew my job status. But they had no clue about the latest occurrence in my personal life.

I grabbed my gear without talking to anyone, the liner to my patrol jacket, my skis and boots and gloves and helmet.

When I got back to the Wagoneer, a cop was already writing me a ticket. I had left the car running, but when the cop saw me he tore the ticket up. I recognized him as a broken wrist on Spar. Stress had narrowed my vision to a tunnel as I sped along Main Street and I had to slam on the brakes to avoid hitting a couple of skiers in the crosswalk. When I reached the roundabout, I took the exit that led to the Aspen Highlands.

There was no line at the bottom, so I rode the chair by myself, my goggles steaming with banked tears of disappointment and fury. Thinking I'd found a special kind of happiness only to have it thrown back at me in such a bizarre manner had taken me to the edge. My mind was a mélange of contradictions: had I slept with a killer, was I wrong to doubt him, could it be that I loved him?

There was a line at the second chair to the top, so I had to share with a couple of young boarders, relieved that they had absolutely no interest in the woman who sat with her back to them the entire ride. Once we hit the top, I slid off and tucked to catch speed up the incline to the snow cat pick-up. A virtual snow tank with treads, the snow cat pulls a trailer to the highest point possible before letting its riders off to trek the rest of the way to the legendary Highland Bowl, a huge open space servicing some of the finest expert terrain in the country. From the drop-off point, it's a thirty- to sixty-minute hike, depending on your level of fitness.

The snow cat had just departed with a full load. In no mood to wait the ten minutes for its return, I clicked out of my skis, threw them over my shoulder and followed in its tracks. Fueled by pain and anger, my pace was far quicker than it would normally be as I put one booted foot in front of the other.

The air grew thinner with each step, my breath shallow with the effort of the climb. Step after step after step, thinking of nothing except the physical agony of your heart pounding against your breastplate as if to burst your chest, your lungs searing with bruise-like pain. My head hung low like a chastised puppy as I climbed, taking in none of the savage beauty of the vast white bowl expanding around me. At one point I took a lingering look over the edge at the most narrow point, a point where a mistake meant certain injury if you fell on to the steep, rocky terrain to the side. I pondered if luck might be with me and cause me to fall to my death. But luck was not on my side and I stayed on my feet. Step after heaving step I climbed, trying to vacate my mind, to outrun all thought. There is no Duane, no Warren, no arson, no job loss. Just climb, Greta, climb.

My mouth was parched and I regretted not having brought water for the grueling hike. But then there was something redeeming in the thirst. It served as a distraction from the stronger pain, the heartache I was seeking to escape. I powered past a couple of boarders and heard one of them say, 'That dude must really have to be somewhere.' I kept my head down as the gap between me and the boarders broadened. The next person I passed was a fit middle-aged local who asked if I was going for the record. I didn't even acknowledge him, but forged onwards. I'd pushed beyond physical pain in my life and this was nothing, my feet working like pedals, rotating without stopping, moving, moving, moving.

As I neared the top I came upon a couple of women who were north of middle age, the mountain equivalent of those trucks on the road with the inverted triangles on the back. One was wearing a bright orange parka, the other bright purple. Even with their goggles down I could see the wrinkles etched into their cheeks. They stood aside to let me power past, one saying to the other, 'I couldn't have done that when I *was* her age.'

And then I'd reached the summit, all 12,392 feet of it. The snow platform was filled with scores of skiers in a far better frame of mind than mine, newbies patting each other on the back for making it, veterans yawning at the newbies' exuberant displays. My heart was pounding so hard with effort that I had to bend at the waist to find my breath. Gradually my heart began to slow and I straightened up.

The view from the top of Highland Bowl defies description. The closest I can come is to say it is pure majesty, with snow-capped peaks extending for miles until they fade into distant blurs. The sky beyond the geographic map was painted a vivid blue. For the first time in memory I had absolutely no appreciation for the panorama unfolding before me. For the first time ever, I wondered what it would be like to stop breathing.

I leaned against my skis and stood that way for a while. The two older women who I had dusted along the way chugged up and gave each other high-fives, their smiling faces etched with the weathered lines of long-time locals. They asked me to take a picture of them standing in front of the solitary lift chair set beneath a canopy of colorful prayer flags. Before I could recuse myself, one had handed me her cell phone. And then the other. Despite being owned by physical and mental pain, I somehow found the wherewithal to accommodate them, and took two smiling pictures.

'We have the same birthday and we hike the bowl every year on our birthdays,' said the one in purple, sharing more information than I cared to hear. 'I'm Donna,' she said.

'I'm Barb,' said the orange.

'Greta,' I mumbled begrudgingly. They took their phones back and were critiquing the pictures when I decided to get out of there before they asked for redos. I snapped on my skis, lowered my goggles and set my sweaty body on a downward course towards the G-zones and the steep glades of the North Woods.

While the entirety of the bowl is a skier's Promised Land, with its varying terrain and degrees of steepness, the North Woods is my particular manna. It's the part of the mountain where the snow stays best the longest. North facing and protected from the sun, the snow never gets set-up or cruddy. It's the place where powder stashes can be found weeks after the last snowfall, where the perfectly spaced trees seem to be part of some master plan as if Gaia had created the bowl for the pleasure of skiing gods.

I cut across the slopes horizontally until I reached the glade that was my personal favorite. The sun that managed to breach the tall trees illuminated the sugar-like snow, turning the surface into hundreds of millions of universes, like miniature stars sparkling upon the mountain. The air was so perfectly calm that the snow parted before my skis like butter to a warm knife. There was no bottom to the snow, no rocks to throw you off course, no stumps to bring you down. The snow, any moisture sucked out of it in the subzero temperatures of the night, was so light it earned the name champagne powder.

I was floating, my legs and feet in unison over the skis like the tail of a mermaid as they conquered the gravity, drawing me downhill. They stretched out to find no bottom, only the marshmallow pillows that propped me above the surface. Streams of snow hitting my face were love taps and my arms reached out, alternately flicking my poles to embrace my downhill course. My mind was cleansed of all things negative, dialed into the mountain and nature, to the elements and beauty, to my own physicality and my body's response to the challenge of each turn or circumnavigating the trees like a race car driver around cones. There was nothing other than the skiing. I was unstoppable, invincible, one with nature, a creature unique in this world, reveling in my solitary existence, all troubles reduced by the purity of the snow.

Having skied without stopping for fifteen elated minutes and seen no other skiers, my legs and lungs were burning, but in a good way. I had segued further to skier's right and one of the heaviest gladed areas when I stopped to take a breather. Glad to be the sole person present, I raised my goggles to wipe the sweat off my forehead and in that one movement couldn't help but notice a flash of blue peeping out from the well of a nearby tree. My nervous system responded, sending an alarm system of arpeggios along my spine.

Being a ski patroller, aside from an avid nature enthusiast, it wasn't difficult to ascertain this was not a color found in nature. A lost glove or an abandoned article of clothing? Perhaps. But my gut told me otherwise.

# THIRTY-TWO

The tree well was uphill and to skier's right, so I side-stepped until I was level with it and then slid on over. I swore aloud upon looking down and seeing the blue jacket of a snowboarder headfirst in the tree well. During seasons such as this one, with an abundance of snow, the trees create huge snowless sections around their trunks, creating danger for any skier or boarder who ventures too close. Tree wells were the quicksand of skiing and once in one it was close to impossible to get out of it on your own.

From what I could tell, the boarder was a young male. He was lucky that his jacket was blue, because his pants were black and his board army green – colors that don't easily stand out amid the spruce in the glades. Then again, maybe he wasn't lucky, because he wasn't moving.

I skied as close to him as possible, anchoring myself by using my skis as a secure platform. I reached down and tried to pull him out by the back of his jacket, but only managed to move him enough to get his face out of the snow. The smooth skin beneath the snow-filled goggles told me he wasn't even a teenager. I kept tugging on his jacket, but was unable to do much more than jiggle him, he was so near to the tree. My skis were impeding me from getting closer, so I took them off and dropped into the less deep snow near the base.

He wasn't particularly large, but he sure wasn't small, and with my legs post-holing every inch of the way, hauling him up and out was going to be a challenge. I'm strong for a woman, but there are situations when the strength of one woman or man is not enough. And this was one of those situations. Had I been on duty instead of suspended, I would have had tools, such as a rope, to help me in extracting dead weight from below me. But as things stood, it was me and my hands and we weren't getting the job done alone.

I continued trying to pull him out, relentlessly fighting

against time and oxygen deprivation with no idea how much time had passed since he'd fallen into the well. Like a mother lifting a car off her child, I found strength I never knew I had but every time I got him halfway up the tree well, his dead weight fell against me and I lost him. I had no radio and knew if I left him to find help, he would undoubtedly be dead before we returned. If he wasn't already.

And then from above I caught sight of movement in the trees, two skiers making slow, strong turns, one in orange and one in purple. It was as if God had sent two angels from heaven. I took off my gloves, shoved both pointers into my mouth and let out a piercing whistle.

The two skiers stopped and looked for the source of the whistle. When they saw me they skied in my direction. As they drew closer I recognized that they were the two older women I had passed on my way up, the two locals who climbed the bowl every birthday, the two who had asked me to take their picture.

The moment they saw the boarder in the tree well, they needed no explanation of what needed to be done. Without losing a beat they clicked out of their skis and knelt in the snow to either side of me. The three of us grabbed the back of the boarder's jacket. I could only hope they were as strong as women who spend their lives outdoors usually are.

'On three,' I commanded. 'One, two . . .'

I counted three and we pulled together with all of our might. What had been impossible for one person was easy work now, and we had him out of the tree well in an instant. I laid him flat on his back in the snow and his still-connected snowboard tipped to the left. Training had taught me that moving an injured person wasn't the brightest thing to do until you know the extent of the injuries. Well, I didn't know the extent of his injuries, but I did know the extent of one thing: he wasn't breathing. Given the circumstances there was no time to waste doing an exam.

'We gotta lose that snowboard, ladies,' I commanded.

While the two women gently unstrapped the snowboard from his unmoving feet, I pulled off his right glove and held a finger to his wrist. 'There's a pulse,' I announced. They watched in patient silence as I took off his helmet and pried his mouth open. There was a ball of solid ice blocking his windpipe, probably inhaled in panic when he fell into the tree well. I wrapped my fingers around the ice ball and pulled it out. Then I opened his jacket in preparation to do CPR.

'What are your names again?' I asked quickly.

'Barb,' said the orange.

'Donna,' said the purple.

'Barb, could you go down to the lift and radio for help? Donna, can you assist me in CPR?'

Before I could say another word Barb was back on her skis and speeding down the last part of the woods. She was skiing faster than she had been before and I prayed she wouldn't get in trouble herself. Once she cleared the woods it was only a short run-out to the chair where a lift operator could radio for assistance and a sled.

I bent over the boy and started working to revive him. Pressing on his sternum with the flat of my hand, I gave him compressions, counting to a hundred and then starting over again.

'You're going to have to give mouth to mouth, you know,' said Donna, adding, 'I was a nurse at AVH.'

'I was planning on mouth to mouth, but I wanted to start with the compressions.'

I was getting no results with the compressions, so I held his nostrils closed and forced breath into his open mouth. Five breaths later I returned to the compressions.

'You look like you know what you're doing,' she said.

'I'm patrol on Ajax,' I informed her.

'That explains it. Let me know if you want me to relieve you,' she said, falling silently on to her knees beside me.

I kept at work, giving him hundreds of compressions to five breaths. While only about five minutes had passed since we'd pulled him out of the tree well, I was beginning to tire. It was tough work. His helmet and goggles were off and his smooth face put him around ten years old, though he was large for his age with the game-boy fat typical of many tourist kids. His hair and brows were dark brown and his blue oxygen-starved lips were full and generous. He looked so young and innocent, it troubled me to think of the pain his parents might have to suffer later this day. I worked harder.

Another few minutes had passed and my lips were to his, trying to breathe life into death, when I felt him pull back slightly. It took me by surprise at first, this sudden acceptance of my expired breath. And then it happened a second time and a third and within seconds the boy was breathing on his own. I looked up at Donna and she was smiling broadly. As his breaths became more and more regular, his color began to return, the blue of his lips ceding to white and finally to pink. His eyes popped open and, just as I had guessed, they were a dark brown.

He took in the two of us hovering over him in one long glance. Then he saw his snowboard off to the side. 'What happened?' he asked with undue calm as if finding two strange women over you in a snow-covered tree glade wasn't an extraordinary event.

'What happened is you fell into a tree well,' I informed him. 'What are you doing boarding back here all alone anyhow?'

'I wasn't. I was with my dad. I kept calling for him, but couldn't find him anywhere.' He tried to stand, but I settled him back down. 'I'm cold,' he complained.

I took off my parka and placed it over him, hoping my adrenaline would keep me warm. I put my gloves back on and beat my hands together to keep them warm. 'Help will be here soon,' I assured him. 'What's your name?'

'Richie,' he said.

'I'm Greta.'

'That's a nice name,' he said. I thought of the way Duane Larsen had said my name. *I used to think so too.*

The mounties arrived five minutes later, first a male ski patroller who'd been in the area when the call came in, then a pair of patrollers, male and female, coming from the top with a sled. They checked his vitals and after feeling secure there was no back or spinal injury, they transferred him to the toboggan and prepared to take him down to the chair where he would be uploaded to the top before taking the long slide down to the lodge and an ambulance.

I'd tried to stay out of things, but one of the patrollers corralled me and asked me what had happened. I explained about coming upon him in the tree well and the other ladies arriving in time to help out. Since I worked Aspen Mountain, I didn't know many of the patrollers on Highland, and I was hoping to make a quiet exit when a fourth patroller, a helmet-less woman with a long braid, came skiing up. I'd known Cindy Forman over ten years, going back to when we were both instructors. She stared at me in my civilian ski garb. 'What are you doing slumming here, Westerlind?'

'Was just looking for a change of pace.'

'Hmmm, guess you got a busman's holiday. Got this one on the radio. Father said he'd lost his son somewhere in the North Woods. I understand the old man is frantic, waiting at the lift.'

After the kid was wrapped up, the two patrollers with the sled skied out and started their descent as slowly as you had to in this steepness. Cindy and the other patrolman followed behind. Donna and I waited until they were out of the way and then started down ourselves. The sun felt good on my back after so much time in the shade without my jacket. We arrived at the chair just behind the sled.

Barb was standing beside a tall, dark-olive-skinned man in expensive black ski clothes. His face was lined and his thinning grey hair receded, but there was an assurance to him that comple-mented his good looks. He looked like the imaginary grandfather you always wished you had. He was clearly significantly older than the boy, maybe old enough to be that grandfather, but that's nothing new in the land of second, third and fourth wives. He dropped to his knees beside the sled, his face wearing the look of someone who has pulled off a bluff against all odds in a poker game.

'Richie, are you all right?' he asked, his voice constrained by worry.

'I'm cold, Dad.'

'I told you to stay with me,' he berated the boy, more out of his own fear than anger.

'I tried. You were too fast. I didn't know where you went.'

The man got to his feet and the patrollers pulled the sled up to the chair. 'We've got to ride up with him, sir. You can take the next chair.' The chairlift stopped and the liftie helped the two patrolmen strap the toboggan across the seat back and the armrest, so the ends were sticking out front and center. Then the patrollers took seats either side of it, holding it secure with their hands. The lift started up again.

This kind of evacuation was new to me. On Aspen Mountain you didn't have to go up before going down. Unless someone like Zuzana McGovern freaked out on a run and we had to take her back up to the top on a snowmobile so she could catch the gondola down. She always took the gondola down.

The silver-haired man loaded solo on to the next chair. As the chair swung around behind him, he sat down and turned to Barb. 'Once again. I can't thank you enough. I waited and waited. And then when he didn't join me here I just kept calling. They should really have better cell service here.'

'Don't thank me,' said Barb, shoving a gloved hand in my direction as the chair swept him away. 'Greta found him.'

'Yeah, you have to thank Greta,' Donna chimed in.

'Thank you all,' he said, adding, 'you'll hear from me.'

I rode up with Cindy, the patrol who had been there with us, while the birthday girls took the chair behind us. 'That's one lucky kid,' I said.

'You don't know the half of it,' said Cindy, flicking her braid with her gloved hand. 'That kid was born lucky. You know who his father is?'

'That guy there. Haven't a clue.'

'Pablo Alvarez.'

My shrug was indifferent. I neither knew nor cared.

'Big Mexican developer. Owns about twenty acres in Starwood.'

'Still never heard of him,' I said, lowering my goggles as we neared the top. The toboggan was already on its way to the base, and Cindy skied off for further duty in the bowl. Barb and Donna were the next people to unload and the three of us stood to the side of the lift huddled in conference.

'Real pleasure to meet you girls,' I said to my new friends. 'That kid wouldn't be alive without your help. So I have this one question for you before we part.'

'And what's that?' Donna asked.
'What birthday is it?'
They smiled at each other and said in unison, 'Eighty.'
Aspen women just rock.

# THIRTY-THREE

The afternoon was still young, so I skied a couple more loops of the bowl without any interruptions from boarders in tree wells or otherwise. My spirits had improved significantly despite the disarray in my life. That's what skiing does for you. It's the safe opiate. It elevates you above all things negative and depressing. Skiing wipes out bad vibes and replaces them with positive. And while my troubles were still significant, they didn't seem quite as large as they had in the morning. Skiing is truth.

Needless to say, Duane dominated my thoughts on the lonely chair rides between runs. By the end of the day, I'd decided there was no getting around a stop at the courthouse to check out his status, hoping a great mistake had been made. It hadn't. In fact, things had worsened. More evidence had presented itself. Dan told me they were thinking of transferring Duane down to the more secure prison in Glenwood. I'm no expert at criminal justice, but the move seemed a little extreme to me, and I told the sheriff so.

'It's not extreme if you knew what I know.' After looking around to make sure no one was listening, the sheriff leaned in to me like he was doing me a big favor and said, 'Now this is completely confidential, but it just so happens there are a couple of other Western Slope girls gone missing since Duane Larsen relocated out this way. One in Breck and one in Vail.'

'So what makes you think he has anything to do with them?'

'Timing. They both went missing on his days off. We've checked his work schedule. You know, neither resort is more than a couple hours from Basalt. He could make either in a day. And he's a pretty good-looking guy. He'd have no trouble getting women to talk to him and who knows where he took it from there. I think we might just have a new Ted Bundy.'

'Do you have the bodies of these girls?'

'No, but they're missing just the same.'

I didn't find that a very convincing reason to transfer him from the Aspen prison, which was renowned for being pretty comfortable as far as detention facilities are concerned, to the more institutional-type prison like the one in Glenwood. During my first ski season in Aspen, I knew a guy who managed to get himself arrested for public drunkenness whenever he was between residences in Aspen in order to have a warm bed that night and a good breakfast the following morning.

'So if he's a serial murderer, you're saying the valley is safer if he's in Glenwood.'

'Yes, I'm saying it's better that he's in Glenwood.'

'Sorry, Dan, but didn't Ted Bundy climb out a heat duct from the Glenwood prison back in seventy-seven and head down to Florida to murder a couple more girls?'

He leveled his head at me, his fleshy jowls falling in my direction, his pupils slightly dilated in his hazel eyes. 'Greta, you should be feeling pretty lucky that this guy is locked up. What if he had gotten you alone somewhere?'

I let that one drop. 'I'd like to see him,' I said.

Dan's eyes flicked to his Timex and back at me. 'Suit yourself. Visiting hours just started. I'll go over with you.'

On the short walk between the courthouse and the county jail, he let loose with his opinion again. 'I hope you weren't thinking of getting serious about this guy.'

'I'm not quite sure what I am,' was my honest reply.

After being IDed and passing muster for visitation, I was escorted through some glass doors into a small room with a few tables and chairs. There were already a couple of people in there, a Latina woman talking to a far younger man wearing an orange jumpsuit. From the age difference, I assumed the young man to be her son. They were speaking Spanish so I couldn't understand what they were saying, but it was abundantly clear that she wasn't happy that either one of them was there. I tried not to look in their direction, but it was hard to keep my eyes from wandering to the orange jumpsuit. The realization that Duane would be wearing the same garb when he entered came with a sharp sting.

And then the truth of the orange jumpsuit presented itself

as Duane was escorted into the room by a deputy. It was so contrary to the green scrubs he'd worn when he was tending to me in the hospital. The deputy's body language told me Duane had already been tried and convicted in his eyes. While the look on Duane's face was severe and the ever-ready smile absent, even the prison garb didn't take away from his beauty. When he saw me, the corners of his lips curled up weakly.

He took a seat opposite me as the deputy retreated to a corner. I couldn't tell if it was embarrassment, shame or admission, but at first he had trouble meeting my eyes. When he did raise his eyes to mine, I found myself unable to find any words. It was really hard not knowing if I wanted to assure him that I believed there was no way he had done this heinous crime, or ask him if he had. I sat silently, afraid whatever I might say would be wrong.

And then he solved my problem by articulating it. 'You're not sure, are you?'

'Sure of what?' I said, deflecting his question with another one.

'Sure that I didn't do this thing.' His words were sharp, his voice nothing like the soft one whispering into my ear in the dark.

'No, Duane, it's not that. It's just that . . .'

The eyes that had made visual love to my body long before the physical act now sharpened into a hostile stare. 'I don't want to hear "It's just that . . ." I'm in trouble here, and I was sure you were the one person I could count as my ally, Greta. I thought there was something special between us. You know, the soulmate sort of fucking bullshit. Obviously, I was mistaken.' The words hurt because he'd only said kind things to me before, and I was taken aback at his use of vulgarity. It occurred to me I hadn't heard him swear before, and I must have grimaced, because he started on me again. 'Wow, was I wrong. If you can even suspect for one millisecond that I could possibly kill the daughter of my good friends, much less do the heinous things that whoever did to her, you obviously have no sense for who I am. This really hurts. Maybe worse than being falsely imprisoned.' He pushed his seat back and signaled for the guard. 'I guess this is it, Greta. I've got bigger things to worry about than a friend who has no faith in me.'

I wanted to argue my side, to tell him I wasn't sure, to ask him about the blood in his house, the blood in his car. But I felt anything I said now would just bury me deeper. He stood up and the deputy was on him like cold on ice. My eyes were welling with tears of sadness and anger at life's curveballs as the deputy unlocked the door to the other side. It may have been a nice prison, but it was still a prison.

'I'm sure you'll be out soon,' I said, but it was too little and too late. I wasn't even really sure how I came up with those words; they sounded so ridiculous. My next words were even worse, but they were the truth. 'I only wish the best for you.'

The door closed without him even looking back.

Dan was waiting in the lobby when I walked back into the free world.

'How did it go?' he asked.

'What do you think? He thinks that I question his innocence.' I searched Dan's face for an answer to my next question. It was as hard and fixed as I'd ever seen it in the fifteen years I'd known him. 'Should I question his innocence?'

'Look, Greta, there's something rotten in Denmark with this guy. One, he's the last to see her alive. Two, there are traces of her blood at his house and in his car.'

I asked Dan the question I'd wanted to ask Duane. 'Did he give you any explanation about the blood?'

'Some story about her cutting her hand on loose nail scissors in her purse after he picked her up at Eagle-Vail. And then stopping at his place in Basalt to wrap it, because it was bleeding so bad.'

This was news to me. 'Did he pick her up in Eagle?'

'Yep. We've confirmed that. She flew into Eagle because that was the best airfare and then she met her friend here in Aspen.'

'So maybe that is what happened,' I said, arguing his case. 'She cut her hand and that explains why there was blood in his house and in his car.'

'Greta, get real. It's not like she's around to explain it. So just to take that doubt out of your mind, I'm going to share another piece of information with you.' Dan paused for ultimate effect before the delivery. 'This is confidential. The real nail in his coffin is we have two witnesses who said they saw the doctor and a pretty blond girl fighting in a Porsche SUV in the parking lot at the Snowflake. That she tried to get out of the car and he pulled her back in. That they drove away together.'

'So why didn't they report it?'

'Said it looked more like a lover's quarrel than anything else and they didn't want to get involved. They didn't think much of it until they read about her death.'

'Who are these witnesses?'

'A couple of guests at the hotel. And that's all I'm telling you. I've told you too much already. Violated confidences. But I just don't want you mooning around for some guy who's a bad egg.'

I was conflicted, and not only from Dan's use of clichés. I wanted to say Duane didn't do it, that he was a great guy. But there were so many contradictions zinging around in my head, I couldn't have said it with any assurance. So I changed my tactics and asked him, 'Are you still planning on posting a deputy at the end of my street tonight?'

'Do you think it's necessary now, in light of Duane Larsen being in prison and all?'

I didn't see how Duane Larsen, maniac or no, would have prospered by burning me alive in my house. Regardless of his innocence or lack thereof, I still feared there was someone dark out there trying to get to me. I thought about staying with Judy and Gene, but after what had just transpired with Dr Duane Larsen, I wanted to be alone to lick my wounds.

'I'd sleep much more soundly knowing there's a squad car parked at the entrance to my street,' I said.

'You got it, Greta.'

The drive home was empty, the feeling of loss crushing. I was so wrapped in my own world, it wasn't until I was pulling off Highway 82 that I noticed the Pitkin County Sheriff's car following me. It was a female deputy and she smiled and waved as she pulled over to the side of the road. I know I should have felt reassured by her presence, but I didn't.

# THIRTY-FOUR

Once home, I opened my front door to a dark room. My memory was still trained to expect Kayla greeting me and the recurring wave of guilt and disappointment I'd suffered since putting her down surged through me. The promise of newfound love had served as a distraction, but now her absence came pounding back harder than ever. The very thought that the man who'd made love to me only a couple of nights before was sitting in a prison cell, maybe or maybe not responsible for the disappearance of two women and the death of a third, was mind boggling. Nothing about him remotely hinted that he was anything other than kind and admirable. Then again, there are dozens of stories of women taken in by an evil person and ending up on the losing end of the equation.

I felt that I was in a pit and wondered where the bottom was. Warren was dead. His widow was solitary in her pregnancy. Toby was in Afghanistan and in constant danger. Someone was trying to do me harm, and my newfound love was possibly a serial killer.

I was loveless, jobless, dogless. I wondered how I would support myself if my job was gone for good. I could always teach skiing – if they'd even hire me back. The very thought of doing slow wide turns down the front of Ruthie's with a class of penguins following behind me depressed me beyond words. Ever since starting on patrol the freedom to go wherever my skis took me had been mine. Losing that freedom would be a big step backwards.

I was overcome with self-pity and started to cry. I have never been a crier. Like I've said, the entire time my mom was sick I never cried once. But just as they had way back on that first day in Aspen, the tears started flowing now. They grew in intensity and soon they were splashing over my lower lashes and flowing in self-serving pity down my cheeks. The combination of grief and shock and pain and disappointment was overwhelming. I was back in that place of not having anything or anyone. There was no bottom beneath me, which was a good thing in skiing, but a bad thing in life. I plopped down into the Barcalounger and buried my face in the crook of my arm.

My breath caught in my throat at the sound of an approaching car. At first I thought it was my imagination playing tricks on me. But the unmistakable sound of snow crunching beneath tires was evidence that someone was nearing my residence. Wasn't there supposed to be a deputy keeping watch at the end of the street? Movie scenes of the female cop sitting in a sheriff's car with her throat slit permeated my brain. I ran to Sam's closet where I'd hidden the Remington before leaving this morning. It was ready and loaded by the time the high beams penetrated the dark of the cul-de-sac.

I peered out the window at the approaching vehicle. If it was a murderer coming, it was a rich one. The car was the mountain version of a limousine, a stretch Humvee with an extra set of doors on either side. Curiosity overruled fear as it stopped in front of my door. I watched the car's driver jump out from behind the wheel and open one of the passenger doors in the back. My eyes widened as Richie and Pablo Alvarez got out of the vehicle. The driver closed the door behind them and took an at-ease stance beside the car like there was some risk of it being towed away. As the father and son walked on to my deck, I couldn't help but think how ridiculous I must look from crying.

I stepped outside, protecting the sanctity of my home from the invaders.

'Greta Westerlind?' Pablo Alvarez questioned. In a ski town, one cannot always be quite sure the person you are addressing is the same person you may have seen earlier in the day. Helmets, goggles and body-covering ski clothes are great disguises, and with my hair down around my shoulders and my eyes puffy and red, I'm sure I looked different from the person he'd glimpsed at the bottom of the ski lift. He was even more handsome than earlier in the day, his salt and pepper hair combed off his forehead, the collar of his brown suede shirt poking out from some mighty fine-looking leather.

'The one and only,' I replied. And then taking back possession of my residence, I asked, 'How did you know where I live?'

'I asked around. I'm a close friend to the owner of the ski company.'

Of course he was. My question as to what he was doing on my doorstep was answered before the words could even beg their way out of my mouth.

'I apologize for not sufficiently thanking you for saving my son's life this afternoon. I would like to do something to express my gratitude.'

A large check wrote itself in my brain. I mean, I am probably one of the least mercenary people you will ever meet, but suddenly Everest was looking closer. I wondered if it was in bad taste to accept money for saving a life. Then again, it wasn't like I went out looking for someone in a tree well to make a buck. My action had been spontaneous. As a gift can be.

I looked down at Richie hovering shyly, half behind his father. Contentment that this kid was breathing was reward enough for me. I took back my poisonous mercenary thoughts and gave him a smile. 'That's not necessary. Helping Richie is part of what I do every day. I'm ski patrol.'

'Yes, I know.' Of course he did. He was after all a billionaire, and when he was making inquiries as to who I was and where I lived, my current job status must have come up. 'But it's come to my attention that you have some time off, so I want to make you an offer and I will not accept an answer of no.'

I couldn't imagine what he was going to say, so I stood silently waiting to hear what this offer might be.

'My wife and I had a lengthy discussion as to what we might do to thank you. And then Richie actually came up with the idea himself. We are leaving tomorrow for St Moritz and we would like you to join us as our guest. No expense to you, of course.'

I couldn't say if I was pleased or disappointed. The idea of joining this billionaire family on vacation felt on one hand a little weird. On the other it held appeal. I'd only skied in Europe once, at St Anton and on a budget. The thought of racing down the famed slopes of St Moritz held appeal. Yes, it was the place of the rich and privileged, but then again, so was Aspen and that sure didn't take anything away from the skiing.

I thought about it further. There was nothing to lose and only skiing to gain. Timing wise the offer couldn't be better. There was nothing going on here for me at present. And then I just thought, why not? From the loss of Warren to Duane's deceit, from my recent shortcomings and mistakes to the fear of someone trying to enter my house, why not just get up and leave it behind? Take a brain vacation. With my life basically in the trash bin, a change of scenery could only make things better.

I thought about commitments. There was my coat-check shift at the Bug on Saturday, but covering that was as easy as giving away white lightning on Skid Row. Class on Monday – I'd just have to make it up. There was Warren's service, but I was banned from that anyhow. There was nothing to lose. In fact, maybe in fresh surroundings, my buried memory might come back to me.

'What time do we leave?'

He smiled an elegant broad smile. 'We leave from the private terminal at noon. My driver will pick you up at eleven forty-five.'

I was going to ask if that would allow enough time for security and all and then it dawned on me that TSA wouldn't be a big issue on a private jet. He and Richie said goodnight and stepped down the stairs. The driver had the door to the Humvee open before you could even think about it. Just as he started to close the door, a last question occurred to me.

'Hey,' I called out. Pablo Alvarez stuck his head out the door. 'Was there a sheriff's car stationed at the end of the road?'

'Yes, Greta, there was. The deputy performed her duty, but when we explained the reason for our visit, she let us pass.'

'Thanks.' Maybe I was going to have a good night's sleep after all.

# THIRTY-FIVE

The next morning I called Judy to bring her up to date on my life. She was packing for a week in Palm Beach with Gene's family. Why anyone in their right mind would want to leave Aspen in the middle of the winter to go someplace warm was beyond me. Not when you could be skiing. I hadn't talked to her in a couple of days and I filled her in on the sorry state of my life and what had happened with Dr Larsen. She'd already seen news of his arrest in the paper and told me in no uncertain terms I'd dodged a bullet. Then I told her about how I'd been invited to go to St Moritz. She was more excited about the trip than I was.

'Nice,' she said. 'I love St Moritz. I can't believe you're flying with Pablo Alvarez. I think he's one of the richest men in Mexico. Gene thinks he's one of the cagiest investors around. Let me know if he drops any tips.'

'Right. As if I care. A change of scenery just seemed like a good idea. Do I need to pack anything special?' I asked, wondering how my Thrift Shop wardrobe would play in Switzerland.

'Just bring a lot of black. No one can tell what it cost.'

The Alvarez Humvee pulled up in front at exactly 11:45. The driver was alone this time, and he took my quickly packed duffel and my ski gear from me and loaded it into the back. I climbed into the front seat and belted myself in. He stood outside the car on his side and stared at me, obviously not accustomed to having passengers sit next to him, and when I explained I wasn't comfortable having someone drive me around, he looked perplexed. After further consideration it dawned on me that he didn't speak English. The drive to the airport was a quiet one.

We arrived at the airport at exactly noon. We bypassed the entrance to the terminal used by the common folk, and pulled into the entrance for the private operations, a low-key structure with a covered turnaround in the front. It was my first ever visit there. For all the years I'd lived in Aspen, for all the Fourth of Julys and Christmases that I'd driven past the airport and seen the tarmac heavy with private aircraft – so much so that some pilots had to drop their passengers off and fly to Rifle to park the plane – I'd never set foot in the private terminal. I hadn't been invited. Then again, I didn't run with the type of people who would have offered the invitation.

There were three people waiting in the lounge, a comfortable room with a stone fireplace, upholstered chairs and free coffee. Richie was playing a game on his phone alongside a sullen-looking teenager with a handsome face that was a younger version of Pablo's.

'Hi Greta,' said Richie, barely looking up before going back to his game.

The teenager looked up longer. He stopped texting and smiled an ironic smile. 'So you're the one who saved my lame half-brother.'

This prompted a response from the third person in the lounge, a remarkably beautiful young woman with smooth, tanned skin and shoulder-length black hair. She had been looking out the window at an arriving commercial jet, but upon hearing the boys she leapt up from her chair and ran to me, surprising me by drawing me close in a very personal hug.

'I'm Maria Alvarez,' she said, practically in tears. 'I can't thank you enough for saving my son's life.'

I was stunned at first, having assumed all three to be Pablo's children. When I recovered enough from the fact that she was Pablo's wife and not his daughter, I awkwardly accepted her thanks. 'You're welcome.' Now how lame did that sound? Like 'Pass the butter, please. Thank you. You're welcome.' 'I mean, anyone would have done the same.' Now I sounded even stupider. I wondered if being around such significant wealth was unnerving me. I told myself to chill.

I mean, Aspen has had people of immeasurable wealth practically from its conception as a silver-mining town. When I first moved here, it was hard not to feel out of place with all the fur and the glitz and the expensive restaurants. But once I started working, especially teaching skiing, it all fell into perspective for me. Money can't buy a better experience out in nature. Hiking. Cross-country skiing in the backcountry. Floating through waist-deep powder. Although financial security is always a consideration, I had little interest in the trappings of wealth. And since I'd already beaten the housing issue when Sam left me the A-frame, and my ski pass was covered by my job, I was wanting for little. Not like the immigrant population who bust their butts and have to drive an hour and a half in to work from Rifle where the rich house their jets.

I have this credo I try to live by. And that is: no one is better than me, and no one is lesser. Our circumstances are just different.

'God put you there,' Maria Alvarez was saying. 'I told Pablo I didn't want Richie doing that bowl, that he was too young. He said it would build character, that it would be good for him. Anyhow, it's done and all is good. My boy is safe.'

Her head turned towards the entry as the senior Alvarez stepped into the waiting area, emerging from down the hall, ostensibly from the restroom. The mood in the room changed immediately, his presence like that of a king arriving to greet his subjects. It wasn't intentional or off-putting; he just had that aura about him. I studied his handsome face, smooth and aristocratic framed in attractively graying hair. It occurred to me that despite being Mexican, there was little Indian blood in him if any, that his heritage was most likely pure Spanish with perhaps a little Anglo thrown in.

'I see you've met Maria,' he said. 'And you know Richie.' He gestured to the teen immersed in some attraction on his phone, oblivious to the rest of the world. 'And this is my oldest son, Carlos. King Charles.' The teen looked up and grunted a hello. Getting a better look at his face, I could see he was at the north end of his teen years, his chin and upper lip dusted with dark stubble, his dark eyes even more penetrating than his father's.

Before we could exchange any more pleasantries, the door leading to the tarmac opened and a tall man wearing a leather flight jacket and a captain's hat walked inside. My mind registered something peculiar about his appearance, but it wasn't until I focused on him that it became evident he had been badly burned. The entire right side of his face was mottled, the corner of his lashless eye fused shut, his right ear missing completely with an open orifice where the cartilage would have been. He held a clipboard with paperwork in his right hand, which was missing the ends of several fingers. I worked my face to not register shock.

He addressed Pablo with familiarity and respect. 'Everything is in order, sir.' Turning his one-and-a-half-eyed gaze on me, he added, 'I see you've got a stowaway. A good-looking one, I might add.' Now I had to fight giving him an indignant glare. I hate it when men make stupid comments like that as if my looks said anything about me. Then he further aggravated me when he said, 'I'll need to see your passport, *young lady.*'

Now there are three stages to a woman's life as far as I'm concerned. Young lady, ma'am, and young lady. Knowing I was past the first 'young lady' but nowhere near the second, I found the expression demeaning. Being ma'am was bad enough. I was in no hurry to be young lady for a second time.

Pablo introduced him as Captain Chris Calloway. I got my name in as quickly as I could before he deigned to drop any more cutesy remarks.

'I'm Greta Westerlind,' I said, offering up the passport I'd pulled out in a panic last night to make sure it was current. He didn't bother flicking through the stamped pages evidencing my travel of the last years, but rather turned to the first page to check the expiration date and then held it up to compare my passport photo with my face. Instead of handing it back to me, he held on to it.

'I'll need this for customs in Switzerland,' he said, all business now.

Then without further ceremony, he turned back to the Alvarez family. 'Your carriage awaits.'

Astounded is not a strong enough word for how I felt when I stepped into that plane. I'd been told that a G5 is an amazing aircraft, but I was in no way prepared for what revealed itself upon entry. The first thing I saw was the co-pilot seated in the cockpit. To even begin to describe the dashboard with its numerous instruments and gauges would be a challenge, but suffice to say it was impressive. An attractive brown-haired woman with a frequent smile stood to the side of the cockpit door in front of a large and modern-looking galley with cabinets made of shiny wood. She introduced herself as Kelly and told us she was there to attend to any of our needs as well as our safety.

And as if things could have gotten any more otherworldly, I turned and looked the rest of the way into the plane. Before Judy met Gene, she and I did a trip to Florence once during the off season. Everyone we knew told us we simply had to see Michelangelo's David. Being on a budget, I remember thinking it was a waste of time and money to stand in line just to see one statue. That changed the moment we entered the museum and turned the corner into the gallery where David was displayed. When I saw the statue I understood. You didn't need to know squat about art to appreciate the masterpiece. The statue was exquisite, commanding and breathtaking, all in one.

Well, that's what it felt like looking down the length of the jet's fuselage. Like the statue of David, it was a masterpiece. The wide seats were upholstered in cream-colored leather with grey leather pinstripes and shiny-hued tables sat between them. Further along was an actual sofa, also leather, with a flat-screen television over a dining table opposite it. Toward the end of the aisle more seats were situated in front of a partition. On the other side was a sleeping area with a half-dozen seats that could be reclined into beds with a privacy wall and reading lamp at each one. A door at the end led to what I assumed was a bathroom.

I was speechless. I turned back to my host to find out what the protocol was. 'Make yourself at home,' he said. 'The flight takes about ten hours, putting us in St Moritz between five and six in the morning. There is plenty of food. Just ask Kelly. And I suggest trying to get as much sleep as you can, if you want to be fresh to ski when we arrive.' He then took a seat at the front of the plane near the cockpit and pulled out his cellphone. The two boys had taken seats across from each other and were intent on texting or surfing the internet. Maria was talking to Kelly up front, ordering up lunch no doubt. I plopped into a single seat next to the window and my first thought was I never knew such soft leather existed. My second thought was the Barcalounger was never going to be the same again.

Captain Calloway announced over an intercom that we should fasten our seat belts. That was it. No safety demonstration, though Kelly did point out where we might find life vests. After a short taxi, we were racing down Sardy Field's only runway, the whole process from embarking to take-off less than five minutes. Seconds later we were leaving the snow-covered mountains behind as we rose through the gray clouds and emerged above them, looking down at fluffy white mountains of an entirely different kind.

# THIRTY-SIX

A dinner-sized lunch was served shortly after take-off, a smorgasbord of shellfish and salmon, slices of tenderloin, roast potatoes, spinach and goat cheese salad, brioche rolls and sourdough bread. The food would have been amazing served in a home, much less an airplane. There was even champagne offered, which I declined. It was enough to be going against my small-to-no-lunch mantra. I didn't want to be drunk on top of it.

I helped myself to more food than anyone should ever eat in the middle of the day and sat down at the table with the family. That is everyone except for Pablo, who was intent on work, on his cellphone deep in conversation. Evidently, the ban on using cell phones on aircraft didn't apply here.

Carlos started teasing Richie for taking too much food. And when I took a look at his plate I could see why. It was heaped high with beef and fish and potatoes, a couple of brioche floating on top like a pair of breasts.

'Think you have enough bread there, oh fat one?' Carlos said. His plate probably held about half as much as his younger brother's, though I did notice he had helped himself to the champagne.

'Carlos, be nice to your brother,' Maria reprimanded him. Clearly her words held little sway with Carlos, because he continued to berate his half-brother. I'm sure his next comments were meant for my benefit.

'How long did it take you to get up the bowl, you pile of mush?'

'Carlos,' Maria said, sharper this time.

Pablo's ear parted from his phone for an instant. 'Carlos,' he echoed and then went back to his conversation. This time his older son listened. He went back to eating his lunch in silence. Richie turned back to his plate, looking at his iPad while he ate, which appeared to be his regular escape. I felt sorry for the kid living in Carlos's shadow.

I decided to test some conversation of my own. 'Do you boys like St Moritz?' I asked.

'They do,' Carlos responded, indicating his father and stepmother and his half-brother. 'It's way too dull for me.'

'You're the one who's dull,' Richie inserted between bites.

'Right, champ,' said Carlos, patting his brother none-too-fondly on the head.

Eager to change the subject, Maria turned the conversation back to me. 'Now, Greta, how long have you been on the ski patrol?'

'Long time. Around ten years,' I replied.

'Around one week too long,' I heard Carlos muttering under his breath. It didn't take a genius to figure out what that was supposed to mean.

In one meal I learned the Alvarez family, like all families, had a rhythm of its own. When I was a ski instructor and had private lessons with rich Latinos from Mexico City, there was often a dynamic where the husband appeared to be the one in charge, but in actuality it was the wife. In this case, from what I could tell it was the opposite. Pablo was at the same time polite and deferential to his wife, but it was clear that he was the one in charge. He was also demanding. When I say demanding, I don't mean as far as waiting on him or performing tasks was concerned, but it was at another level. An unspoken expectation that lingered in the air of how she was to act and present herself. She had probably ventured outside acceptable behavior when she confided in me that she hadn't wanted Richie to board in the bowl.

Richie, as I'd perceived before, was a shy kid who needed to be drawn out, perfectly content to watch movies or play video games in his own universe on his iPad. No wonder he was carrying the extra weight. King Charles, or Carlos rather, was an entirely different story. Clearly the son of a previous wife, he was lean and fit with a lot of the privileged persona of his father, talking to people when and where he felt like it. He didn't care for his younger brother and made no secret of it.

When we'd finished eating, I paid a quick visit to the head, more out of curiosity than need. And my curiosity was rewarded. The room was larger than my bathroom at home with not only a toilet and vanity, but a shower with a window. I tried to imagine what it would be like soaping up among the clouds.

I returned to my seat and went back to Ovid and the story of Io, the unlucky mortal who had taken Jove's fancy while drawing water from a stream. The supreme god had pulled some of his usual hijinks to have his way with her, casting the world into darkness so his wife wouldn't catch him in the act. After Jove had his way with her, he turned the unfortunate woman into a white heifer to throw his jealous wife off the trail. Smelling a rat, Juno one-upped Jove by asking for the cow as a gift. Juno then went on to torment the poor cow in myriad ways, to include setting a gadfly upon her, nearly driving her mad.

Unlike the other myths we'd covered, this one had a happy ending. Jove took pity on Io and begged his wife to let up, promising to never wander her lush fields again. Io was returned to human form and gave birth to a son who most likely bore Jove's DNA.

This set me to wondering if Pablo's first wife hadn't wished she could have turned Maria into a cow.

We flew into twilight and the cabin lights were dimmed. I moved to the back of the plane where the seats reclined flat for sleeping and sat alone reading. The boys were still occupied with video games and Maria was watching a movie on one of the monitors, her headphones blocking out all noise. Pablo was still up front, on the phone hovering over papers.

Kelly appeared out of nowhere to ask if I would like my bed made up. While she worked her magic, I paid another visit to the bathroom. When I returned to my seat it was still upright, but a sheet and down comforter had been fit over the smooth leather. I was just getting ready to lower it to sleeping position when the door to the cockpit opened and the captain walked out. His silhouette dominated the aisle as he walked toward the aft of the plane, his broad shoulders hunched so as not to hit his head on the ceiling.

He nodded politely as he passed me and went into the head.

On his way back to the cockpit he stopped beside my seat. I swear I was ready to kneecap him if he called me young lady again. He was hatless and the melted side of his head looked like candle wax. He stood in contemplation for a minute, and then took the seat across from me and leaned in to talk.

'First time in a G-Five?' he asked.

'First time in a private jet period. It'll be hard flying commercial after this. Not to mention sitting on any chair in my house.'

He laughed, stretching taut the smooth burnt flesh on the lipless side of his mouth. He tipped his head to the right and for a moment only the untouched left side of his face was visible. He had obviously been quite a handsome man before being burned.

'So your last name is Westerlind?' he queried.

'That's what it says on my passport.'

'There was an Army Ranger named Westerlind in Afghanistan when I was there ten years ago. Hell of a guy. Took risks no sane person would.'

'Please don't tell me his name was Tobjorn.'

'He went by Toby. Any relation?'

'My brother.'

He was speechless for a minute as if he was musing over whether to share his next words with me or not. 'Well, your brother saved my life. Dragged me out of an inferno after the CH-Forty-Seven I was flying from Bagrum to Jalalabad was hit by an RPG.' He read the question mark on my face and clarified: 'Grenade. Rocket propelled. We were brought down smack in the middle of terrain filled with IEDs.' He stopped again. 'Improvised explosive devices. Your brother was driving past in a Humvee when he saw us come down. He turned straight across the minefield to get to us. The helicopter was a conflagration, but he climbed in to evac anyone he could. Dragged me out with my skin slipping off in his hand and went back for one more guy from the force. The rest were hopeless. Lost my co-pilot and three other men.' He was silent with the pause that goes into significant thought. 'Threw me over his back and got me to his vehicle. Not many men would do that. He's a true hero in my eyes.'

Ten years ago. I pictured my then twenty-five-year-old brother carrying the enormous man across from me on his back. Though I'd never for an instant doubted my brother's bravery, it troubled me to know just the kind of risks he took. I couldn't help but look at the captain's mottled right arm and imagine Toby's hand slick with his missing skin. I appealed to the same power that watched over me while I was buried under the snow. *Please don't let any harm come to my brother.*

'What's he doing now, anyhow? He still in the service?'

'He's still in. For all I know he's married by now. To a woman with one leg.'

The captain didn't quite know how to respond to that. He stood up and smoothed his slacks with his palms. His right hand with the missing fingers looked incomplete next to the left. 'Great guy, your brother,' he said, turning back toward the cockpit. 'Now you get some sleep.'

I tried to sleep after he'd gone, but the talk of my brother left me troubled; the image of him entering a burning plane refused to leave my brain. What if the plane had exploded? What if he had gotten burned like Chris Calloway, his face destroyed?

I turned back to Ovid for distraction. The next story was that of Phaethon, Apollo's son, who in the spirit of most teenage boys basically borrowed his dad's chariot without telling him. Anyhow, he was exceeding the speed limit while driving the sun across the sky and crashed and burned, nearly setting the world on fire. Sound familiar? Teenagers then. Teenagers now. Is there really any difference?

I was awakened from a sound sleep by a gentle hand on my shoulder. I opened my eyes to see Kelly hovering over me. 'I'm sorry to disturb you, Miss Westerlind, but we're going to be landing soon. Can I get you anything?'

I told her a coffee would be nice, and reluctantly roused myself from my down featherbed and silky linens and went into the bathroom. There were toiletries laid out, so I washed my face and brushed my teeth making use of the expensive inventory on the counter. My hair was an unruly mess of blond frizz, but that's its natural state so it was nothing out of the ordinary. I ran a comb through it in hopes of restoring some order and went back out into the cabin. My bed had already been stripped of the linens, the seat returned to upright. A cappuccino rested on the table next to it. The thought ran through my mind that a person could get used to this sort of treatment. On further reflection I decided it would get old fast.

The co-pilot appeared and came down the aisle. Much shorter than Captain Calloway, with a full head of jet-black hair, he nodded as he walked past me. I realized I hadn't seen him at all during the flight, which told me how soundly I had slept. Shortly after he returned to the cockpit, there was an announcement to make sure we had our seatbelts fastened as we were on approach to landing.

My face was glued to the window at the sight of the Alps. They appeared more rugged than the Rockies, the treeless snowcapped peaks with greater rises from base to apex than at home. As the plane descended and the mountains drew closer, nowhere did I see evidence of a town, much less an airport. And then there was the sound of the landing gear lowering just as a highway and a four-circle exchange came into view. A strong gust of wind jogged the plane to the left and the captain pivoted right to compensate, the plane vibrating like it wanted to break up as he crabbed it through the wind to the landing strip. After a landing that would have most people grabbing for the air-sickness bag, not one of us so much as blinked an eye. After years of flying into Aspen and the same frivolous winds, we were all used to it.

A stretch Rolls-Royce, something I never even knew existed, awaited us on the tarmac. We were escorted to the car while Captain Calloway went in to clear us through customs. It wasn't long before he came back and handed us our passports. The door was shut and the driver started into the ski resort of St Moritz. Evidently the crew rated less exclusive transportation.

When we entered the town, I was overwhelmed by its unique beauty and the way it nestled in the snow-covered peaks of the Alps just like Aspen did in the Rockies. It was as dysfunctional as Aspen too, with charming Swiss chalets juxtaposed alongside metallic modern-day condominium buildings. The streets were lined with expensive boutiques of the same ilk as Aspen and, judging by the dress of the pedestrians and skiers we passed along the way, the town dripped money just like my home.

We pulled up in front of a Gothic edifice, a regal stone hotel situated up the hill with a five-star view of the frozen lake. I'd done a little research on the internet before leaving Aspen and learned that until the 1890s, St Moritz had been primarily a summer destination for wealthy English. That is until 1864 when Johannes Badrutt made a bet with four British tourists that if they didn't like St Moritz in the winter he would pay all their travel costs. They evidently enjoyed themselves enough to come back and St Moritz as a winter sports mecca was born. Johannes's son, Casper, later built a huge palace, which he eponymously named Badrutt's Palace Hotel.

I'd pretty much assumed that we were sitting in front of that hotel, my suspicions confirmed when the car doors opened and two uniformed doormen said simultaneously, 'Welcome to Badrutt's Palace.'

'And here we are,' Pablo announced. 'Home for the next week.'

We left our bags behind for the valets to deal with and were ushered into the lobby, a massive room of marble floors and high ceilings with grand hallways stretching to either side of us. And at this point, it came as no surprise to me that we didn't have to check in. We were escorted directly to an elevator and then to our rooms with baggage mysteriously having appeared right behind us, except for skis which I am sure went to a home all their own. Our rooms were lined up along the same hallway, Señor and Señora Alvarez taking one, the two boys another and the third was mine.

'Maria and I are going to take a rest,' Pablo informed me. 'We never ski on arrival day. And the boys are most likely going to rest as well. If you find you have the energy to ski, just stop at the front desk. All the arrangements are made.'

I thanked him and followed the bell captain into my room. He put my duffel bag on a rack and asked me if I would like it unpacked. I declined his offer and reached into my backpack for my wallet to give him a tip. He raised a hand that said it was not necessary. Of course not, I surmised. Everything would be taken care of by Señor.

After he had gone, I took a good look at my room for the first time. Before we had a house, when Toby and I had shared a room in a rental apartment, I had dreams of being a princess. One day I found a packing crate near the dumpster and dragged it up to our room, using it to divide the room in half. My half of the room became my palace with a canopy of sheets over my bed and my pillow a fluffed throne beneath it. I begged my mother for a satin princess gown and crown for my birthday and she went over budget to deliver it. Dressed in my princess garb, I would sit in my private quarters for hours, addressing my loyal subjects, a collection of dolls and stuffed animals.

When I scoped out what was to be my quarters for the next week, my visions of royalty were fulfilled. The suite was easily the size of my home and then some. There was a huge bed framed in gold with a real canopy over it. And while I'm not well versed in period pieces, something told me that what I was looking at was the real deal, though from what period was anybody's guess. Lack of knowledge didn't stop me from enjoying my new digs any. I took a running start and leapt on to the bed like a child and lay there enjoying the views of the mountains from my new kingdom.

For the first time in my life, I was truly a princess.

# THIRTY-SEVEN

P ablo Alvarez assumed right when he thought I might want to ski. I'd gotten enough sleep on the plane and was ready to hit the lifts as soon as they opened. But it was still too early, so I took the time to unpack my duffel bag and arrange my small plastic bag of toiletries in the apartment-sized bathroom. After hanging my lonely jeans in the closet, I ventured down to the lobby to get the lay of the land. The concierge jumped to service, more than happy to make arrangements for me to be taken to the main lift by the hotel shuttle.

'Would you like a guide, Miss Westerlind? It's often wise to ski with someone who knows the ropes.'

My polite but firm *no thank you* was ready before his last words were out of his mouth. After all the pressure in the last week, there was nothing I wanted more than to be alone without obligation to talk to anyone. This was my day to explore uncharted territory, to let my legs and skis carry me to places never visited, to glory in the rugged beauty of the Alps.

'Very well, Miss Westerlind. But please know that we here at the hotel are at your service. If there is anything you want, please don't hesitate to ask.'

I thanked him and took the stairs back up to my fourth-floor suite. I had just finished putting on my Thrift Shop Bogner ski suit when there was a knock at the door. I opened it to see Maria and Richie Alvarez standing in the hall, Richie in winter gear, his mother in street clothes. She smiled, her teeth gleaming white in her comely face while her plump son hung his round head shyly.

'I hate to disturb you.' Somehow that statement didn't seem to have any teeth to it. 'Neither Pablo nor I plan to ski today, and Richie really wants to snowboard. I don't want him to go alone.' Her eyes glossed over my ski pants and turtleneck. 'Would you mind if he joins you?'

I recalled a Steve Martin routine my mother used to get a

kick out of. Do you mind if I smoke? No, do you mind if I fart? Now I like kids, but I didn't feel like sharing my first day on the slopes of Corviglia with anyone I hadn't vetted, much less a ten-year-old. Not to mention I was entertaining the notion of some off-piste skiing, and although there aren't really tree wells like in the Rockies, keeping an eye on Richie would still be a downer. Of course I minded. I minded a lot. My mind scrolled my files in search of other options.

'Don't you think he'd have more fun with his brother?'

'Carlos is sleeping in and then he's going to do the Cresta Run.'

I'd seen pictures of the track, a run of packed snow which people screamed down head first on a sleigh, instead of feet first like the luge. The track was part of a private club which still excluded women, but I had no doubt Pablo Alvarez was a member.

'Richie, don't you want to do the Cresta with your brother? I hear it's really exciting,' I suggested.

No sale. He looked at me timidly and said, 'I did it last year.'

'How about a guide for Richie?' I tossed in as a last-ditch effort, recalling my conversation with the concierge. No doubt a guide was expensive, but the last thing the Alvarezes needed to worry about was money.

'I want to go with Greta,' he said, turning his appeal to his mother, ignoring me for all intents and purposes as if his mother held sway over my decision. Then he turned his round brown, dark-lashed eyes up towards me, and I revisited watching them pop open in the glades and the reward of knowing a potential death had been averted. My stance softened. Perhaps the two of us had a special bond. Besides, his family had given me one hell of a ride here, and they were picking up my shelter, nutrition and entertainment. What else could I do?

'OK, Richie. We're on. Bus leaves in ten minutes.' I looked at my watch for emphasis. So much for being a princess.

An hour and a half later, we were boarding the shuttle to Corviglia after spending the better part of the morning in the downstairs ski shop getting adjustments made to Richie's equipment. He had insisted on trying out a new board, and so we'd had to deal with rentals, which took forever because Richie couldn't make up his mind on what color he wanted.

After a scenic ride past expensive boutiques along winding snow-banked streets, we finally arrived at the funicular at eleven o'clock, a full three hours later than my intended start. As the lift moved out of the station and gained elevation, my mood turned upbeat. The view of the town and the lake was breathtaking. It was hard to believe that only hours ago I had been in Aspen and now I was in Switzerland about to ski Corviglia, which I had heard so much about. I looked at my young charge. Well, I *hoped* I was going to ski.

After his harrowing experience in the bowl, Richie was understandably gun-shy and he asked if we could start out on one of the gentler slopes. 'Sure, kid,' I said, my eyes venturing up the mountain to the expert terrain. After a few runs in intermediate terrain I broached the subject of trying something a little more challenging.

Richie bucked at that idea. 'I like where we are,' he said.

'You don't like something a little more difficult?' I said, gazing longingly at the legendary Piz Nair above us.

'No,' he whined. And then he dealt the fatal blow. 'I'm hungry. Can we have lunch now?'

WTF. Don't tell me he wanted to stop for lunch. It wasn't even noon. I shared my mantra with him. 'Lunch is for wimps.'

The look he gave me was the visual equivalent of the F-bomb followed by 'you'. The brown eyes that I found so needy earlier changed to resolute orbs, a member of the privileged class used to getting his way. No matter my feelings about this, it occurred to me that I had neither choice nor voice as far as lunch was concerned. Like it or not, my role had diminished from lifesaver to babysitter.

*There's always tomorrow*, I told myself as we slid into a mountain chalet overlooking the broad white slopes for what I told myself would be a quick snack. As things turned out the restaurant only offered table service and the prices were exorbitant. Richie ordered with gusto, while I settled for some salmon and a green salad. Richie was finishing up dessert, a Black Forest cake, as the regular lunch crowd started to gather. Sleek and slim, dressed in fur ski outfits or expensive designer wear, they were glossy and monied, the elegant people, a class apart. Now I'm not one to ever think of another person as my better, but there was no doubting they might have a different opinion about me. Polite and composed, they were bred to think they were superior, and there was no doubting they bought into it. Aspen may have its rich, but many of them play down their wealth. Here they flaunted it.

The check came, and naturally Richie didn't have any money, so I put the meal on my credit card hoping his parents would ask about lunch and at least reimburse me for what their human vacuum cleaner had consumed. But at least lunch was over and I could once again feel the crisp cold Alpine air on my skin and the smooth corn snow at my feet.

After waiting fifteen minutes for Richie to finish in the bath-room, I finally managed to steer him back on to the slopes. The outside temperature had dropped and the sky had clouded over, turning the light flat so that it was difficult to read the terrain. While this posed no problem to me, it didn't meet with Richie's approval. When the light is flat, I usually ski in the trees where the definition is better. But unlike Aspen Mountain, Corviglia is relatively treeless, so skiing the trees is not an option. Richie kept falling until finally one time he simply lay on the ground waiting while I side-stepped back up the mountain to him.

'Are you all right?'

'I'm done,' he said, and by his tone of voice, I knew there was no debating it.

It was two thirty and my first day of skiing in the Alps was coming to a close. I'd spent more time in the restaurant than on the mountain. Richie refused to slide down, so we took the funicular. I tried fighting through my aggravation. After all, one can't completely blame a spoiled child for his actions. A child is a reflection of his upbringing. Still, I wanted to strangle him.

I thought of Tantalus, the human who cut up one of his kids and put him in a stew that he served to the gods as a trick. When I'd first read the myth I was appalled, wondering how the ancient mind could come up with anything so vile. Now I was beginning to think the author was on to something.

# THIRTY-EIGHT

I t wasn't even three when the shuttle dropped us back off at Badrutt's. We checked our gear at the ski shop and headed up into the lobby. Richie had turned from petulant to cheery now that he was warm, fed, and near a bed and his iPad.

Even though there was time to still be wrung out of the ski day, après-ski appeared to already be under way in Le Grand Hall that stretched practically the length of the hotel. It was quite a scene, the people lean and stylish and, well, rich. Dressed in my Thrift Shop skiwear, I felt the polar opposite of the people around me, the women coiffed and made up, the men sporting expensive watches and slicked-back hair over soft cashmere blazers. The pelts of dead animals were in abundance, sleek coats draped over the backs of chairs, trimmed vests and hats, boas wrapped around necks, even fur boots. If I thought a couple of Texans in raccoon coats was a big deal, it was nothing compared to this scene. The only place I have ever seen more fur was the zoo. Any self-respecting PETA member would have immolated his or herself in one of the fireplaces in protest.

When we got to our floor, Richie disappeared into his room without even a thank you. I closed the door gratefully behind me, falling on to my gold princess bed, not in exhaustion but in frustration at the wasted day. Wondering what to do next to amuse myself in this most decadent town I picked up the Badrutt's guide on the nightstand and started leafing through it. My fingers came to a halt at a full-page picture of an indoor swimming pool with a rock deck and windows looking out over the Alps. A swim could be nice. The only problem was I hadn't thought to pack a swimsuit for my trip to wintry St Moritz. Then the words of the concierge from this morning echoed in my memory. 'If we can do anything for you . . .'

A call to the desk rendered a sleek red maillot delivered to my door five minutes later.

\*    \*    \*

My entry into the pool area wearing a hotel bathrobe and a pair of Merrells drew a few indifferent glances from the couples luxuriating in the churning waters of a steaming Jacuzzi. The panorama that met me out the windows was breathtaking, almost like a painting, the frozen lake banked by white-dusted fir trees that diminished as they moved up the surrounding mountains to the treeless peaks.

The Jacuzzi may have been full, but my interest lay more in the pool with its granite diving platform, its aqua blue water beckoning. I slipped out of the robe and dropped it on a chaise, kicked off the Merrells, and feeling both sleek and chic in the red maillot, I dove into the pool. The water was body temperature warm, circumventing any shock of dry body meeting wet cold. Having grown up in the Midwest and spent a lot of time in lakes, it's my opinion that you are either a water person or a mountain person. Moving to Colorado was tough at first because it meant choosing between languid summers floating on blow-up rafts in lazy lakes versus the challenge of the arid Rockies. A year later the mountains won out, hands down. I wouldn't trade the mountains for anything.

But that doesn't mean water isn't good from time to time. I started doing laps and after a while my hostility over having to virtually babysit Richie began to drain away. After all, he was a kid and his mother probably had no comprehension of what a let-down the day had been for me. Besides, I'm better than that. Truly.

At least I am when there aren't so many things weighing on my mind. I'd been avoiding thinking about Duane in the hours since leaving Aspen, and maybe that was the right thing to do. Forcing my mind to go blank in the soothing silk of the water, my troubles fell away for the time being, much the way they do when I'm skiing. By the time I climbed out of the pool my frame of mind was much improved.

I dried off with a plush towel handed to me by an attendant who had materialized out of nowhere and slipped back into the robe and Merrells. I was on my way out the door when I heard my name called. I turned to see Carlos nestled in the Jacuzzi between two blonds.

'Greta,' he said. 'C'mon over.' His arrogance never took a

break, it seemed, but nevertheless, I walked over to the lip of the Jacuzzi. The air between us smelled of warm chlorine. 'Why don't you come in?' he said in a voice far too suggestive for his eighteen or nineteen years.

'Looks like you've already got your hands full, Carlos,' I said, and without another word I turned on the heels of my Merrells and walked away.

Back in the room, I had showered and dried my hair and was lying on my stomach making more work of Ovid when the phone rang. I picked up to hear Pablo's warm voice. They were going to a party and he wondered if I wanted to join them. The last thing I wanted to do was face a bunch of people I didn't know who didn't want to know me, so I begged off, saying I was tired. His relief at not having to look after me was clear in his voice.

Having not seen him since getting off the plane this morning, I was getting the feeling he wasn't quite sure what to do with me now that we were all here together. He told me to feel free to dine in one of the restaurants or to order in room service – which is exactly what I did. Content in my hideaway, I ordered up a hamburger and a beer, watched a pay-per-view movie and was blissfully asleep before nine o'clock.

# THIRTY-NINE

The next morning I was up and out the door by seven, wanting to thwart any invitations to ski with young Ricardo again. The lobby was practically empty, most of the hotel guests apparently sleeping it off. I stopped at the concierge to ask where the best off-piste skiing could be found and he suggested Diavolezza, translated as she-devil, twenty kilometers away in Bernina. When I asked about the best transport, he suggested I take a private car. Knowing full well the price was probably prohibitive, I did something quite out of character for me. I signed on for the ride. I figured Pablo Alvarez could afford it, and after babysitting his son the day before, I sort of felt he owed me.

The driver of the shuttle was fourth-generation St Moritz. As we drove along the winding mountain road to Bernina, he lamented the changes that had taken place in his birthplace, both in the physical town itself and in the caliber of the tourist.

'Of course, St Moritz has always drawn the wealthy,' he said to me in German-accented English, 'but the nature of the visitor has changed. It's all new money these days, and the new money people can be so tiresome. And now the Russians, so many Russians. No class, the Russians, spraying bottles of champagne all over themselves as if it were free. Having money is new to them and it shows. You never would have seen anything like that forty years ago.'

'I come from Aspen. I can share your pain,' I said as we pulled up to the lift station. 'We have the same growing pains in Aspen but not so much from Russians.'

'Just wait,' he said as he pulled away.

The cable car was half-filled at the early hour with other hardcore skiers. The mountains were magical in the morning light, almost pink in the vestiges of the January dawn. It had snowed a few inches the night before, but in this Swiss Camelot the sky was already clear. As the lift rose higher, my excitement about attacking this mountain grew. I was ready to see what it could show me and what I could show it.

There was casual conversation among the skiers in the car, dominated by a large group of English complete with their witticisms as well as a healthy dose of entitlement. They were clearly impressed upon learning I was from Aspen, though they did give my Thrift Shop ski suit the once over. Even if it was a Bogner. When I asked what runs they recommended they were quick to suggest the upper part of the mountain.

'With last night's fresh snow, it should be divine,' said one of the women.

'What about off-piste?' I asked.

'You definitely want to take the glacier run from the top. It's about forty-five minutes all in and ends in front of the railway. We always do it at the end of day and hop on the train back to the base. Just be sure you know where you are going. There can be some deep crevices if you get too far off track.'

Once up top I skied inbounds for the early part of the day, taking advantage of the sort of steep, challenging terrain I had been cheated out of the day before. The slopes were wide open as I swept back and forth in the fresh snow, my legs oiled pistons beneath my hips. As the day turned into afternoon, I decided it was time to give the off-piste the British had told me about a try.

The signage leading to the glacier run was clear enough, and as I stood at the boundary trying to decide whether to venture into unknown terrain alone, the group of Brits I'd ridden with earlier skied past me on to the run. Now I'm a pretty good skier. And I'm usually a smart one. But I think because I was feeling so cheated about the skiing I missed the day before, I did something not so brilliant. I skied off on to terrain completely unfamiliar to me – alone. Well, I wasn't entirely alone. At first. The Brits were there, and I just figured I'd tail them.

The problem was they kept stopping, and that isn't how I like to ski. So when they made one of their infernal stops I just blew right past them and kept going. The snow was fabulous, putting to rest, at least for that day, the idea that if you ski in the Rockies you won't like the Alps. It was light and untracked and the terrain quite different from what I'm used to. I felt insignificant in the shadow of the savage peaks that rose to either side of me like heaped tufts of beaten egg whites. I was one drop in all the oceans, one grain of sand on all shores.

There was not one other person in sight as I floated downwards under the power of my legs. I was Diana the huntress chasing her prey. I was Hermes on winged feet. I was Apollo driving his chariot across the sky. The skiing was fabulous and I didn't have a care in the world.

I must have been a half-hour out when I finally came to an exhausted stop. The sky was a bluebird and the sun warm on my back as I took in the valley below me. There were crevasses in the distance, but they didn't worry me as they were quite evident and avoidable. Of course I had no idea where I was, and I knew I'd travelled quite a ways. But I wasn't overly concerned since the Brits had said the run took about forty-five minutes, which meant I would reach the end of the run in another fifteen minutes, give or take. I sipped some water from my Camelbak and planted my skis downhill again.

Another half-hour passed without seeing any sign of the end of the glacier run. I stopped and looked around. There were no landmarks, nothing stretching ahead of me but white fields of empty terrain. I told myself there was no need to panic. Yet. It was only around two o'clock, which left me plenty of daylight to find my way back. I was getting hungry, so I pulled out a few of the ever-present Snickers from the inner pocket of the insulated jacket that I always wore under my ski patrol uniform. I hydrated myself from the Camelbak and, feeling refreshed, started back downhill, confident that I would find the base sooner or later.

An hour later the open terrain had ended and I found myself in a forest with no idea where I was. The sun was ducking lower in the sky and it wouldn't be long until it was dusk. It wasn't wise to keep skiing unknown terrain if the visibility wasn't good. While the likelihood of a crevasse in the woods was low, there might be cliffs or a gulley that might suck me in. I knew I'd been lost since my first stop, but now was the time to admit it.

It started getting dark more rapidly, the winter sun weak and the sky grey. I knew that I was in trouble. The first rule in a situation like this is to keep your head and not panic. I parked myself on the large root of an ancient pine and decided to take inventory.

My Camelbak was nearly empty and I cursed myself for not filling it before starting out on this folly. The large pocket of my inner jacket held a baggie with ten mini Snickers. Another pocket relinquished lip protector and sun block, and a cloth for cleaning googles. A second baggie in that pocket served as a makeshift first-aid kit with aspirin and Tylenol and an array of different sized Band-Aids, and – yes, there is a god – the lighter I confiscated from the pot-smoking boarders on Aspen Mountain. I gave it a flick and almost knelt in worship at the flame. A final interior pocket gave up four chemical handwarmers, the kind that you snap to activate before you stick it in your gloves.

And I had my phone. I turned it on and switched it to roaming and was instantly rewarded with an all-caps NO SERVICE.

I decided to try shouting in case there was someone in the area. I shouted and waited, shouted and waited, moving forward cautiously on my skis the whole time. I cursed myself out for not bringing the whistle that was always in my patrol jacket. And then since my attention was focused on listening and not skiing, one of my skis went into a rut and I fell sideways, smacking my thigh on a rock. Hard. It stung like hell, but there was no blood, so at least that was a blessing.

It was getting dark at an alarming rate and the reality set in. I had to prepare to bivouac. The two biggest enemies to survival in the cold are hypothermia and frostbite. Hypothermia happens when your core body temperature drops too low. Besides causing shivering, hypothermia can lead to confusion which means bad decisions. Frostbite can cost toes, fingers, noses, and even limbs. I thought about the snowboarder who was lost for days in the High Sierras years ago. He'd survived by his wits but still had to undergo a double amputation of his legs. I didn't even want to think of going there.

The first thing to do while there was some light was prepare a bed and find wood to start a fire. I collected some fir branches and made myself a natural mattress. I found some other branches to use as a covering. And then I set out to build a fire.

Night was really upon me now and I used the lighter intermittently to help me collect branches to fuel the fire. I gathered up as much as I could and tried to light it, but the wood was too moist and the fire didn't take. The best I could do was get the needles to burn, but they burnt out quickly. I needed to find small pieces of wood to use as kindling. I was in complete darkness now, except for when I flicked the lighter to search for more kindling. My bruised thigh was throbbing and a sudden debilitating pain shot down my leg as I ran into a low branch. When I reached out reflexively to grab my injured leg, the lighter flew from my hand into the night.

Thus far I had avoided panic, but losing the lighter set me near the edge. I got on my hands and knees and pawed around for it, but in the pitch dark the task proved impossible. I didn't want to move too far from my makeshift mattress, because if I couldn't find it and had to lay on the bare ground, I would be in real trouble. So I stayed put, reaching out for the lighter now and then in hopes of scoring a win. No such luck.

I was dressed for cold weather and moving around had kept me warm, but now the temperature was dropping. I was tiring and beginning to shiver. I decided to eat half the Snickers and drink half the water and try and get some sleep on my bed of branches. My hands and feet were already cold and I thought of the chemical hand warmers in my pocket, deciding they would serve me better in my boots than in my gloves. I could take my hands out of my gloves and warm them against my body, but my feet were too remote. I unbuckled my boots and pulled the tongues out. I located the hand warmers in my jacket pocket and snapped two of them into service. Then I shoved one deep into each boot.

It wasn't long before the insides of my boots started to warm, and I found myself thanking God for chemicals. I lay on the pine branches huddled into the fetal position beneath a couple more branches I pulled on top of me, praying for sleep and for the dawn to come quickly.

It was peculiar, but just like when I was buried in the slide outside Ruthie's an odd peace came over me. It wasn't that I was succumbing to giving up, but it was more an acceptance of where Fate and bad decisions can bring you. I wondered what the Alvarezes would be thinking at Badrutt's about now. Were they wondering where I was? Would they send out a search party? But in the vastness of the ski area where could they search? I hadn't told them where I'd gone.

The Greeks believed our lives are predetermined. I prefer to think we are in charge of our fate to a certain degree. Fate had brought me to the mountains and for that I was grateful. If my mother hadn't been who she was, if she hadn't died and I hadn't heard those people talk about what a wonderful place Aspen was, I would probably be working some dumbass job in Milwaukee with a couple of kids and a redneck husband. I'm not saying that would be bad necessarily. But it wouldn't be the life I'd built for myself in the mountains.

With the exception of the last two weeks, my life had been as good as it got. Living outdoors and skiing and hiking and communing with nature fed most of my needs. Friends, school and reading filled almost all the rest. The only true gap remained having that significant other, something not so pressing in earlier years, but as I moved deeper into middle age the desire to have another person in the picture had grown. But it didn't own me, and I wasn't going to settle.

And then laying in the cold in the dark in some Swiss forest not sure where, not sure what my situation would be when morning came, my thoughts turned to Duane. In my heart I knew I had been wrong not to believe in him. He was a good man, and had I not turned my back on him, I wouldn't be lying on a bed of branches thousands of miles from home. I'd be in Aspen, helping him find the right attorney, giving him all the moral support I could muster, maybe even helping to find the person who was truly responsible for Kimmy's death.

I drifted in and out of sleep and dreamt of being warm under down and wool in my loft, even as my body shivered out valuable heat. I tried to remain still, to preserve energy needed to keep me warm. My feet had frozen again, so I took out the last two hand warmers and stuffed them deep into my boots. This time the chemical warmth burnt my frozen flesh and I almost cried out at the pain of the circulation partially returning. I wiggled my toes as best I could, hoping to force nourishing blood into the tiny ventricles. It helped a little, but not completely. I lay on my side thinking that losing a couple of toes might be acceptable, but a leg was not.

# FORTY

The dawn came slowly, the deep black sky giving way to dark gray to lighter gray to welkin blue. I was curled in a ball, barely able to feel my feet. My core and my head seemed OK, my torso insulated by good ski gear and my head by my helmet. I sat up on my bed of branches, shivering as I tried thinking of the best course to take. The lighter was in clear sight in the daylight, laying atop the snow just a foot away from me. I cursed myself out for losing it in the dark. A fire sure would have meant a better night. But I was grateful to have it now. It meant I could build a fire to warm myself before making any other choices.

My hands felt like blocks as I gathered wood, but I could move my fingers – a good sign. And though my fingers were white when I took off my gloves to examine them, there was no black, which meant I'd avoided frostbite so far. My feet encased in the ski boots were solid blocks too, but I had to walk to gather the wood so I put their condition out of my mind and went about doing what needed to be done. When I'd piled enough wood into a stack, I used some small branches with pine needles as kindling this time and when I applied the lighter my heart leapt with hope as they broke into flame that spread to the larger branches. It wasn't long before I had a roaring fire. I moved in close to the crackling warmth, practically hugging it with my frozen hands.

I was careful enough not to warm my hands too quickly, however, and even warming them slowly made me want to cry out as the blood painfully found its way back into closed-off circuitry. But gradually all feeling came back and I flexed my fingers back and forth with the glee of a prisoner having a death sentence sent to appeal. It's amazing how encouraging small victories can be when your life hangs in the balance.

I had been holding my booted feet to the fire as well, and the warmth was working its way slowly through the plastic shells. Just as with my hands, there was the mixed victory of warming, of excruciating but encouraging pain. The boots had been frozen almost solid, so it was difficult to manipulate them, but as they warmed they grew more pliable and eventually I managed to move the tongue enough to slide them off. Then I literally held my feet to the fire. They felt alien to me, lifeless blocks somehow connected to me. I slowly peeled off the thin wool socks that are protocol for skiing. A huge wave of relief swept me at the sight of my white-as-ivory toes. Though they were frozen solid, just like my fingers, they were free of any black. Frostbite had not found them in the night either.

I thanked the heavens.

I sat in front of the fire until the sun was mid-morning high in the sky, and the day had warmed into the 20s. I decided it was time to get moving. My stomach was an empty cavern, but rationing was in order, so I only ate a couple of the Snickers. Wanting to retain what water was left in my Camelbak, I sipped as much of the melted snow around the fire as I could. When the last of the fire had burnt out, I put my thawed feet back into my boots, clicked into my skis and let gravity take over again.

The terrain was tight and treed, and I had to be super careful picking my way through the obstacles thrown at me. The only good news about that was the effort of skiing these conditions kept me warm, even as it depleted my energy. My thirst was growing out of control. When it was noon according to my watch, I allowed myself the luxury of eating the last Snickers and draining the last drops from the Camelbak.

I continued my trek through the woods, worrying about what would happen if I had to spend another night in the cold, wondering if another day of travel would be possible without food. My only consolation was the lighter, but without nourishment and water would a fire be enough?

I forced myself to forge onward, hoping that just beyond every few turns signs of civilization would occur. But as the afternoon wore on I began to feel I was deeper into the woods than ever.

And then the first hint of dusk began to level, hope began to wear thin and I resigned myself to another night of bivouacking. My legs felt like every turn was a newborn effort itself, but since I didn't see a good place to put down I forced myself to go just a bit farther in search of a better place to spend the night. I probably made another hundred yards when I spotted what appeared to be an opening in the woods. I gravitated toward it and with immeasurable relief realized it was a trail. Trails lead to towns.

I was going to live after all.

# FORTY-ONE

It's pretty amazing how one can be at the banks of the River Styx one minute and in the lobby of a five-star hotel not long afterwards. The trail had taken me down to a small roadside café where I bought a couple of liters of water and two ham and gruyere sandwiches. I hitched a ride from a restaurant worker on his way into town. Evidently people must use the trail often because he made no inquiries as to how I had gotten there, just threw my skis in the back of his truck. His English was limited, so we didn't have much conversation, though he did look at me oddly when I asked him to take me to Badrutt's.

My adventure had left me pretty exhausted, not to mention banged up, and I practically crawled into my fancy digs. Le Grand Hall was abuzz with the same sort of chic people as two days prior, absorbed in themselves and their furs, totally oblivious to my near-death experience. As I dragged my battered body toward the elevators, I'm sure I looked like the ski version of a street person. Just shy of the elevators, in one of the many alcove seating areas along the lobby, I noticed a bald-headed man with a half-melted face sitting alone on an upholstered sofa. It was Chris Calloway, the pilot of the G5. His jeans and a pullover black sweater made him look almost as out of place in that lobby as I did in my dirty ski suit and gnarled hair. He happened to look up just then and saw me staring at him. He leaned forward in his chair and smiled. Though his smile was disfigured it was genuine, and I couldn't help but notice how perfectly his white teeth were aligned in his mottled face.

'Join me for a drink?'

I thought about it. I was tired, but I was safe and warm and there didn't seem to be any clothes police in the area. 'Why not?' I said.

My bottom had barely touched the chair when a waiter

appeared. 'What would madam's pleasure be?' I hadn't been
called madam since . . . well, I actually don't recall ever
being called madam, and I wasn't quite sure if I was comfortable with it. The thing I was comfortable with was having a
drink, so I ordered a beer. The beer came promptly and I took
a long bracing sip. The alcohol hit my system right away,
bringing on a much-appreciated sense of wellbeing, my close
encounter with death distancing itself with every sip.

'Good day?' he asked.

'Huh?' I replied, not giving any thought to the point that
he was totally uninformed about my misadventures.

'Did you have a good day?'

'Which one?' He looked at me quizzically, and I smiled,
deciding to forego the tale of my odyssey. Half because I
didn't have the energy to tell it and half because it was over.
Like, why beat a dead horse? 'Long story, but I think I almost
ended up in another country. Next time I'll remember to bring
my passport. What about you?' I asked, intentionally shifting
the conversation off me. 'Did you ski today?'

'I don't ski,' he said. My opinion of him immediately
plummeted, but rebounded when he added, 'I board.'

'Good to hear. I don't usually speak to people who don't
engage in winter sports, and I was thinking I'm way too tired
to change tables.'

He laughed, a musical laugh that invited a listener to sit up
and listen to see what could possibly be so amusing. 'Then I
guess it's a good thing I took up the sport. I only started after
I began flying for the Alvarezes. I got tired of sitting around
in places like this and Aspen with nothing to do.'

'So do you know them well?'

'I suppose about as well as you can know a billionaire who
signs your paycheck. Pablo's a pretty good guy, pretends to
understand the proletariat, but he doesn't. Maria is a sweetheart,
not too demanding. I hear his first wife was a real bitch. Treated
all the employees like they were indentured servants. You can
see her imprint on Carlos. As for Richie, he's a little bit of a
poor rich kid. His dad presses him to do things he can't.'

'Don't you feel subservient working for them?' I wondered
aloud.

'Well, there is a bit of ass-kissing in the job, but in the end it's well worth it. Make a great buck and get to fly the heavy iron. What about you? I've been trying to figure out where you fit in.'

'They didn't tell you?'

He shook his head.

It seemed odd to me that neither Pablo nor Maria had shared the story of Richie's rescue with their pilot. Then again, why would they? He was, after all, just an employee. As it seemed to be turning out, so was I. When I told him about that day skiing the bowl and spotting Richie's blue parka in the tree well, he let out a low whistle.

'That's one lucky kid,' he said. 'And so this trip is your reward?'

'Guess so.'

'Bet you would have appreciated a check more than a family vacation.'

'A little spare cash wouldn't have hurt,' I admitted, my grey matter filling with visions of an Everest climb. I'm sure it was dehydration, but the beer was going straight to my head and I felt a sudden need to lie down. I sensed the waiter hovering someplace unseen and grabbed my ski jacket from the back of the chair before he could make another appearance. 'I'm beat. I need to take a nap.' I said.

'You have plans tonight?'

'I don't know. I imagine I should check in with my hosts. In fact, they are probably wondering why I haven't checked in.' *For over twenty-four hours.*

'I doubt it. They probably will be glad to have you off their hands tonight, if they even remember you're here. I know a great locals' place with a fantastic Wiener schnitzel. You want to join me?'

At the moment, my biggest priority was a nap. And raiding the minibar for food. But the thought of seeing more of St Moritz other than Badrutt's Palace did hold some appeal. After all I was still alive, and besides, Chris Calloway was turning out to be pleasant company.

'Why not?' I said.

\*    \*    \*

There was a message from the Alvarezes waiting for me back in the suite, apologizing that they had plans for the evening, but that I should feel free to dine in any of the hotel's restaurants and charge it to the room. They made no mention of my absence the night before. Just as Chris had implied, they didn't even notice I was missing. They probably assumed I'd gone out to eat on my own. I spoiled myself with a bath in the deep tub, luxuriating in hot water up to my neck. There was a huge bruise on my thigh from where I'd hit the rock, but all things considered I'd come out ahead of the game. I had all ten toes, was breathing, and was going out to dinner in St Moritz.

The bath made me even sleepier and after getting out and toweling off, I lay down on my gold bed and within minutes my eyes were sealed shut. When I next opened them, the last vestiges of daylight had gone from the sky and my view was a black canvas speckled with the lights of the town below. I looked at the bedside clock. It read 20:00. Chris and I had agreed to meet at eight thirty, so I shook myself awake, ran a brush through my unruly hair and put on my dress jeans and the black turtleneck. Hoping I wouldn't send anyone in the lobby into shock, I grabbed my mundane fur-free parka and headed out the door.

He was waiting at the entrance still wearing the same jeans and black turtleneck. 'I see you got the memo on the dress for tonight,' he laughed when he saw we were dressed the same.

'Maybe they'll think we're the entertainment,' I lobbed back.

Walking out the main entrance, we passed on the shuttle and took the winding street into the center of town on foot. It was snowing lightly and the streets had a fairytale feel to them, the lit windows of the elegant shops and the fur-clad people staring into them all part of the set. The air was winter crisp, a phenomenon that usually invigorates me, but this night it set me to shivering, probably prompted by memories of my night in the woods. So I was super pleased when Chris stopped in front of an old-fashioned wood-fronted restaurant at the edge of the village with the word 'Welcome' in several languages in the window. Aside from that, there was no name on the building.

'Here we are,' he said, holding the door open.

The room was jammed, filled with people as polar opposite from the Badrutt's crowd as you could get. For one, most of them were young. There were plenty of tattoos and nary a fur to be seen. Elevated voices floated different languages – German, English, Italian, Dutch, but no Russian as far as I could tell.

There were no tables available, so we grabbed a couple of seats at the bar. The wall behind the bar was plastered with photographs taken locally over time, scenes of ice skating on the frozen lake, celebrities disembarking from airplanes, skiers with long skis rising far above their heads as used to be the custom. The bartender leaned in and asked us what we wanted to drink. We ordered a couple of beers and he moved down the bar to the tap. In his absence I had a good view of the photos on the wall across from me. As my eyes swept them with no particular interest, I froze on one. It was a color shot of a couple standing in front of the restaurant. It couldn't have been too old, because the couple's skis came just past their chins, the current accepted length. The man was tall, the woman diminutive in comparison. She was in profile with a large fur hat encircling her head, cutting out most of the face. Something about the woman's face was disturbing to me.

When the bartender returned with our beers I pointed at the photo and asked, 'Who is that?'

He turned to look at the picture I was referring to and his smile turned somber. 'That was Werner Mayer, one of our greatest local skiers.'

'Was?' He didn't look very old and the photograph appeared to be taken within somewhat recent history.

'Yes. Werner is dead. Far too young. Unfortunately an avalanche took him three years ago.' The look on his face changed from somber to fond remembrance. 'He was probably the most liked man in town. The entire town went into mourning when he died.'

'Who is the woman?'

The look of fond remembrance morphed into unconcealed disdain. 'That was his wife, Inga Lena. No one liked her. No one could understand why he married her.' He turned back to give the picture another look. 'Well, she was very good looking. But she was – what do you call it in America – a gold-digger. She was angry when Werner left the racing circuit to work on the mountain. She thought he was going to go far as a great racer, get the big money and all the endorsements. She used to fight with him about amounting to nothing. But that was Werner. He was a great guy, but he wasn't ambitious. He just lived to ski.'

'Was she from St Moritz too?'

'No. She was Swedish.'

'What happened to her after he died?'

His eyes coasted skyward and then dropped to the floor. 'Who knows – up or down? She was in the avalanche too.'

Another customer was vying for his attention, and he disappeared to care for the patron farther down the bar. Chris was staring at me curiously, wondering what was fueling all the interest in some dead Swiss skiers. The bartender came back and we ordered two more beers and two Wiener schnitzels. I initiated the conversation we both wanted and dreaded.

'Tell me about my brother in Afghanistan,' I said. 'But please don't frighten me.'

'Toby Westerlind?' he said, stopping to compose his voice. 'I literally only saw him twice. The time he dragged me out of the aircraft and one time afterward when he came to visit me in the burn unit.' We were so alike in that regard, I thought. I always had to check on the wellbeing of people I'd brought down the mountain.

Chris smiled a confident smile, the smile of a person who has grown up good looking and knows it. 'I told him his timing couldn't have been better. He got me out before anything below my waist got burned.'

Thankfully, before that conversation could grow legs, our food arrived.

# FORTY-TWO

My dinner with Captain Calloway was more enjoyable than I ever would have thought possible. He was funny and witty and, as off-putting as his appearance was at first, after a while his deformity ceased to exist in my eyes. He told me about growing up in Iowa and how 'little he knew about how little he knew' until his first visit to New York at age twenty where he saw not only gay men holding hands, but actually making out. 'And we thought we had it tough back home with animal jokes,' he said.

And while he kept his distance during dinner, I could tell there was attraction simmering below the surface toward me. Which I must admit was a little bit mutual, but I pushed back. After all, what kind of person could I be to switch affections not once, but twice within a couple of weeks? A mixed-up one, that's for sure. Not to mention the question of Duane Larsen still burning near the surface.

After dinner we walked back up to the hotel. It was still snowing and the streets were magical. With my belly filled and a few potent local beers down the hatch, I was pretty relaxed. Chris regaled me with his early days of flying as a crop duster while my mind kept looping back to the photo of the woman in the fur hat behind the bar. That distraction was replaced when Chris took my gloved hand in his. I slid mine out as delicately as I could. He gave me a 'well I tried' sort of look.

'Hey Chris, don't get me wrong,' I explained. 'You're an attractive, sexy guy. But I've recently been through some complex relationship issues and I'm a little raw right now. OK?'

'Gotcha,' he said, loosening that easy smile. We were nearing the hotel and he slipped an arm inside mine in a less personal manner. 'Can a guy still escort a pretty girl inside?'

God, he was corny. Guess that goes with being brought up an Iowa farm boy.

\*   \*   \*

The lobby was busy as ever, though the evening had a different flavor from the après-ski crowd. There were plenty of tuxedos and floor-length gowns, and chic-looking men and women heading to King's Club at the far end of the lobby. The pulse of music threaded with loud conversation came from the nightclub in bursts each time the door opened.

Chris wanted to have a nightcap, but I decided to pass. I was far too exhausted for another drink. We said our goodnights and I headed towards the elevators as he went into the bar. That's how tired I was. I didn't even have the energy to walk four flights, a strength-building discipline I usually opted for whenever there were steps.

I summoned the elevator and was set back on my heels when the doors opened and young Carlos stepped out. He was accompanied by a brunette who not only appeared to be significantly older than he, but had a face suggesting the heavy make-up she wore could well be a business expense. He was well dressed in wool slacks and what was probably a very expensive blue blazer. His eyes settled on me with a dismissive look that lasted longer than was polite.

'Good to see you too, Carlos,' I said, stepping past him into the elevator.

An hour later, I was lying on top of the bedclothes wearing my Rockies T-shirt that doubled as pajamas, along with a pair of wool socks, revisiting the day. Ovid was open on my lap, but try as I might the ancient words weren't gelling. When there was a knock at the door, I found myself instantly irritated. I'd made it perfectly clear to Chris Calloway that while there could have been possibilities between us, now wasn't the time. I pulled on the plush Bedrutt's bathrobe hanging in the bathroom and opened the door a notch.

It wasn't Chris after all. It was Carlos. He was standing in the empty hall alone, although swaying would have been the better description. His handsome face was marred by a stupid drunken look I should have recognized as trouble. But before I was able to process his presence, he pushed the door open and came into my room, his foot slamming the door shut behind him like an accomplished soccer player.

'You know you're a pretty good-looking babe. I just want to know what you were thinking of, saving my pathetic brother's life.'

'What are you doing here?' I demanded, crossing my arms and staring up at him. Before I could utter another word his hands were upon me, grabbing me by my shoulders and pushing me backwards into the room.

'Stop it,' I demanded, putting menace into my voice this time. Evidently, he felt unthreatened because his response was to attach his wet drooling mouth to mine as his unyielding hands kept driving us closer to the bed.

It didn't take a genius to know what he wanted. I was fighting him, but he was the larger of us and had the strength and speed of a testosterone-filled youth. I was losing the fight. 'Stop it,' I demanded again, managing to free my mouth from his. Still, he continued driving me backwards until the bed was pressing the back of my thighs. In a heartbeat, he had flipped me down on to the bed and was laying upon me. Parting the robe with his knee, he pushed my T-shirt up and put one slimy hand on my breast. His other slimy hand tugged at my panties.

Naturally I was frightened, but I was also angry. The memory of my mother's boyfriend in my bedroom when I was a girl came back with a vengeance. But I was a different person than that young girl my mother's friend had tried to rape. Had my brother not saved me that night, I would have had to carry a bad memory my entire life. But knowing that Toby wouldn't always be there, I had long since learned how to defend myself. Carlos was grappling with his pants, trying to free himself to finish the intended act, when he moved his head back just far enough for me to make my move.

My right hand came up, and I hit him full on in the Adam's apple. The action set him howling and he jumped up, clutching his neck. That's when I hit him in the solar plexus with my foot. He fell to the floor like a rock. He sat there gasping for air with one hand on his torso, the other holding his neck. I calmly tied my robe and went to the door.

'You little shit,' I said, standing in the hallway in case he made a recovery. 'Get the hell out of here before I scream for security.'

He got to his feet and walked past me into the empty hall, choking the entire way. Just outside the door he managed to find his voice. 'Don't even think about telling anyone about this,' he rasped. 'My father does the same thing to all the help.'

And then he was gone.

I lay back down on the princess bed shaking with anger and replayed his words. Did his father really do what he had just tried to do to his employees? I severely doubted it. But what in Carlos's make-up made him think he was entitled to assault me? My first impulse was to tell his father what Carlos had tried to do – but to what end if his words held true? The feeling of violation from all those years back rose up again. Only this time I'd been able to rescue myself. But what about the next woman that Carlos tried to violate?

Unfortunately, I was in no position to solve that problem, being a mere servant in the Kingdom of Alvarez. But there was one problem I could solve and that was to change my venue. I decided right then I'd had enough of St Moritz. It was probably going to cost me a fortune to get home on my own coin, but I was so out of there it wasn't even funny.

# FORTY-THREE

I t was another early-morning wake-up. I was showered and my duffel bag was packed and waiting at the door by six thirty. I would have already made my departure if not for the little detail that my best boards were hostage in the ski shop and it didn't open until seven.

So much for being a princess. Like all things in this world, there's a price to being a princess, one I would never be willing to pay.

The moment the clock ticked seven, I was on the elevator to the lobby after scouting the area to make sure none of the Alvarezes were in sight. Not knowing whether they would even realize I had gone, I left a note for Pablo with the concierge, explaining a family emergency had forced me home. Of course, the note made no mention that the family in the emergency was theirs. I wondered how Carlos would react to my absence, but on second thought I was putting my money on the patriarch not even mentioning it to the others.

The moment the ski shop opened, I picked up my skis and was on a shuttle to the train station faster than a hawk on a field mouse. Once at the station, I went to buy my ticket and was disappointed to learn I would have to wait until later in the day. Though the trains to Zurich were frequent, this was a busy time of year and the early trains were all sold out. I bought a ticket on the eleven o'clock train and wondered what the hay I would do to occupy myself for the next four hours. Having no desire to warm a bench in the train station until my departure, I checked my bags at the depot and walked back into town.

Despite my negative experiences thus far, there was still no denying the beauty of St Moritz and its setting. Like Aspen, every limit had been tried, and like Aspen, some limits held and some hadn't. Many charming lodges and storefronts had been replaced by glitzy multi-level buildings, and I could see the large, empty houses the shuttle driver had spoken of – the ones that were occupied two weeks a year.

The day was sunny and quite pleasant, and as I wandered I was happy to be free of the claustrophobic moneyed atmosphere of Badrutt's. After meandering for forty-five minutes, I found myself on the same street Chris and I dined on the night before. In fact, not only was I on the same street, but the Welcome was directly across from me. I crossed the street and went inside to take another look.

The room was half-filled with people in ski clothes devouring breakfasts of eggs and sausage and apple-filled pancakes and bowls of yogurt and granola in preparation for a day of skiing. The inviting smell of coffee filled the air. I took a seat at the empty bar and studied the photograph that had caught my eye the night before. Last night's bartender had been replaced by a pretty woman with blond shoulder-length hair tied in a neat ponytail. Her cheeks were a natural rosy pink, and her full lips were painted with a lipstick the same rosy color.

'Can I help you?' she asked in English.

I ordered an espresso and while she prepared it, I stared at the picture that had so intrigued me the night before, trying to fill in the face hidden behind the fur hat. Could it really be who I thought it was? When the bartender returned with my coffee, I asked her, 'Do you by chance happen to know anything about the woman in that picture?'

Just as the bartender last night had done, she turned and stared at the photo. Only her face lacked the animosity his had displayed. 'Inga Lena? I knew her well. We worked together in hotel three years ago. We were roommates when I first came to St Moritz. She was married to Werner Mayer. They died together in avalanche.'

'She looks very much like someone I know and I wonder if they could be related. Is she Czech?'

'No, I'm Czech. She was Swede. Before she married, she was Inga Lena Bergstrom.'

'A Swede?' This information baffled me, throwing the thrust of my inquiry off. I looked back at the picture. The resemblance was uncanny, but there was no denying that the woman in the photo was Swedish and dead. Still, something unanswered drove me to learn more. 'Where in Sweden was she from?'

'She came from very north of Sweden, a town called Falun. She would tell me how she hated winters there. Nights so long and days so short.' There was a barely audible sigh as she added, 'It's shame they choose such dangerous piste that day.'

'What do you mean?' I asked.

'Avalanche risk high,' she replied.

'I'm Greta Westerlind,' I volunteered unasked.

'Christina Schmidt. My pleasure to meet you. You are American?'

'Yes. From Aspen.'

'Aspen,' she echoed, her eyes filled with a wistful sort of recognition. 'I wanted to go there some years ago. But passport was stolen right before. All that work to get visa and I never made trip. I married Jan instead. We talk about going next year.'

'Probably better off staying here the way things are in my country these days,' I said, letting a rare political opinion drop. I finished my coffee and paid the bill. Then I headed out the door, stopping to pick up one of the restaurant's cards on my way out.

The Glacier Express is most likely one of the most stunning train rides in the world, but it was basically lost on me. As the train wound along impossible mountain passes across imposing terrain, my mind was wrapped around Inga Lena Bergstrom Mayer, dead three years ago in an avalanche that took both her life and her husband's. As I peered down at small towns banked on both sides by peaks so high they probably enjoyed no more than two hours of sun a day at this time of year, I kept trying to work out what it was about Inga Lena Mayer that was making me crazy. The fact that her husband died in the same avalanche as she did was disturbing. Was I drawing a parallel between Inga Lena and Werner and me and Warren somewhere in my head? Or was I looking for something more? The great peaks of the white-capped mountains towered over me, and my thoughts turned inward in a blur. Then the truth hit me like a ton of bolts.

Suddenly Aspen was looking far away and my Everest climb even farther. Instead of being Odysseus on the way home, I was Jason in search of the golden calf. And though it was way out of budget, something told me the answers to my questions were waiting in Falun.

# FORTY-FOUR

It was dark when my flight from Zurich landed in Stockholm and darker still on the train north. Falun, it seems, is poised on the edge of the planet. There is no nearby airport, but for some reason enough people want to go there that the trains run regularly. What that reason is, I have no idea, but I asked myself that question a number of times as we pulled into the station and I disembarked on to a platform whipped by a raw wind and encircled with flat white.

There were taxis queued up so I got into one and asked to be taken to a reasonably priced hotel. Ten minutes later we pulled up in front of a modest low-slung red-brick building that looked more like a home than a hotel. There was a reason. Turns out it was a home turned into a B&B and was owned by a most delightful widow named Agneta Aronsson. She was blond and blue-eyed – no surprise there – over six feet tall and rail thin. Probably the age my grandmother would be, if I had one. When I dragged myself into the front door of the inn carrying my skis and my bag and told her that I needed a room, she took one look at me and decided I needed some looking after as well.

'Where are you coming from?' she asked, eying my tired face as she looked at my passport and handed it back to me.

'I was in St Moritz this morning.'

'You came all the way from Switzerland today? You poor girl, you must be exhausted. We'll get you a warm meal and a warm bed and you can tell me your story tomorrow.'

She led me to a small but comfortable room with a pair of twin beds side by side and a wooden writing desk poised in front of a darkened window. I was in the process of washing up when there was a knock on the door and it was Agneta carrying a tray with a bowl of steaming soup and a small stack of knäckebröd, the preferred Swedish breadstuff my mother would eat whenever she could find it. I was so hungry I barely tasted the soup and ate the entire pile of knäckebröd. Then I pulled on my T-shirt, lay down on the bed and fell into a deep, dreamless sleep.

When I awoke the next morning at nine o'clock it was still dark. I don't know what else I would have expected in January in the north of Sweden. No wonder my mother said her child-hood winters had depressed her. They'd probably depressed Inga Lena as well. I dressed and went into the main room. There were several other guests sitting at scattered tables, drinking coffee and eating bread and herring. I took a table by myself and Agneta appeared with a pot of coffee.

'Did you sleep well?' she asked.

'Like a rock,' I admitted. 'What time does the sun come up anyway?'

'In January around nine thirty. But this is not so bad. December is the bad month.'

I reminded myself to never visit Sweden for the holidays. Then, with little to lose, I decided to lob a question her way regarding Inga Lena Bergstrom. After all, it was a small town.

'I'm actually here trying to get some information on a woman from Falun who moved to St Moritz years ago. Inga Lena Bergstrom. She would be in her early thirties. Did you know her?'

'Inga Lena Bergstrom, you say?' She paused long enough to build up my hopes before saying. 'I don't believe I know of her.'

*Darn*, I thought. Then who ever said it was going to be easy? But rather than try to track down a person I didn't know in a country where I didn't speak the language, I decided to enlist Agneta's help.

'The reason I've come to Falun is to find anyone who knew her. I have some questions to ask about her. I don't suppose you have a phone book?'

Being a hotel of sorts, she kept a phone book for the guests and when she brought it out I thumbed through the alphabetical listings. As it turned out, Bergstroms were plentiful. At least twenty, but no Inga Lena. Agneta's eagle eye was glued on me and she could see my disappointment at the number of names listed. She took the book from me and pulled out her cell phone.

'Here, let me help.' Moving her fingers down the list of Bergstroms, she started dialing. Seven times, I heard her blabber something in Swedish followed by the name Inga Lena. Seven times I heard her say '*tack sa mycket*' and hang up. On the eighth try, she stopped mid call and raised a thumb in the air. The conversation went on a bit longer before she hung up. Her face was unsmiling as she said, 'She was married to their deceased son, Magnus. They weren't too pleased when I mentioned her name, but they agreed to see you. At one o'clock. And they invited you to lunch. They live in the old town. I will take you.'

When we left the B&B around noon the sun was up and overhead making it hard to believe that dawn had broken only two hours before. There was an hour before my lunch date at the Bergstroms', so Agneta insisted I allow her to show me around. Riding in her Volvo – no surprise there – her pride in her hometown shone through.

Our first stop was a large scaled-back patch of earth, a massive pit which she explained had been an operating copper mine until recent years and was now part of UNESCO. Though the pit was brushed white with snow, the red earth showed through – Falun red, she explained. She informed me that there was a tour to where miners went daily nearly a century ago and asked if I was interested. I took a pass on the tour. My interest in being deep underground is somewhere on a par with my interest in investment banking.

The next landmark we visited was the Lugnet sports complex with its famous ski jump. There were two jumps actually, side by side, and they were visible from a great distance, like the old-fashioned water towers had been in Milwaukee. As we drew near, the ski jumps looked like they probably rose as far above ground as the mine descended below. I was far more interested in the jumps than the mine, having never witnessed a ski jump before. As it was a Saturday, there was a competition going on and when Agneta asked if I wanted to watch for a while, I quickly agreed.

We stood next to the car watching from the parking lot. There was a jumper up top waiting on a bar perpendicular to the run itself. I asked Agneta how high the jump was and she told me fifty-two meters. Even from a distance, I could sense the energy coiled in the red spandex-clad figure waiting his turn on high. And then the signal came and the jumper was on his skis, racing downwards from the height of a fifteen-story building, faster and faster, gaining speed until he hit the end of the jump and flew free of anything attached to Sweden, or this earth, for that matter. His long skis were spread in a 'V' with his body centered in between as he sailed effortlessly through the air.

After travelling what seemed a football field, he floated downward until his skis united gracefully with terra firma. People standing near the jump started shouting in Swedish. Agneta turned to me with a smile. 'That's a local woman and she's just broken her personal best.' It wasn't until that moment that I realized the *he* was a *she*. She had coasted to a stop and people were running up to congratulate her as we climbed back into the Volvo.

'And now on to the Bergstrom house,' said Agneta.

# FORTY-FIVE

The Bergstrom house was surprisingly reminiscent of an American farmhouse, down to the picket fence, but instead of being painted white it was painted Falun red. My knock was answered immediately by a couple standing together in the doorway. Lars and Margaretha Bergstrom were in their late sixties, he a mere stick of a man, she a sturdy woman who had clearly once been a beauty.

'You are Greta,' the woman said in accented English. 'Welcome into our house. I hope you are hungry. We've planned lunch.'

I could tell by their enthusiasm that visitors were rare and my staying for lunch posed no imposition. They led me to a simple square table that was total Ikea dating back to before Ikea existed. It was evident that they were simple frugal people.

'So you are American?' Lars asked.

'Yes. From Colorado. Aspen. It's a ski town.'

'Yes, we know of it. Skiing is a particular love of the Swedes.'

'And there are a lot of Swedes who have made Aspen their home.'

They both nodded knowingly at this information, as if living in a ski area was the master plan of all Swedes. We talked a little polite talk, avoiding politics, though they did pose a questioning statement about the current president, which I managed to sidestep. 'There's always another election,' I said and let it drop at that.

Margaretha disappeared into the kitchen and came out with three large bowls. 'You like herring?' she asked. I nodded, not really knowing the answer to that question. Herring was something I'd managed to avoid thus far in my life, as evidenced by my abstinence of the fish at breakfast earlier. But as I was the guest of these lovely people, I felt I had no option but to accept. When I took a bite of the fish, it surprised me.

Something in my psyche had informed me that that herring was going to be unpleasant and strong tasting. That something had been wrong.

'Your friend said on the phone that you wanted to talk about Magnus?' Lars asked as he tucked into his fish.

'Actually, it was more about your former daughter-in-law. Can you tell me about her?' Knots appeared in both their jaws and dislike colored their faces. Not quite sure myself what I wanted from them, I recovered quickly and said, 'But first tell me about Magnus.'

With joy and enthusiasm, they told me all about their only child, who was the perfect son, a good student and an accomplished athlete. 'He was the best jumper in town,' said Lars. 'He was destined to break world records.' Then, with heads hung low, they went on to tell me about the beautiful girl with whom their son had fallen absolutely 'sommarmorgon'. 'He lost all sanity. She was a beautiful-looking girl, but underneath she was a witch who put him under a spell. Her parents were dead and she was looking for someone to take care of her. They got married and from the beginning all she wanted was more, more, more,' Margaretha said. 'She thought Magnus would bring her riches as a famous jumper.'

'Until he missed a landing one day and broke his . . .' Lars struggled for the word and finally found it: 'Femur. He broke his femur. They told him he would never jump again. Or ski.'

'She changed toward him after that,' Margaretha chimed in. 'He was no longer the promise. She started to treat him poorly. And then, Inga Lena . . .' Margaretha paused as if letting the name slide across her tongue pained her: 'She had an affair with one of the owners of the mine. It nearly killed Magnus.'

Which brought me to the reason for my visit. I didn't want to exacerbate their grief by telling them that Inga Lena had ended up in St Moritz, but I needed to know about Magnus's death. 'How did your son die?'

Lars stoically told me of the freakish house fire that occurred shortly after Inga Lena's affair had come to light. An open can of paint left too close to the fire had ignited. Inga Lena had been at the movies with girlfriends the night of the fire.

She disappeared shortly afterwards, taking what little savings they had with her.

'And as the Americans say, "good riddance",' he added.

Margaretha went into the kitchen and brought out the next course along with a bottle of schnapps. For the next hour we ate and drank schnapps and talked about kinder things. Just before dessert, they brought out pictures of their son.

He was a handsome man with a strong jaw and tousled brownish hair. There were pictures of him in his skintight jumping suit and pictures of him as a child on skis. Finally, the album turned to the page of his wedding day, he a smiling proud groom in a suit, she in a white dress with flowers in her hair. And there was the proof, clear as Rocky Mountain air on a crisp winter day.

Somewhere along the line, Inga Lena Bergstrom had become Inga Lena Mayer had become Zuzana McGovern.

Back at the B&B I paced my room, trying to put the pieces of the puzzle together. And then, even though it would cost me a fortune, I set my phone to roaming and placed a call to the Welcome restaurant in St Moritz. The noise level told me the restaurant was busy, après-ski in full swing. I cringed at being on hold at international rates while I waited for Christina to come to the phone. When she finally picked up, I could tell she was harried. I reminded her of our meeting the day before and asked if she might answer a couple of quick questions.

'Yes? What is it?'

'Where is Inga Lena Mayer buried?'

'She is buried somewhere on mountain,' she replied in accented English, omitting all use of *a* and *the* as Eastern Europeans are prone to do, the use of the article being unnatural for them. 'They never find body.'

'But they found Werner's?'

'Yes, he is buried in local cemetery.'

Her exasperation with all my questions was coming across the line. But the ton of bolts was beginning to make sense and I couldn't let it go now. 'I'm sorry. I know you're busy, but just a couple more things. When you lost your passport, was it around the time of the avalanche?'

'I lose it couple weeks before,' she said, astonishment coloring her voice. 'How do you know?'

'Just a weird guess. One more question, my last I promise.' I could sense her frustration over the line. 'What is your middle name?'

'Zuzana,' she replied.

I hung up, thinking that while Zuzana McGovern had a pronounced Czech accent, unlike most Eastern Europeans she always employed the articles *a* and *the*.

# FORTY-SIX

My mind was so caught up with my discovery the entire flight back to the US, I hardly noticed that I was squished in a middle seat between two people who hadn't missed a meal in like a thousand years. The one-way flight to Aspen via New York and Denver cost the better part of the halfway mark to Everest's 29,029 feet summit, but there was no choice but to lay out the dough if I wanted to get home quickly – which I did. Along the way I worked out exactly what to do and only hoped I could pull it off. While I was no closer to filling in the remaining blanks of what had happened the day the wall of snow pounded me twice, I felt closer to getting the answer to what Warren McGovern and I had been doing out of bounds that fateful day.

Then there was that other matter taking up space in my brain: Dr Duane Larsen. After my solitary meditation during the cold night in the forest, I was certain he hadn't killed Kim Woods. I owed him an apology and the promise of support. But that was going to have to wait until after my first task was out of the way.

I landed in Denver at three p.m., which was eleven at night on my body clock. My connection to Aspen didn't leave until six, so I found a seat in a deserted boarding area and tried to catch a little shuteye. But I was so wired that sleep evaded me.

I turned on my phone for the first time in days. There was a call from Judy in Palm Beach asking about my trip and one from the sheriff asking me to call him. I ignored both messages and lobbed in a call to Neverman to check my status with patrol. I could tell from the noise that he was in the hut, could hear Reininger in the background telling one of his bad jokes. There was a communal moan as he hit the punch line.

'Westerlind, is that you? Where in hell are you?'

'Denver. Waiting for a flight to Aspen.'

'Hell, there's no way you're getting in here tonight. It's snowing like a mother. Flights are all cancelled.'

That's the thing with Aspen and Denver. It can be perfectly sunny in one and blizzard conditions in the other. I stood up to check the board behind me, and sure enough my six o'clock flight had been cancelled. As well as every other flight to Aspen for the rest of the day. I call it Aspen roulette.

Usually when there is a weather situation, the airline books you out the next day for free. And while they aren't responsible for putting you up for the night, they hand out discount slips for a local hotel. My problem was that, discount slip or not, hotels cost money. As do rental cars if I wanted to drive. In the wake of my recent European travel, to include the obscenely expensive lunch with young Richie for which I would probably never be reimbursed, my credit card was maxed out.

'Shoot,' I said in reaction, really meaning that stronger and similar sounding word. What this all meant was I'd most likely be spending the night on a chair in Denver International. I turned the discussion back to the true reason for the call. 'I just want to know if I can come back to work.'

Neverman paused in that way I was so used to, the way that told me something had irritated him. His tone of voice confirmed it. 'You're off suspension. It seems some higher-up intervened with the owners on your behalf.'

It didn't take much noodling to figure out who the intervening 'higher-up' might be. Well, I guess there was something to thank Pablo Alvarez for aside from the ride in his fancy plane. I hoped the suspension wouldn't be reinstated after I had that little conversation with him about Carlos. 'And actually, we could use you ASAP. We're short. Cole broke his leg when some yahoo ran into him at the bottom of Spar and Meghan's out with the flu.'

'Cole broke his leg?' I couldn't imagine anything worse than being housebound during such an epic season. 'That's awful.'

'Just be glad you're not his wife. Can you imagine putting up with him on the couch all day? Anyhow, we could use you tomorrow.'

'I'll be there the moment I get in,' I promised.

\* \* \*

The jet landed on Sardy Field's solitary runway nearly twenty-four hours after my departure from Stockholm. My neck had a huge kink in it from sleeping curled up in an airport chair, but otherwise I was no worse for wear. I saw a guy I know from the Bugaboo at the baggage pick-up and he gave me a ride home. Needless to say, I was much relieved to round the bend and see the A-frame still standing.

It was a balmy forty degrees inside my house, the thermostat having been left at just above freezing while I was out of town. I changed into my patrol duds as quickly as I could and went out to fire up the Wagoneer. She didn't want to start at first after a week of rest, but finally came around. I drove straight into town, parked in my usual place and headed to the gondola. A woman on a mission, my adrenaline was pumping so hard I didn't even notice my lack of sleep.

Since it was already mid-morning, the first tracks mob had already dispersed and I rode the bucket up alone, my preoccupation taking away from the usual pleasure of the magnificent view. I got off up top, put on my boards and slid over to the patrol hut. Singh was out front, just clicking into his skis. He smiled when he saw me.

'Hey Greta. You back in good graces?'

'Appears that way.'

'Glad to know it. I've missed you. Word was out you took a pretty nice trip.'

'It was OK,' I said, racking my skis and heading inside to check in with the boss. Most of the patrol was out on the mountain, but Reininger, Lucy and a few others were in back, drinking coffee in front of the fireplace. They all offered hearty greetings of 'welcome back' except for Reininger who was still probably pissed about me nearly blowing us all up. Or maybe it was because I didn't laugh at his jokes.

Neverman sent me out to mark some obstacles and the hours dragged as I waited for the morning to pass. I should have been enjoying the hell out of myself – the snow was sublime and it was great to be back on familiar turf. But my stomach was churning in anticipation of the confrontation that was soon to be executed.

And then finally the lunch hour was upon us. And I knew exactly where she would be.

One o'clock is the time the fancy people all hit the Mountain Club. They hang their expensive parkas and trade in their ski boots for slippers. The women head to the ladies' room to fix their helmet hair, as do some of the men. The sweaters and the ski pants are all elegant and perfectly fitted, the size of some of the women's diamonds so close in size to a bird's egg, it's a wonder they fit them in their gloves.

Non-members are forbidden from going any further than the entry desk without a member, even ski patrol, but luckily the restrooms are just inside the door, before the desk. There's a cloak room outside the bathrooms, and so I parked myself on a bench over a row of ski boots attached to boot warmers and waited.

I didn't have to wait very long. She waltzed into the room, hooked her green parka on to one of the hooks and went straight into the ladies' room without noticing me. I gave it a few minutes and then followed her inside. She was standing in front of the mirror putting on fresh lipstick when I came up behind her, positioning myself so that I was over her shoulder in the mirror. Her focus flicked from her own image to mine and then back to hers again. The look on her face was that of someone who has just seen a ghost – which is what I am sure she wanted me to be.

'I didn't know you were a member, Greta,' she said as she continued putting on her lipstick.

'Oh, I belong,' I said, my face a perfect deadpan. 'But I'm not so sure about you,' adding after a perfectly timed pause, 'Inga Lena.'

Her recovery was more challenged this time. Her eyes flashed from privileged to terrified before they managed to regain privileged again. The way she stared at me in the mirror was like she wished she could will me away. But having to will me away wasn't necessary. I was going.

My plan was to drag it out of her over time. To drop the information I'd gathered slowly, bit by bit. Mention the Bergstroms' small house. Magnus's death. Christina at the Welcome restaurant. I'd torment her until she came clean about who she was. Or until she left town. I really didn't care which. I didn't know what she had done or how, but I did know she was the enemy.

I backed out of the restroom leaving her gape-mouthed with her lipstick in her hand.

The rest of the day kept us busy. With so much snow, we were seeing our share of maimed knees and dislocated shoulders. One skier had torn his Achilles tendon and was writhing in pain until I administered a healthy dose of ketamine. I thought of Achilles the warrior, so invincible until he wasn't. And his mother who knew he was doomed to die in battle, a result of dipping him into immortal waters with her hand covering the very tendon that was giving the fallen skier so much grief.

It was getting near to the end of the day and I was back at the top of Ruthie's, near the scene of the crime, putting some equipment away in the shed that patrol keeps there. Reininger came skiing up as out of breath as I'd ever seen him.

'Don't close that,' he huffed. 'We need a sled. Just got a radio call about an injury on Traynor's.'

'Traynor's? Is it even open?' I queried.

'Nope. Some ying yang ducked the rope and he's down. Called from his cell. Sounds like an AFK. Neverman told me to get you.'

Instead of being irritated by the late-in-the-day rescue, I was stoked. Traynor's was the most difficult terrain on Aspen Mountain, the only part of the area rated 'extreme'. The steep, rock-studded part of the mountain was named Traynor's for the mine it sat upon. This part of the mountain was seldom open and even when it was could be a challenge to the best of skiers. The rescue promised to be a greater challenge than usual. The good news was, it wasn't a heart attack. The injury was just another run-of-the-mill torn anterior cruciate ligament.

Reininger pulled out the sled and headed down the catwalk adjacent to Ruthie's. I followed right behind him to the Traynor's entrance. Sure enough the ropes were up in addition to signs warning that it was dangerous terrain.

'Damn poachers,' said Reininger, watching me untie the

rope so the toboggan could pass through. We entered the closed area and proceeded cautiously along the trail. There hadn't been any avi work done in days, though luckily the area was heavily treed which limited the risk of a slide. Still the terrain was tricky with the tight trees and we moved carefully in the deep snow.

'Was he able to tell anybody where he is?' I asked, as we skied towards the far end of the ridge.

'Yeah. He said he was at the north end and hadn't gone down too far, so he's got to be somewhere in here.'

It had started snowing hard again, and the visibility was limited as we stared into the falling white.

'Don't see any tracks,' I said. 'I hope he's conscious. Maybe we should call for some back-up to sweep.'

'Wait,' said Reininger, pointing towards a stand of trees further down the hill. 'I think I see something moving over there.'

'Probably a rodent,' I said, skiing ahead of him through a glade to get a better look. I stopped at the edge of the glade and peered into the stand. I was ready to call out that I didn't see anything when the snow in the stand started to move like an eruption coming to life. First the shape of a white arm followed by a white leg. And then a white mound that could have been a head. The experience was otherworldly, as if the injured skier had been absorbed by the mountain and was being spit back out. Little by little the skier took shape with his back to me. He was small and dressed entirely in white, which was why I hadn't seen him in the first place. And then the white fur hood turned toward me and icy blue eyes glared at me from within.

'Zuzana,' I uttered, too shocked to call her Inga Lena, puzzled as to why she was in Traynor's and why she had called for help.

'Hello Greta,' she said in a voice as icy as her eyes.

'I was right. It was a rodent,' I called back to Reininger.

And then, like a bolt of winter lightning crackling down a gulley, my memory came back.

# FORTY-SEVEN

I was in the ski patrol shack at the top of Ruthie's. Neverman had sent me over to clean up the mess made by abandoned markers and coils of rope. It seemed he always gave us women the clean-up details. I had just finished getting things perfectly arranged and was locking up the shack when I saw Warren sliding off the Ruthie's chair by himself.

Since the normal route would take him past me, I raised my arm to wave hello. But he seemed distracted and didn't even look my way. Instead he skied up to the rope that marked the area boundary. He stood there for a minute peering down into the Castle Creek Valley, and then, to my absolute horror, he ducked the rope and skied out of sight.

I yelled at him to stop and was over there faster than a mother bear protecting its cub. It was snowing hard and from my vantage point at the ski area boundary I could see him below making his way across the mountain. He appeared to be looking for somebody, stopping every so often to call out a name. Then his figure shrunk in the storm.

I wondered if he'd lost his mind. The aspect he was skiing was dangerous enough under normal circumstances, but considering the present conditions the danger was amplified. The pattern of melt and freeze and winds racking the open terrain followed by more snow and melt and freeze made the layers like concrete on ball bearings. But what could I do? Watch him ski to his death? My heart was on that hill with him. If I caught up to him at least I could direct him into the trees where the likelihood of a slide was lessened. I ducked the rope myself and followed him into the chute, staying light on my skis, praying with every turn that the mountain would hold.

I was halfway to him when he stopped and I called out his name as loudly as I could. He turned at the sound of my voice and then raised his arm to point at something behind me. I heard the crack and turned toward the sound. And there she was, standing atop the fracturing snow. Dressed in white she blended into the landscape as the snow below her crumbled into a wave.

Even though my goggles were down she must have read the revelation in my eyes, because her lips curled and her cheeks rose in a facial shrug. 'Now you remember,' she said. 'It's really so sad that you decided to follow Warren that day. And now it's too bad that you decided to kill yourself over him, all alone on an isolated ski run.'

'Kill myself? Are you crazy? I have no intention of killing myself.'

'That's what they all thought until they found your body.'

The absurdity of the situation wasn't lost on me. Here was a woman who had intentionally triggered an avalanche to kill her husband, and she was telling me I was going to kill myself. Right. In front of Reininger, a fellow ski patroller.

'Yeah? And how am I going to do it? The snow in here isn't about to slide.'

'You're going to shoot yourself, Greta.'

The voice I was hearing wasn't Zuzana's. It came from above, a man's voice. My head wheeled round and one final image from the day of the avalanche slipped into place, completing the picture. A tall, dark figure with bowed legs standing on the upside of the fracture beside her. I turned back to the woman I knew as Zuzana. She was holding a gun, smiling with all the attraction of Medusa.

'You two?' I didn't need to finish the sentence. I thought back to the day early in the season when Zuzana had turned her ankle on Silver Bell and took a toboggan down. Reininger was the patrolman on the scene. Had they been in cahoots before or had they started up then? 'I just hope you can handle the bad jokes.'

'I'm not worried about his jokes,' said Medusa and without missing a beat she pivoted and shot Reininger right through the forehead. His face seemed to explode in his helmet and blood began to seep out even before he crumpled to the ground, his hands still on the grip of the toboggan.

Right then I started to take her seriously. My natural defenses jumped into gear as my mind quickly assessed the situation. It didn't take much to figure out that I was in the grips of a murderous woman, a sociopath with absolutely no concern for anyone but herself. I knew sociopaths were chronic liars, but they also had huge egos and were eager to prove themselves.

'Did you just kill the father of your child?' I asked, trying to buy myself some time.

Her laugh was even more demon-like than her smile. 'My God. There's no child. I just invented one to keep Warren around until I could get the job done. I was worried he might just leave me. You see, his true interest lay elsewhere.' She paused before throwing me the bone. 'I knew he was getting ready to tell me his feelings toward you, to break things off with me. That's when I invented the child. It was probably the only reason he followed me out of bounds.'

'So did you put the bird's nest in my chimney?' I asked, wanting to keep her talking, trying not to think about what her words implied.

'Of course. We were afraid you might remember seeing us cause the slide. We had plenty of time while you were in the hospital. It was my idea. He,' she said, giving a nod to the body bleeding out in the snow, 'was too stupid to think up anything so brilliant. As brilliant as an open paint can near a fire, don't you think?'

I scrolled through the other incidents. 'The toboggan?'

'Stu had removed a critical screw. Nothing you would notice on the flat, but a problem on a steep slope.'

'And was he responsible for the bomb that could have killed Singh and me?'

'Now you're showing how smart you are,' she cackled. 'He found a fast-burning fuse to replace yours. But unfortunately you didn't die in any of the mishaps. We would have tried burning you up sooner, but there always seemed to be a man in the house. Which reminds me. You forgot one.'

'You've lost me,' I said in all honesty.

'The dead car battery. We turned your lights on. The plan was Stu was going to offer you a ride home, but then the doctor got in the way. He's cute, by the way. Maybe he'll be my next conquest.'

For some reason a jealous streak ran up my spine. 'He's in jail and you know it.'

She studied me for a moment and then broke out into a laugh. 'You don't know?'

'Know what?'

She ignored me and glanced dismissively at Reininger's limp body, the snow around it a bloody snow cone. She turned her attention back to me, the gun still trained at my head. 'What some people won't do for sex and the promise of money. Men are such fools. Make them feel good and you own them. I've never known it to fail. They think they are in love with you, but they are really in love with themselves and how you make their bodies feel. We women are so much smarter, don't you agree?'

While I would wholeheartedly agree that we women are smarter, in Zuzana's case I would have to add more treacherous and cunning as well. She coldly murdered her first two husbands when they failed to live up to her aspirations. Magnus Bergstrom died because of his career-ending accident, Werner Mayer for lack of ambition. And then there was Warren, prematurely taken for a reason I didn't want to think about.

I looked at Reininger all crumpled on the ground. He must have thought he was finally getting out of that van. All that effort for naught. And while I would have loved to debate her on the frailties of men versus the intelligence of women, I was thinking with her true confessions coming to an end, it was high time for me to get the hell out of there.

'What's that?' I said, looking off behind her in the oldest ruse of all time. She bit and looked over her shoulder, but only for a second. I took advantage of the second to do a side kick turn and take off through the woods.

She was on me in an instant; she was that good. But with Zuzana having just demonstrated that she had no compunction about cold-blooded murder, I had to do something to better my odds. At least I was moving instead of waiting to be put down like a lame horse. I was skiing like a mad woman, breaking every rule in the book, skiing too close to the trees, gaining speed I didn't want as I held off on making a turn, at certain points out of control, staying on my skis by leg strength alone.

We were crushing it though the glades, throwing it down as we shredded the snow, moving in synchronicity as she mirrored my every move. I tried to shake her, to outski her, but she was a better skier, even with a gun in one hand, even without her poles.

The snow was deep and the terrain studded with obstacles. Once I felt my ski brush a stump, but I kept going, driven forward by the knowledge that a gun was pointed at my back. I fought to block the image of a bullet penetrating my helmet and my head blowing up the way Reininger's had.

I tried making unexpected turns in an attempt to shake her. She followed my every move, so close that I could hear her breathing, see the gun raising in my peripheral vision. I heard a shot and felt hot iron rip at my shoulder, tearing at the flesh like a fishhook. I could feel warm liquid seeping out and running down my arm. Then another shot. This one through my side. I pressed on through the pain, knowing if I stopped it was certain death. I couldn't outski her, so I was going to have to outsmart her. And then it came to me, and I knew what to do.

Making impossibly tight turns, I segued towards the edge of Traynor's where ropes delineated the out of bounds area. I'd done trail work a couple of summers back and knew the terrain on the other side of the boundary markers. I skied straight for the rope, ducking low at the last minute to clear it. Getting under the rope slowed her, putting more space between us than there had been since the chase started.

And then without warning, I smacked into a stump hidden under the snow. My bindings released and I ejected onto the mountain, rolling head over heels until I came to a stop twenty yards downhill from her. She had stopped too, of her own volition, and was glaring down at me. In no hurry now, she began a leisurely slide toward where I lay in the snow unprotected. As the real estate between us grew narrower, she raised the gun and pointed it at my head. I cowered and closed my eyes, certain the breath I was taking was my last.

Then I heard a surprised gasp and opened my eyes just in time to see Zuzana disappear from sight, gun and all. Her screams were like those of a Tasmanian devil, echoing evil across the mountain until they came to an abrupt stop when she hit the bottom. This part of the mountain was riddled with abandoned mineshafts you could only see when there wasn't any snow. Thank god I remembered this particular open shaft from doing clearing work in the summer. Actually, my calculations had been off a few feet and if I hadn't hit the stump and ejected I would have gone in before her.

# FORTY-EIGHT

By the time I limped down to the gondola there were only a few people in the locker room. Neverman was one of them. He took one look at all the blood and called an ambulance. I insisted I was fine and then fainted on to the floor. Evidently, I had gone into shock.

And so I was wheeled into the emergency room for the third time in as many weeks. By now the overhead lights and the Spartan rooms were familiar to me, as was half of the staff. My favorite nurse, Adam, had hooked up an IV and was asking me if I had any allergies.

'You mean after all my time here you don't have it in my chart?' I challenged him.

'We always ask. As long as you're awake.'

My shoulder was beginning to throb and I closed my eyes against the pain. 'This really hurts,' I confessed.

'I'll get you some morphine,' he said, leaving me alone in the room.

I squeezed my eyes shut, trying to figure out how soldiers shot in the field survive the pain since the hole in my shoulder was probably only a flesh wound. Flesh wound or not, it hurt like a mother. The gunshot in my abdomen hurt less. Go figure.

I squeezed my eyes shut against the pain and thought about how Duane Larsen had attended to me on my two previous visits. The first thing I was going to do when I was released was find him and tell him how sorry I was to let him down. Evil did exist in this world. Zuzana was a perfect example. Reininger not so much. He was just dumb. But Duane? There was no evil in him anywhere, I was certain.

The door opened and someone came into my room. I peeled my eyes back the tiniest bit expecting Adam with the happy juice. But the next breath I drew was one of disbelief. Dr Duane Larsen was standing in the room wearing his familiar green scrubs. The last time I had seen him he'd been wearing orange. A rush of adrenaline surged through me, like when you barely miss being in an accident or you walk into a room full of people yelling 'surprise'.

'You just can't stay away from here, can you? You really are going for the frequent flyer discount.'

I was injured and I was in pain, but I wasn't dead and I needed an answer. 'You're out. What happened?'

'You didn't see it in the paper?' he said, his voice holding a degree of accusation.

'I just got back from overseas.'

He sat down on the edge of the bed and looked at me with those earnest eyes, one green and one brown. 'They got the guys who killed Kimmy. Sadly, she wasn't the only one. There were two others. The missing girl from Breckenridge and the missing girl from Vail. It's all on tapes that the sickos made. Kimmy had broken away from them and ran. That's how she ended up in Castle Creek with a broken neck. She was the only one to get away.'

'But who? How?'

'It was those creeps doing the Ted Bundy documentary. They'd entice young women into their van under the auspices of seeing themselves on film and then they'd drug them and tape themselves doing . . . well you don't want to know. They were staying in the room next to Kimmy's at the Snowflake and grabbed her before she went inside. They were the two "witnesses" who saw me fight with her. Which of course never happened.'

'But the blood in your house?'

The look he gave me was both forgiving and final. 'Like I told the cops. She cut her hand in my car and we stopped at my home to bandage it up.' He didn't ask me why I didn't believe him before, and his eyes told me there was no swimming up that stream again. He was lost to me forever.

Surgery went well and I'm on the mend. Should be back at work in a couple of weeks. Like Duane said, 'Who needs a spleen anyway?' I did my best to try and assuage him, to let him know in the end that I did have faith in him. But it was too little too late. He left town shortly after he was sure I was doing OK. He said he wasn't comfortable living here anymore after what had happened to him. And I couldn't blame him.

Life in the A-frame is back to normal. No more fear of intruders like Zuzana and Reininger putting a bird's nest down my chimney or tampering with sleds or changing fuses or burning me out of my house or running down my car battery. The Remington is back in the closet, and I don't know if it will ever come back out again. I would never think of using it on an animal and the human ones seem to be at bay for the time being.

And there's one other good thing coming in my life. Next Monday I go to get my new dog.

# EPILOGUE

The sun has yet to crack the mountains and the morning sky is a weak gray. The gondola sits still while the lifties curl their gloved hands around steaming cups of coffee and share stories of the previous night's debauchery. I wrap my skins around my skis and head straight up the front of the mountain. Though the snow cats gave the run a last pass a half hour before, an inch or so of freshie has accumulated before the last of the storm lifted. Overall, a foot plus of new snow has fallen since the lifts closed the evening before.

As I climb higher the new snow gets deeper and soon the snow I am climbing through is nearly knee deep. But the bitter cold keeps the snow light, making the task less arduous. I move in solitude in the shadow of the treed slopes to either side of me, each breath preceding me in a gray plume that floats upwards.

The sun has risen higher as I near the top, my armpits soaked and rivulets of sweat running down my back. It breaches Independence Pass in a golden globe just as I reach the top and rolls across the new snow like a curtain coming up on billions of earthly stars, a sparkling galaxy. And I am the only one in the audience.

I take the skins off my skis and fold them into my backpack before starting down. The snow parts before me as gravity carries me along, a wake of powdered sugar rising to either side of me, settling behind me. I plunge into the virgin snow with the enthusiasm of a bridegroom.

I never wear a helmet on these solitary runs and my braid streams out from beneath my hat. My screams of ecstasy are only heard by the winter animals in their burrows as I continue downwards through open meadows and ancient trees, unencumbered, unstopping. My legs are screaming for a break, but I refuse to listen. There is plenty of time to rest afterwards.

And then I'm ripping down Jackpot, my legs unfolding to

bottomless snow, my body propped up by the mountain. My mouth is frozen in a smile as I pass beneath the still-unmoving gondola, and I think that the only thing that comes close to this sensation is sex, but it would have to be multiple orgasms. And then I reconsider. Even sex isn't as good as this.

And then I come to a stop at the top of Little Nell where I can see the line that has formed at the base of the mountain. It stretches down the steps of Gondola Plaza to Durant Street as hopeful skiers wait to get a first crack at the untouched snow I have so selfishly devoured by my lonesome. And I make no apologies.

It doesn't get any better than this.